TOUGH TIMES ON CORONATION CLOSE

LIZZIE LANE

Boldwood

First published in Great Britain in 2025 by Boldwood Books Ltd.

Copyright © Lizzie Lane, 2025

Cover Design by Colin Thomas

Cover Images: Colin Thomas and Alamy

The moral right of Lizzie Lane to be identified as the author of this work has been asserted in accordance with the Copyright, Designs and Patents Act 1988.

Every effort has been made to obtain the necessary permissions with reference to copyright material, both illustrative and quoted. We apologise for any omissions in this respect and will be pleased to make the appropriate acknowledgements in any future edition.

A CIP catalogue record for this book is available from the British Library.

Paperback ISBN 978-1-80483-436-7

Large Print ISBN 978-1-80483-435-0

Hardback ISBN 978-1-80483-438-1

Ebook ISBN 978-1-80483-434-3

Kindle ISBN 978-1-80483-433-6

Audio CD ISBN 978-1-80483-441-1

MP3 CD ISBN 978-1-80483-442-8

Digital audio download ISBN 978-1-80483-437-4

This book is printed on certified sustainable paper. Boldwood Books is dedicated to putting sustainability at the heart of our business. For more information please visit https://www.boldwoodbooks.com/about-us/sustainability/

Boldwood Books Ltd, 23 Bowerdean Street, London, SW6 3TN

www.boldwoodbooks.com

1

JUNE 1941

It was Friday night, the weekend had arrived, and a tidal wave of girls poured out of the tobacco factory in East Street, Bedminster. The factory was a red-brick affair, its windows set into gothic arches reminiscent of a fairy-tale palace from medieval times. Not that the mainly female labour force cared about that. They did their work and, regardless that some had to work Saturday, at least up until lunchtime, Friday night signified the beginning of the weekend. A fun time beckoned.

'Anyone fancy a Woodbine?' somebody shouted.

'No thanks. I've been with them all day,' came the prompt reply amid hoots of laughter.

By day, they worked churning out millions of Wills' Woodbines, a cigarette smoked by many, including those who had declared they'd had enough of them for one day. For eight or more hours, they stripped tobacco leaves, tended the production line, packed cigarettes into tins for selling or sending as part of a serviceman's daily ration. Tobacco dust floated in the air, thanks to endless production and the necessary sweeping up that followed, most of which went back into use.

The married women couldn't wait to get home, have a cuppa and attack life on the home front. The laundry, housework and putting a meal on the table were top priority. So was catching up with their children, who, like everyone in this war, were expected to contribute by way of helping with household chores. The unmarried girls, eyes sparkling, spoke of going to a dance, the pictures or on a date with a young man who might – just might – be the one.

Mary Dawson whisked the turban from her hair and tossed her mane of auburn tresses, sending it falling like fiery rain onto her shoulders.

Eldest daughter of Thelma Dawson who lived at number twelve Coronation Close, Knowle West, she was one of those looking forward to a good night out, and a date with a young man she'd only just met. Beau was Canadian and lived in one of the hundreds of brown khaki tents in a field adjacent to the airport. He worked in logistics, which he told her meant maintaining the supply line of everything from nuts and bolts to tins of beans.

'It's an important task,' he'd assured her.

'I have read that an army marches on its belly,' she'd responded. 'And everything is held together with nuts and bolts.'

Flushed in the face and bristling with excitement, her closest mate at work, Pauline Chambers, a dusky-skinned beauty with a mass of black silky hair, walked with her to the bus stop, a moony look on her face.

It struck Mary that if it hadn't been for her heavy-duty work shoes, her friend might have been floating on air.

The continuous sighing was being done for a reason. Pauline wanted her to ask what was ailing her. Mary finally gave in.

'Go on. Tell me what's on your mind.'

Pauline's eyes sparkled. 'I reckon tonight might be the night when Jeffrey pops the question, we set the date and I'm out of here.'

'You're really sure?'

'Absolutely.'

'You sound as though you're already making plans.'

'I know exactly what I want. And I know what my dress will look like. And my bridesmaids. White for me – obviously. Shocking pink for my bridesmaids. You'll be one of my bridesmaids, won't you?'

Mary shuddered at the thought of her, a redhead, wearing something in shocking pink. The two did not go. She wouldn't say so, of course, though hoped that at some point she'd find a way to wriggle out of her friend's plan. Being a bridesmaid was all well and good but not when hair and outfit colour clashed.

'It seems as if you've got everything planned,' she said brightly. She reserved saying anything about the shocking pink. Surely Pauline could work that out for herself?

'Oh, I have,' returned Pauline without the least sign of accepting that auburn hair would not mix with her choice of colour for the bridesmaids' dresses. She held her hand against her heart, the moony look still in her eyes. 'Even down to the flowers.'

Mary believed her. Some people kept a diary of their day-to-day lives or jotted down important dates onto paper. Pauline had a vivid imagination and carried her wedding plans around in her head.

She thought of Snow White or some other fairy-tale princess, delicate little hand on heart, the prince – in this case Jeff – on his knees offering an engagement ring set with a huge diamond presented in a blue velvet box. Butterflies and bluebirds would be circling her head and petals, the precursor to the big day, floating down from a ridiculously blue sky.

'You'll be like a princess,' Mary remarked in a kindly manner.

'Oh yes.'

'A fond farewell to the tobacco factory? How could you bear to leave it all behind!' Her tone was sarcastic, but she laughed so Pauline would know she was joking.

Whether she noticed or not, Pauline didn't bat an eyelid. The wistfully faraway look remained as her voice floated around with the dreams she held in her mind.

'My own front door. My own house. That's what I want.'

Mary didn't let her see the grimace on her face. She and Pauline were the same age, had left school at fourteen and were now seventeen and eighteen respectively, Pauline having celebrated her birthday just a few days ago, a few months ahead of Mary. She'd been flattered when someone as popular as the raven-haired Pauline had befriended her within a week of starting work. Others had followed, of course. Mary was easy going and likeable. Sassy was also a word used to describe her. Saucy might be too.

She was also sincere both to family and friends.

'I can't wait,' murmured Pauline.

Mary's smile was warm, her words truly meant. 'I hope your dream comes true.'

It was Pauline's greatest wish but wouldn't suit Mary. Not yet anyway. In her opinion, there were too many fun times to be had before thinking about a husband, a house and kids. Funny, but it seemed to be what most women wanted.

'I'm going to have fun before I settle down,' Mary stated firmly and not for the first time. She accompanied the statement with a resolute toss of her head.

'Don't believe you,' said Pauline, enviously eyeing the tumbling red hair, the pale skin and slender figure. 'No matter what you say, I can see you married by the time you're twenty-one – if not before.' Pauline giggled before lowering her voice. 'Might 'ave to if you get a bun in the oven.'

'I might want a baby and not a husband,' Mary said with a cheeky grin as she combed her fine white fingers through her silky tresses.

Pauline gasped and held her hand over her mouth. 'You can't do that. Think of what people would say.'

'I don't care what people say. Where's the law that says a woman should be tied to a man for life?'

She'd said it loudly enough for heads to turn and thought she heard the word 'tart' mentioned, and 'fast'. Not that it worried her. She'd always been a resilient type of girl, one who went her own way.

'So, getting married might not be your dream?' Pauline pressed.

'Might not,' Mary said tartly. 'And you won't be staying on at work once you're married?'

'Certainly not. You're an old maid if you're not married by the time you're nineteen.'

Mary didn't agree with this and said so.

Pauline was adamant. 'I dream of it every night. He's only got three days' leave and then he's gone again, so he'd better do the deed right now.'

'Hope your dream comes true, Pauline, and you and him live happily ever after.'

Pauline cocked her head. Sooty lashes brushed her cheeks, along with her look of disbelief. 'Ain't you got the same dream? Sometimes. Just sometimes. Isn't there anyone you'd walk down the aisle with at the drop of a hat?'

Mary shook her head. 'Not even if they dropped a golden crown at my feet. Anyway, there's no one I fancy – not like you. I'm not engaged. Not even close to it.'

'Don't you worry about being an old maid?'

Mary shook her head adamantly. 'No. Free to do as I please, go where I want and no dirty socks to wash.' Dimples appeared alongside the wide smile on her pink lips.

'Marry in haste and repent at leisure,' said one of the women in the queue.

'Where's this perishing bus,' cried someone else. 'A tram would 'ave been yer by now.'

'Well, there ain't none of them any more!'

It was true. Bristol tramways had been bombed back in the Good Friday raid and were gone forever.

'I blame Lord Haw-Haw meself. I 'eard 'im on the wireless. Said they'd 'eard the council wanted to do away with the trams, but the Luftwaffe would do the job for them.'

'And they did,' muttered another arrival in the general conversation.

'That Lord Haw-Haw should be 'anged for blowing up our trams when they finally get 'old of 'im,' said a gravelly female voice through a fug of cigarette smoke.

'Yur right there. 'Eard on the wireless that we've got to look out for traitors like 'im. Fifth columnists they call them. Be careful of any bloke asking too many questions.'

'Might not just be men,' suggested Mary.

'It's mostly blokes,' said the gravelly voiced woman. 'Better watch out for them.'

'Better look out for any bloke,' said another with a dirty laugh. 'They're all after something.'

They laughed and joked, but somehow a small kernel of

serious truth stayed in the overall atmosphere accounting in a small way for what happened next.

2

As a green double-decker bus came into view coming from the direction of Bedminster Bridge, the queue shuffled forward on aching feet, ready to pile on and get home.

'Inside only. Standing room only,' shouted the conductress, a middle-aged woman, her hair caught in a hairnet beneath her regulation cap.

Work-weary bodies crammed upstairs and down, too many really for one bus to take, but the conductress turned a blind eye.

The smell of body odour was strong mixed as it was with that of cigarettes and poverty. Mary held her breath when she could, turning her head away from sweaty armpits and fetid breath.

One bus stop after another came up, more and more passengers getting off. By the time they got to the end of St John's Lane, she and Pauline managed to nab a couple of the side seats close to the open platform at the back of the bus. If you wanted fresh air – and Mary most definitely did – this was the best place to be.

She sighed blissfully as she slid off one shoe, then the other. Even young feet got tired. She welcomed the fact that Pauline was seated in one of the side seats immediately opposite. Talk about Jeff popping the question would be curtailed – at least until they got off the bus at Melvin Square.

After slipping her shoes back on Mary took great gulps of the air coming through from the open platform at the end of the bus. Her brain thus refuelled and, not able to easily converse with Pauline, she studied the other passengers – not that there was anyone special on board; the same collection of men and women coming home from a long shift. Everyone worked a long shift nowadays.

That was until the man in the brown trilby and khaki trench coat got on.

It struck her that it was too warm a day to be wearing a trench coat. Unless he felt the cold. Or unless he had need of the extra pockets – to carry things. Things that wouldn't fit into the brown suitcase he was carrying. He did look uncommonly bulky.

Smokers tended to go upstairs on the bus. That was what he seemed inclined to do at first until he caught her eye and smiled at her.

'Fancies you,' Pauline mouthed silently from her seat.

Mary flapped a hand dismissively and mouthed back, 'Silly cow.'

Whether he did or not, he seemed to be making a decision, upstairs on the bus or down. He settled for upstairs, possibly because he wanted to smoke.

His feet clumped heavily up the stairs to the upper deck. They could hear him greet the other passengers up there before he loudly remarked, 'Good grief. Bit smoky up here. Think I might go downstairs.'

Posh voice, she thought. Or fairly posh. He wasn't a local that's for sure.

The bus conductress had been on her way upstairs to collect more fares but stood back to give him room as he came down.

'Sorry, my dear,' he said, politely touching the brim of his trilby hat. 'Too much smoke for me upstairs. It's bad for my chest.'

He coughed and patted the front of his khaki trench coat, the belt of which was cinched tightly around his waist.

To Mary's ears, the cough sounded put on, like the kind she'd used as a child when she'd not wanted to go to school. Unfortunately, her mother was not easily fooled. A clip around the ear had healed her cough in double quick time and got her racing for the school gates. One clip around the ear was more than enough.

The conductress didn't seem to care one way or the other. She was one of those who'd heeded the call to fill jobs usually done by men, thus releasing them for fighting. With the calm efficiency of a mature woman whose aim was to prove her worth, she got ready to punch a ticket from the metal machine hanging on a strap around her neck.

'Right, sir. How far do you want to go? And before you turn cheeky, I mean where do you want to get off.'

Risqué chuckles erupted from some quarters. Disapproving frowns from others.

'Leinster Avenue.'

'All the way,' she asked, readying a purple ticket for punching.

'All the way suits me,' he said, winking as he handed her two copper pennies.

Bang went the punch into the correct ticket. The conductress demurred, though there was a shot of amusement in her eyes. 'Don't be so bleedin' cheeky. I'm old enough to be yer mother.'

After she'd handed him his ticket, he backed away from the stairs and stepped through to the lower deck.

Behind him came the sound of the conductress's feet clumping up the stairs before her voice resonated down from the upper deck. 'Any more fares up yer?'

Mary often occupied herself during the journey by trying to guess what people were like, where they lived, where they worked and whether they had odd habits. Sometimes her musings were works of pure fiction. Had that woman sitting next to Pauline been a dancer in her youth? Had that man been a hero in the Great War – the war they were now calling the First World War? Was that young man with the staring blue eyes and wisp of dark hair on his upper lip related to Adolf Hitler?

The man in the trench coat stood in the gangway between the side bench where she sat, with Pauline on the opposite bench. He didn't resemble anyone famous or otherwise. One thing she did notice was that there wasn't a trace of body odour. It was hard to work out what he did smell of. Cigarette smoke of course, but a rather sweetish tobacco, one she didn't recognise. Certainly not Woodbines! Something expensive? Could she also smell lemon? She couldn't be sure.

His appearance intrigued her more than anything. She was reminded of Robert Donat who had played Richard Hannay in the film *The 39 Steps*.

Had Pauline noticed the man? It didn't seem likely. No doubt she was still mooning about Jeff and whether he would pop the question before he went back to his unit. He was in the army, stationed in East Anglia near a place called Ipswich. It seemed that absence had made the heart grow fonder if a proposal of marriage was on the cards. Unless Pauline was reaching for the moon of course.

It was fleeting, but for a moment Mary's eyes met those peering out from beneath the brim of the clay-coloured trilby hat. It was an odd look – at first open and then suddenly closed. He had an unrelenting smile that neither increased nor diminished. It was, she thought, as though it was fixed there by glue and might crack if he stopped doing it.

Catching her looking, he winked. 'Good evening, young lady. You have a nice smile.'

'Thank you.'

'Is this bus always so full?'

Mary answered without hesitation. 'Everyone's going home from work or from shopping. You should have caught it earlier – or later.'

'Ah. My fault then. I should have planned to catch the early one.' He said it with good humour and a jerk of his chin.

'So should I,' grumbled a woman. 'Working all day, then getting what I can to make a decent meal tonight. Bloomin' rationing!'

The man looked sympathetic and seemed enthused to have provoked conversation. 'I feel for you, madam. It must be very difficult. I have to say I admire you women. Queuing for food for hours and then carrying it all home. Do you shop every day, or just one day a week?'

He smiled as he said it, white teeth beneath a thin dark moustache that looked to Mary as though it had been drawn on. Surely nobody could trim and shape a moustache so finely?

'Three times a week,' said a woman in the first seat on the right-hand side, her knitting needles pausing for a moment as she tilted her head and looked over her shoulder.

'Even though your men are away fighting?' he enquired.

'Still have to shop.'

'Some of us have children. Can't see them starve.'

'Of course not. I take it some of you ladies work for the war effort.'

'Some.'

The man in the trench coat carried on. 'Bet you need plenty of sleep then. Good job there's been no bombing of late. That must have interrupted your beauty sleep.'

'It ain't been easy for any of us,' said one of the men, his head hunched into his shoulders. 'Twelve-hour days. It ain't no joke. Craters and potholes, flattened 'ouses and fire duty and whatnot on top. It's a dog's life, it is. A bloody dog's life.'

The knitting needles stopped their racket as the woman in the third seat threw the man a look of disapproval.

'Sorry, missus. Bloomin' is what I should 'ave said.' He tapped the side of his nose with a grubby finger. 'Careless words.'

Daft thing to say, thought Mary. Careless words only applied to giving away the country's secrets. It had never applied to using bad language.

Other people gave their view on their own experiences of the working day; little titbits of what they did, complaints about how it could be done better – or not at all.

The man in the khaki trench coat responded to each and every one. He was attentive as a parent listening to a child relating what had happened at school that day.

Mary listened. The man was like a ringmaster at the circus, drawing everyone into the conversation, people who, for the most part, would have remained silent until the bus came to their stop and they got off and toddled home. She couldn't help becoming suspicious. A more reserved young woman might have said nothing, but Mary had never been reserved.

'Careless talk costs lives,' she blurted suddenly. He should know better. The posters warning about giving away even the smallest secrets were everywhere.

Her sudden outburst attracted his attention. She studied his face as his gaze met hers. His eyes were dark and deep set, his cheekbones angular, his jaw was square and he had a dimple in his chin. He saw her looking and flashed her another of his white-toothed smiles. An act of reassurance.

'Everyone's been touched by the war,' he remarked and winked at her again.

It was a saying she'd heard a hundred times. To her mind, such exclamations should have ended there and then, but the man in the trench coat pedalled on.

A red stone flashed in a gold signet ring on his wedding finger, its presence taking her by surprise.

Seeing her looking, he suddenly covered the ring with the fingers of his other hand. A suspicious gesture. Or was it? Was she overreacting?

Mary looked away, pretended it was nothing, but in fact his actions and the things he said were making her feel uncomfortable.

Her discomfort increased when he went on to say that he hoped they were well protected from bombing raids and presumed there was an anti-aircraft gunnery post close by, especially seeing as Bristol Airport was located at Whitchurch and adjacent to the housing estate.

He wasn't exactly asking whether there were such things, but more as though he was seeking confirmation.

It was no good. She was only young, but warnings were given out in newspapers, on the wireless and at the pictures.

Mary's voice rang out. 'We shouldn't be talking about things like that.'

The sound of the knitting needles ceased. Passengers who, up until now, had taken no notice, turned their heads and looked at the man with suspicion in their eyes. Especially the women.

Mary pointed to the warning notice above the window. *Beware of strangers asking questions about military matters.*

Other passengers followed the direction in which her finger was pointing.

Weariness forgotten, their mood changed. They now looked at the man in the trench coat with outright hostility.

He gave a light laugh, as though it was all a joke. 'I'm just asking. I'm new round here and looking for digs...'

A woman wearing a knitted pixie hood – far too warm in this weather, thought Mary – turned fully round in her seat, and asked, 'Are you foreign? You sound foreign.'

Mary pointed out that there were plenty of foreign troops from the Empire around, some of whom spoke English with a foreign accent. 'Though they are easily identifiable by their uniforms.'

'True,' said the woman in the pixie hood.

But the woman had a point. 'You're not in uniform. Why is that?' There was a boldness in Mary's voice beyond what was normally expected of a young girl of seventeen.

'Reserved occupation. I'm an engineer.'

His explanation, glib and swiftly rendered, should have sufficed, but Mary had sowed the seeds of suspicion. Awakened from turpitude, the passengers weren't going back to a state of ignorance.

It was, thought Mary, like a pack of dogs had been roused from their slumber, pricked with patriotism dormant until now.

Mary too felt a flush of patriotism. She had no intention of letting go now. 'Where are you from then?'

He gave no hint in his expression that she'd unnerved him. In fact, he laughed it off. 'Now why would you want to know that?'

'You've got a funny accent.' She wasn't sure whether he did or not but throwing out this question – one not really based on fact – seemed the sort of thing a suspicious person would ask.

'I'm from the Channel Islands.'

'But you *parlez-vous Français*.'

'Some of us do. Guernsey is part of the Channel Islands.' From where he was standing, he half turned and addressed them all, 'Though, of course, it's fallen into German hands, so I suppose you could say that there are now three languages spoken there.'

Glib tongue, she thought, and was about to pry a bit more when a man further down the bus who'd been hunched into his collar waded into the conversation. He coughed and spluttered a bit before saying, 'You asks too many questions.'

'He does that,' remarked the lady who knitted.

Mary met the scared look in Pauline's eyes and the whiteness of her knuckles clutching a patchwork handbag made from bits of felt. Normally, Pauline would have got off the bus at Melvin Square, but instead she sprang to her feet at the one before, squeezed past the man and got off without looking back. She hadn't asked Mary to join her. Determined to see this through to the end, Mary would not have gone with her friend. The bus journey home was no longer mundane. She felt inspired and in charge.

Her voice, full of confidence, rang out. 'Call the conductress. Call 'er now. And get some of the men from up top down here.'

The woman with the knitting needles was having none of it. 'Oy. We don't need the men. Do you think us women aren't capable of coping with a fifth columnist?'

The bus trundled on towards Melvin Square.

Looking a bit rattled, the man began pushing towards the entrance. 'My stop, I think.'

Mary got to her feet, barring his way to the platform and escape. 'This isn't Leinster Avenue. That's where you said you were getting off. That's what you told the conductress.'

A wall of working-class women and their shopping bags stood between him and the bus platform.

Mary felt a sense of pride. Too young to join up, she congratulated herself that she might – just might – have contributed something useful to the war effort – if he was a spy. What a feather in her cap that would be.

The conductress swung from the stairs and into the fray. 'What's going on 'ere then?'

Primed with courage, Mary told her what had been going on. 'This bloke 'ere is asking questions about the airport and whether there's ack-ack guns close by. I reckon he's a spy.'

The conductress pulled in her chin as she thought about it.

'Right.' She stood on tiptoe. 'Someone up in the front seat get the driver's attention. Get 'im to stop the bus. Don't let it pull away from this stop.'

A loud banging on the glass partition between the lower deck and the driver's cubbyhole ensued. The driver obviously got the message – the sound reverberating around his tiny cabin – and brought the bus to a juddering halt.

'Hold him there,' ordered the conductress to the motley band of women who'd formed a barrier between the man and the rear platform of the bus – the only way off.

The driver, a grey-haired man with a broad stomach,

stepped onto the platform. He looked nonplussed as he tried to figure out who was doing what to whom and why all these women in headscarf turbans and heaving shopping bags had corralled the smart-looking man in the trench coat and brown trilby hat.

The conductress explained. 'This bloke's been asking questions about the airport and other stuff. This lot reckon he's a fifth columnist.'

'And he speaks with a funny accent.'

The driver looked taken aback at the mention of a funny accent. 'Right,' he said slowly. 'Can you 'old 'im here whilst I call for a copper?' He ambled off on short legs that should probably have been retired some while ago. But the war – the blasted war – had called for retirees to step forward and lend a hand whilst younger men went off to fight.

'Ladies,' said the man, looking confident despite being cornered. 'You must believe me. I was only making polite conversation. I am a stranger here.'

'Don't you move,' said the woman with the lethal-looking knitting needles, brandishing one only inches from the man's right eye.

'Now, look here... let me through.'

The women crowded in on him.

'You ain't going anywhere.'

As one, they pushed him to the ground. He found himself surrounded by thick legs, stout shoes and heavy bags of King Edward potatoes – heavy and lethal – only inches from his head.

Feeling she'd done her bit and keen to get home, washed, dressed and out on her date, Mary alighted from the bus. She'd done her bit arousing everyone to what might be going on. The man was surrounded and the conductress and heavyweight driver looked perfectly capable of taking charge.

The shops on Melvin Square were still open. Pauline lived just off the square in Broad Walk. Mary had been surprised at her getting off before her usual stop and concerned that she'd been frightened by events. It wouldn't hurt to hang around a while until she appeared, just to see how she was. She had to come this way, her usual stop unless she was that scared, she'd scampered along the lane at the top of the Novers.

With that in mind, Mary found a warm niche between a red telephone box and a solid wooden police box at the end of the terrace of shops, a comfortable enough place to wait for Pauline. Even if she didn't turn up, there was the chance of seeing what happened to the man in the trench coat. If anything.

3

Police Constable Percy Routledge, who lived at number five Coronation Close with his wife Margaret and their three children, believed himself suited for better things than patrolling the roads of the Knowle West council estate. There was a war on, and he truly believed he could contribute something worthwhile to the war effort. Like Mary Dawson, he'd seen *The 39 Steps.* He'd seen many other films where a man of duty, of resource and physical skill had given great service to their country. Conceited to the core, he saw himself as the sort of man capable of becoming a national hero, like Gordon of Khartoum or Lawrence of Arabia. Destiny would find him some day; of that, he was sure. It was just a case of waiting for the right circumstances and the right contacts.

But when? It was the question he continually asked himself and felt hard done by that the answer was taking a long time coming. What he did know was that when the moment came, he would grab it with both hands.

Today had proceeded like any other day. He had been marching purposefully towards the blue police box at the corner of Leinster Avenue and Melvin Square when he saw a figure in some kind of dark uniform waving at him franticly. Beyond him, Percy saw a green double-decker bus – a common enough sight, seeing as many of the Bristol transport fleet terminated or passed through the area, but a crowd had gathered round it.

His high forehead fell into wrinkles above brows as thick as hairy caterpillars. These people were not following the rules. Well, he couldn't have that. People were not supposed to congregate and cause trouble. He had no reason to think they were causing trouble, but Percy had long ago built a high wall between the public and his duty as an upholder of law and order.

The bus driver clasped his hand against his chest as his breath laboured.

'Something up, driver?'

The man was in his fifties, his hair was iron grey, and his face was criss-crossed with purplish veins, like that of a cider drinker who doesn't know when to call time.

'The women on that bus...' It was a rush of words that left him breathless. 'They've cornered a bloke – a foreigner, I think. He was asking about the airport and ack-ack defences...'

'Was he now! Lead on, driver.'

Percy had been prepared for something far more mundane, like a drunk causing trouble and refusing to leave the bus, or a woman gone into labour and nobody with the necessary experience being on board. Mention of women having cornered a man asking about the airport and defence batteries was something he could get his teeth into, though he knew how daft women could be, after all he was married to one.

Shoulders braced and the light of battle in his eyes, Percy's size ten boots thudded over the pavement, his swift pace

causing him to overtake the bus driver and get to the stationary
bus before he did.

'Now then,' he said, fetching his notebook from his pocket
and licking the end of his pencil in readiness. 'What's been
going on here?'

A ring of women escorted the man from the bus, led by a
woman with a very large knitting needle.

'He was asking about the airport and other stuff,' said a
man with a rheumy look in his eyes. He stood slightly back
from the women as if afraid to get too close in case he got a
dose of the same treatment they were giving out to the man in
the trench coat.

Percy gave him the once-over. To his mind, he looked very
respectable, but Percy trusted no one until he'd known them
for some time – and even then, he was wary. If they broke the
law, then no matter if he'd known them for twenty years, they
got no mercy from PC Percy Routledge. But this man looked
respectable, and Percy Routledge prided himself on knowing a
respectable man when he saw one.

'Stand back, ladies. Let the dog see the rabbit.'

Nobody laughed.

'We reckon he's a spy.'

'Do you now. And what do you say to that?' Percy squared
in his shoulders and did his best to look the man in the eye –
but, seeing as he was at least four inches taller, ended up eyes
to nose. Big feet did not equate to great height, even when
encased in a pair of size ten boots, much to Percy's dismay.

The man's eyes flashed over him seeming to evaluate Percy's
stature and general appearance before replying.

Finally, he dropped his voice and glanced at the women
who surrounded him with an air of condescension. He leaned
in close to Percy, an action symbolising a kind of brotherhood

that women simply wouldn't understand. 'As one man to another, what do women know about war, eh?' Percy grunted but did not give any sign that he agreed with his comment. Inside, what with the man looking respectable and all, he was inclined to think the same. He wrote the date and time on his notebook in handwriting that he was justly proud of.

'First things first. I need your name.'

The man leaned in closer. 'Can I have a word with you in private.' He threw a disparaging look over those keeping close and attempting to hear every word that was uttered.

'Why would that be, sir?'

The man slid an identity card from his pocket. 'I could show you this, but only somewhere we won't be seen or overheard. I'm sure you understand.'

He said the last bit with an air of secrecy that sent a spear of thrill through Percy's conceited heart.

After telling the women to go about their business, Percy nodded. 'Follow me, sir.'

He took him to the blue police box, for which he had a key. From there, he could phone through to the local station, tell them where he was and what he was doing. Warn them of enemy subterfuge, should this man's actions be less than honourable. Not that he thought there was a problem. After all, the man seemed more than willing to talk to him. Whichever way things went he couldn't help thinking that he had at last reached a crossroads in his career – even in his life.

The blue police box was next to the red telephone box. They were close together but left a narrow gap where Mary was waiting for Pauline. On seeing them approach, she drew back in as far as she could, her shoulders brushing against the obstructions on both sides. They wouldn't see her.

'My name's Quentin Appleyard. The Honourable Quentin

Appleyard, as a matter of fact. My people have an estate in Devon. It's where I was born. My father is Sir Algernon Appleyard. We reside at Hargreave Hall. Have you heard of it?'

'Vaguely, sir,' Percy answered, though didn't really know for sure. He'd heard a few names of landed gentry hereabouts, but Devon was a long way away. Still, one stately home was much like another. And landed gentry expected and received due respect. He couldn't argue with that.

'Here's my identity card.'

Having no wish to appear ignorant or cause offence, Percy gave the proffered identity card only the most fleeting inspection. Titles and upper crust impressed him. But what was this chap doing on a bus with common working-class people?

'If you were wondering why I was travelling on a bus, I was testing the waters, so to speak. I wanted to see how the lower classes would react to a man asking the kind of questions I was asking. The kind of experiment those in high places find very useful when it comes to matters of national security.'

It was as though the man had read his mind.

Percy's pigeon chest expanded with pride. He was the man overlooked and sometimes criticised for doing his duty. Now here was someone who claimed to be working on behalf of a government department, who had recognised his attributes – even though they'd only just met.

The Honourable Quentin Appleyard eyed him like a general in the field of battle ordering a lowly ensign to go over the top and head straight for the guns.

'You do understand that, Constable, do you not?'

With toy-soldier stiffness, Percy saluted. 'Of course, sir. You can never be too careful.'

'Exactly,' said Quentin, a gleam of satisfaction adorning his aristocratic face. 'I can see you're an intelligent man and possess an in-depth knowledge of the working class and society in general, I shouldn't think. Is that so, Constable...?'

Flushed with pride, Percy gave another stiff salute. 'Routledge, sir. Police Constable Percy Routledge.'

Percy was flattered. A titled – or almost titled man – had taken him into his confidence, a man of reserved occupation, secret occupation, for that was surely what was being hinted at.

The man offered him a cigarette. 'Percy. May I call you Percy?'

Percy felt a glow of satisfaction from his head to the tips of his toes. Even though he wasn't a habitual smoker, it seemed a companiable thing to do. 'Certainly, sir.'

He spluttered but managed a smile.

Quentin took it all in. In his experience it was not so easy to read the mood or character of a crowd. A man alone was a different matter. This, he decided, was a man who did not accept that his ambition far outweighed his ability.

He knew how to be warm. How to be friendly.

'Percy. You may call me Quentin. But I would appreciate you keeping my identity to yourself. I'm going to trust you with the fact that I work for the government but would stress that also you keep it strictly to yourself.'

Just for once, Percy was dumbstruck. Government officials were on a higher plain than him, one he much aspired to. He couldn't help but be impressed – and to be trusted with a secret! A state secret. That was the way he looked at it.

A hand lay on Percy's shoulder, a sign if it were needed that he was trusted and valued. This, he thought, was his moment of brushing shoulders with those in higher office, those of a world apart from the mundane. He imagined the Prime Minister, Winston Churchill, being the fount of Quentin Appleyard's mission, of Quentin actually reporting back to him. How incredible was that?

Recognising a man almost begging for his patronage, Quentin imparted more information, though only for his own ends. He wanted to be let off the hook. He wanted to fade away into normality. He wanted the police constable standing before him to assume their meeting was a chance encounter – nothing more. Nothing to be concerned about. Giving the impression that he was taking him into his confidence would achieve that. He was good at it.

His fixed smile was tight as rigor mortis on a dead man. Just as cold if Percy had had the gumption to look more carefully. The truth was, he was hooked. This man, a stranger a few minutes before, made him feel important. 'I'm new to the area and here to take up work at the airport and to ensure that its defences are not compromised.' He paused. 'You know what compromised means, do you not? And you know to talk of these things could endanger the security of this country?'

Percy nodded vehemently. 'Of course, sir.' He tapped the side of his nose. 'Mum's the word.'

Percy felt his chest swelling with pride as he looked with something approaching reverence at his new acquaintance. It was as though a halo of light was glowing around the honourable head – or at least around the brim of his hat. Such was the power of title and privilege to the mind of Percy Routledge. Who would have thought he would have ever met such a man – the Honourable Quentin Appleyard – son of a knight, or baron, earl or duke. He was unsure about which was which. All that mattered was that he belonged to a world of privilege and power. Percy was sure he would fit into that world very well indeed.

Quentin patted Percy's shoulder as someone might pat a

well-trained dog. 'You're a good man. Perhaps I might beg of your services should I need your help. In fact, Percy, I would go so far as to say that you could be useful to myself and our organisation in future. Have you heard of the department of internal intelligence?'

Percy swelled with pride. 'I don't believe I have, sir... Quentin... but then, it wouldn't be that secretive if I had.'

'Good point, Percy. Damn good point.' Quentin laughed, a big throaty laugh, a lock of lustrous hair falling over his forehead. 'Your country will not forget your helping me, Percy. Diligent duty will reap its just reward.'

Fit to burst, Percy dared to imagine himself at Buckingham Palace walking a red carpet, to where the king was waiting to knight him for services to the British Empire. This man was the key to what he could be, no longer a dream but a reality. He wasn't going to let this go. This was exactly what he wanted, and he envisioned a future out of uniform, plain clothes for the intelligence services. What a feather in his cap that would be.

'Where can I get in touch with you should I learn something threatening to national security?' Percy enquired, his face alive with the enthusiasm of a man desperate to be more than he was. If he sounded boyishly impetuous, he didn't care. This was the opportunity he'd been waiting for.

Quentin smiled. 'Give me your notebook and pencil. I'll write down the address of my lodging house...' He paused. 'But I would stress that you mustn't tell a soul. Can I count on you to do that?'

'Absolutely,' said Percy and saluted for the third time, more smartly than he ever did for the chief inspector, superintendent or even the chief constable.

4

Unseen by either of them, Mary sank back into the gap between the police box and the telephone box.

What a turn-up! Percy Routledge usually stuck to the rules like a sticky toffee to a woollen jumper. But not now. The moment secrets and the possibilities of helping this man in his stated mission of protecting the realm had popped up, raw enthusiasm had entered Percy's tone of voice. His enthusiasm amused her, so much so that she was forced to stuff her fist into her mouth. She could hear it all and got the gist of what was going on. What a turnaround! Percy was no longer interested in taking him to the station for questioning because this man had stroked his ego to an extent that it had never been stroked before.

At the sound of footsteps and the receding of voices, she chanced peering out from her hiding place.

The two men had moved away from where they had been. The man in the trilby slapped Percy on the shoulder in a friendly manner, picked up his suitcase and stalked off towards Daventry Road. She recalled on the bus journey that he'd specifically asked the conductress for a bus ticket for the end of Leinster Avenue. She supposed he'd changed his mind, anything to get away from Police Constable Percy Routledge.

'I don't blame him,' she whispered.

Percy, for his part, glowed with self-satisfaction. He truly believed something very special had happened today, something that could change his life forever and place him where he belonged.

'Thank you again, Percy,' the man shouted. He jerked his chin tellingly at the bus. 'Sorry for the misunderstanding and rousing those women to action.'

Percy, who had no idea that Mary Dawson was close by listening to every word, shook his head and reiterated what they'd agreed earlier, 'Women. What do they know about war. Once this war is over, it's back to the kitchen sink for all of them.'

He didn't see the satisfied smile on the face of the man in the trilby hat as he left Melvin Square and turned into Daventry Road. Neither did he see Mary in her hiding place, seething in response to their comments about women. It only served to strengthen her resolve to run her own life stronger than ever.

The two men had set off in diagonally opposing corners of Melvin Square. The Honourable Quentin Appleyard towards Daventry Road and Percy off on the last leg of his beat before heading for home in Coronation Close.

Once she was sure both were unlikely to see her, she came out from her hiding place, brushing off the spiders' webs adhered to her shoulders. She took her time assessing what she'd heard and what was going on. First, she looked to where Percy was a black silhouette against the setting sun at the far west end of Leinster Avenue. His disappearing figure made her feel quite relieved. If he'd discovered her eavesdropping, she would have got some kind of warning – he'd pulled her up a few times when he'd caught her hurrying home in the blackout and flashing her torch at bedroom windows. Only because she'd been a bit tipsy and thought it funny. But Percy didn't have a sense of humour. Duty was all he thought of.

Looking in the other direction, she saw that the man called Quentin hadn't got very far along Daventry Road. He looked bundled up in his coat with his brown suitcase banging against his side. She saw him take off his hat and mop his brow. If he was that hot, why didn't he take off his trench coat? It was far too warm a day for it anyway. He might make faster progress if he did.

Mary crossed the road and stood in the middle of the grass at the centre of the square for a while as she digested what had happened. Having disgorged the workforce from the factories, shops and offices, the buses had all gone. The square was empty.

A sudden breeze ruffled Mary's hair and reminded her that she was off out tonight with Beau, and she'd be late if she didn't get a move on. Pauline hadn't turned up. She guessed she'd taken a short cut.

She broke into a run, as fast as her shoes would let her, though her speed slowed as she entered the close, more so when she found herself being overtaken by another running figure. She recognised the dowdy figure of Margaret Routledge, wife of Police Constable Routledge.

'Mrs Routledge. You're in a bigger hurry than I am.' She said it in a jovial manner though there was no jollity on the face of Percy's wife.

'I had to get something for Percy's supper. He wanted a kipper tonight. I forgot.'

'Wouldn't he be satisfied with something else? Woolton pie perhaps? Sausage? I do like a sausage myself – a lot more than a kipper.'

A horrified, scared expression appeared on a face unadorned by make-up. Her purple lips had a pinched look and were dry around the edges. Her mousy hair was strained back from her face in a bun, not a curl, not a single wispy tress of hair, allowed to alleviate the stern blandness that bordered her face. She was, thought Mary, like a downtrodden character from *Jane Eyre*, sent away by a family that didn't want her and not allowed to stray far in the world.

'Oh no. Woolton pie is for Tuesday. It's fish on Friday. Always fish and preferably kipper.'

Mary watched as Percy's wife dashed off as though the Hound of the Baskerville was snapping at her heels.

'Poor woman,' said Mary's mother when Mary told her, shaking her head sadly. 'I don't think he's an easy man for a woman to live with.'

'I think the whole of Coronation Close thinks the same,' Mary added.

She might have gone on to tell her mother about the stranger on the bus and the conversation she'd overheard between him and PC Routledge, but she was off to meet Beau. It could keep. That's what she told herself. Then forgot – at least for the time being – at least until the time came when she had to tell what she knew.

5

Quentin thanked the landlady at his lodgings and told her that he would like something to eat, though not a cooked meal in the dining room with the other guests.

'I'm rather tired,' he said. 'A sandwich here in my room would be enough.'

He also declined a pot of tea. He couldn't stand the stuff. Coffee would be better, but in this country, it came in a bottle. Camp it was called. It might have been palatable if chicory wasn't added in the production process.

Once the door was closed and he was left alone to await his sandwich, he gave the room a cursory look. It was basic. A three-quarter bed, a chest of drawers, a single wardrobe with a glass mirror set in the door. The smell of mothballs came out when he opened it. For now, he'd hang clothes on the back of the door. The smell of mothballs he could well do without. And anyway, his plans had changed.

Normally, he would have joined the other lodgers at dinner, but he hadn't foreseen the reaction from the women on the bus. He might have learned some interesting things from the lodgers but couldn't chance the copper turning up. The women and their intense curiosity had been rather unexpected. He might have got away with it if the police hadn't been called, though, hopefully, he'd circumvented that minor problem, recognising a vain man who thought he deserved more from his career.

Giving the policeman the address of his lodgings had been a calculated risk. There had been the distinct chance of Percy Routledge insisting on accompanying him to his lodgings. Over time he might become a nuisance, and besides he really wanted to be closer to the airport without the likes of Percy hassling him there. No. Quentin would stay here a couple of nights, then move on. Somewhere a little less built up. Somewhere there wasn't a telephone. That would be best.

Once his sandwich had arrived, he ate it quickly, washed down with a liberal swig or two from a bottle of Haig whisky. After that, he took off his coat and the extra layer he'd been wearing beneath it and placed the suitcase on the bed, not to pack his clothes in there because there was simply no room. The wireless set had the suitcase all to itself.

6

Robin Hubert had been a part of Jenny Crawford's life when they were at school. Things had happened to push them apart, but since his separation from Doreen and the death of Roy Crawford, they had got back together. Their relationship was fairly casual but loving all the same. Only Robin's matrimonial circumstances were keeping them apart.

On the Friday evening following the incident on the bus, Jenny Crawford went out with Robin for a quick drink at the pub. That was when he informed her that his son, Simon, would be visiting within the next couple of days.

'Before he takes up 'is apprenticeship.'

Jenny knew that in reality it meant he was coming over for some money, possibly to put towards overalls, tools and other kit he might need for his mechanical apprenticeship at Bawns Motors on Coronation Road. Doreen, his mother, Robin's estranged wife, would have put him up to it of course. She could hear that grasping, greedy voice in her head: *Get as much off yer old man as you can.*

That was Doreen all over. She'd married Robin so she

didn't have to work and was still sponging off him now they were separated. It irritated her, made Jenny feel like giving Robin a good shake. She would bite her tongue and say nothing. But she knew there would be an awkward atmosphere in the shop if both she and the boy were there at the same time. Not that Robin would notice – or perhaps he merely pretended not to. It was difficult to know for sure. All the same, her mood at the end of the evening was not as robust as it had been at the beginning. No matter how much she did her bit to make Simon feel at home, it never worked. His hostility to her did not abate. The next day would not be as bright as she'd hoped it would be.

Saturday came. Robin stated his intention to pick Simon up.

'He likes coming with me in the van.'

Jenny gave him a weak smile. 'Off you go then.'

He wore a sheepish expression when he left which made her think he was lying about Simon liking to be picked up in the van. Perhaps yet again it was Doreen behind the boy's demand to be picked up to give her an extra opportunity to tap Robin for some money. It was always money with Doreen.

The shop would only be open until midday. After that she'd spend an hour or so totting up the takings, although there would be a bit of trade in the morning.

Monday and Tuesday were the busiest days of the week when the locals came in to pawn their way to the end of the week. Men got paid on Friday and if a woman wasn't quick to grab her housekeeping, it would go on beer. Women came in with whatever small valuables they could borrow against until the end of the week.

Despite it being Saturday morning, there was business to

be done. One of the regulars had come into the shop before ten o'clock.

'You said half a crown?' The customer's tone was challenging and disbelieving, with a smidgeon of hopefulness thrown in for good measure.

Jenny Crawford, who lived at number two Coronation Close, had worked at the second-hand furniture and pawn shop on Filwood Broadway for long enough to know most of the customers. She was well used to those who tried it on. Her stance was forthright. 'That's what I said.'

Mrs Billings from Torrington Avenue frequently popped in to buy bits and pieces, as well as pawn her wedding ring when the need arose. When it came to purchasing items for the home, she always asked for a bit to be knocked off. Dressed in a panelled coat with nipped-in waist – although she didn't have any waistline to speak of – the same old excuse for being short of cash rolled off her tongue with each visit.

By virtue of her near toothless mouth, her lips made a slapping sound as she prepared to trundle out the same old words she used on every occasion. The fact that Jenny had heard it all before was either forgotten or Mrs Billings hoped yet again to depend on her generous nature and proclaimed sympathy.

'It's my Mabel over in St Werburghs. The place she lives in was bombed and she ain't got a stick of furniture left for the new place – not that it's much of a place. Pig pen, if you ask me. It'll take some effort to make it look half decent. Desperate she is. So, what's a mother to do? I got to 'elp out ain't I?' Her guttural voice, the result of excess smoking, changed to wheedling. 'So, if you could knock a bit off, I'd be ever so grateful...'

Jenny gave her a knowing look. She knew very well that it had been some time since St Werburghs, an area adjacent to the city centre, had got bombed. Rumour shared in the queue at the Co-op on Melvin Square was that old man Billings made a point of coming home more drunk than usual once a month, mainly paid for, it was said, by black market activities. The latest rumour was that him and a few of his mates had fattened and sold a pig at a profit. All meat-producing animals and profit made – except for poultry – had to be kept secret from the Ministry of Food. Getting found out could result in the animal being confiscated and the perpetrators who had dared to think they could profit from the venture, in direct contravention of rationing regulations, sentenced to prison.

Pockets lined with excess cash from black market activities, old man Billings regularly celebrated his ill-gotten gains until he was full of beer all the way to his head and buying drinks for his mates. Every weekend was much the same. By the time he gained the matrimonial home, violence had taken over from bonhomie and he'd smashed things up. Furniture, pots, pans, chairs and table, everything got entirely destroyed or badly battered. This included Mrs Billings who regularly sported a bruised cheekbone and black eye.

Jenny was aware that the two oak dining chairs Mrs Billings wished to buy had been gathering dust for a while. They were a bit too big and heavy for most tastes, but no doubt big and heavy might mean them lasting an onslaught from Mr Billings and Mrs Billings not having to purchase another pair for some while.

She held out her hand, palm open. 'Two bob then. Seeing as you're a regular customer.'

Mrs Billings' beady eyes reminded Jenny of a mouse peering out of its hole – small and unblinking as she assessed whether to push her luck and knock a bit more off or scurry away whilst she was on top. Her thin lips smiled, exposing a rank of oddly shaped teeth interspersed with fleshy pink gums. She was about the same age as Jenny but looked a decade older. 'That's very kind of you, me love. Here you are.'

Jenny had only held one hand out, but it took both hands to receive the twenty-four coppers – two shillings in total – tipped from Mrs Billings' battered brown purse. 'You don't mind coppers, do you?'

'No,' laughed Jenny. 'They're always handy for the gas or electric meter.'

'That's where they came from,' chortled Mrs Billings.

It came as no great surprise to Jenny that Mrs Billings had 'borrowed' the pennies from the meter, somehow jerking it open and sealing it again – though how she hadn't a clue. It was common enough practice roundabout, but nobody ratted on the hard done by if they could help it.

She kept a straight face. 'Would you like a receipt?'

Even before she'd asked, Jenny knew the answer.

'No need, love. I knows I paid you and you knows I paid you. We're honest, God-fearing women, ain't we?'

Not entirely aware such a statement was true for either of them – although the war caught more people praying for divine intervention than in the years of peace – Jenny agreed that they were.

'Would you like Robin to drop them off for you?'

Four Marcel wave curlers, ugly-looking things made of steel and designed to clamp hair into rigid waves, looked as though their metal teeth were embedded in her head.

'No need. I've got the pram outside. I can put them across that.'

'That's a good idea,' said Jenny, the hoard of pennies sliding from her hands and into the cash drawer. 'I can carry one out for you if you want to take the other. They are quite heavy.'

'That would be a big 'elp, me dear.'

Each chair needing both hands, by sheer determination, they headed outside, the brass doorbell jangling like a fire engine behind them.

Mrs Billings led her to a coach-built pram, a splendid beast of shiny chrome and stiff navy-blue canvas. It wasn't unusual for baby prams to be used to transport items too heavy to carry, a sack of coal being the most common or the weekly shop for a growing family. No baby in the pram meant plenty of room for whatever the load, although two chairs were a bit bulky and out of the ordinary. Jenny was ready for anything – except that this pram wasn't empty. A baby of about eight months old or so was inside, sound asleep for now, though not for long.

The pram's springs gave a judder and made a sound like a scalded cat. No wonder the poor little mite woke up, blinking at first, then looking terrified at seeing a pair of chairs being loaded crossways and obstructing its vision. Poor thing, thought Jenny, as she imagined it finding itself behind a cage formed by the chair legs. No wonder it began wailing its head off.

'And you can stop that row an' all,' proclaimed Mrs Billings showing not one iota of sympathy for the terrified child.

Jenny couldn't help voicing her concern. 'Oh dear. Are you sure you don't want Robin to deliver them? It wouldn't be any bother.'

Mrs Billings didn't answer but leaned into the pram. 'Stop that racket or you'll get a fourpenny one!'

Jenny winced. Women around here were tough, and their offspring learned that their rule was law. 'You can't blame your baby for being upset. It can't see its mother.'

'It ain't my baby and I ain't its mother. Tain't nothing to do with me. Borrowed the pram from next door.'

'With the baby?'

'Yeah. Mother needed a break, and the kid needed a bit of fresh air. Killed two birds with one stone, you might say.'

Jenny watched as Mrs Billings bent into her task, one hand on her wobbly load, one on the handle of the baby pram. By the time she took the first step away, the child in the pram was bawling its head off.

'Poor thing,' murmured Jenny, and shook her head.

There was no time for recriminations or running after Mrs Billings and offering to lend her a hand. Robin was back.

His van pulled up beside her and the driver's door slammed as he got out of the driver's side and his son, Simon, out of the passenger side, looking his usual miserable self. Robin had collected him from the flat in Montpelier where he lived with his mother. As usual, he wore a sour smile on his thin features. Jenny said hello to him. As usual, his response was dully delivered, his tone of voice seeming to come from somewhere in his boots.

'Started your apprenticeship at Bawns?' she asked him. Her question, well meant as it was, got no more than a grunt in reply and a look of total disinterest.

There was a look of helplessness and indecision on Robin's face when he glanced at his son. Jenny felt for him. No matter what he did, Doreen had done all in her power to turn their children against their father. Robin sorely needed cheering up.

She adopted a cheerful smile and tone of voice to suit. 'I want to tell you something funny that happened earlier.'

She told him about Mrs Billings, the chairs and the pram complete with baby that she'd borrowed from a next-door neighbour to get her purchases home.

He laughed at the same time as shaking his head. 'I hear he

had a bit of a session on Friday night. Even old Adolf couldn't stop Alf Billings from getting drunk.'

'Very funny,' muttered Simon, who looked daggers at Jenny.

'I take it your mother is her usual vindictive self,' muttered Jenny to herself.

There was buoyancy to the way Robin informed his son that his bed was made and he could go on up if he liked.

Simon didn't need telling a second time. Head bowed, shoulders slumped, he scurried off to the back of the shop and the door which opened on the flight of the stairs that led to the next floor. He didn't go up immediately but stopped and glared angrily at his father.

'Are you coming now?' His tone was petulant.

Jenny thought him a selfish brat but wouldn't say so to Robin. He loved the boy. In fact, he loved both of his children, Simon and his twin sister Susan.

Robin nodded. 'Give me a minute to close the shop.'

Judging by the look on Simon's face, it was not the answer he'd wanted to hear. 'Huh!' he exclaimed, a sound of pure exasperation and wilful demand.

The door slammed and was followed by the thunder of stamping feet going up the stairs.

Robin stared into the interior of the shop to where the door had slammed shut. There was sadness in that look and helplessness. Jenny sensed the soreness of his feelings. No matter how hard he tried to interact with his son, nothing seemed to work.

'When does he begin his apprenticeship?' she asked. He'd already told her, but it wouldn't hurt to indulge him, although the truth was that she'd like to give both Simon and his father a shake. Simon was a weapon for his mother and Robin, adoring of his children, allowed himself to be used as a doormat.

He brightened. 'Next week. It'll give him something to do. He'll be learning a trade that'll stand him in good stead,' he said, a hint of pride creeping into his voice.

He needed that reassurance and more. Jenny helped it along.

'And Susan's doing well?'

Susan had already started her job in Woolworths – a position Doreen would no doubt take full advantage of. All that discounted face powder, cheap perfume and other items that were in short supply. Doreen never went out of the house without wearing face powder and lipstick.

Robin never admitted that he missed his daughter. 'I understand why she don't come visiting. Daughters tend to stick with their mothers, don't they?'

That's what he'd said to her. Jenny hadn't the heart to tell him that it wasn't necessarily so. Her youngest daughter, Gloria, who was eleven years old had doted on her father. Even though he was gone, she sometimes caught her with a faraway look on her face usually preceding the question, 'What would Dad say now that I'm doing so well at school?'

'He'd be very proud of you,' was the off-pat answer, though, quite honestly, she wasn't sure Roy would have noticed. He'd preferred a man's life, firstly getting involved with Sir Oswald Mosley's Blackshirts, then joining the army. His wife and children were a shield against what he was, a predilection shunned by society. Still, she would not besmirch his name in the eyes of his children. A warm memory of him was better than a harsh one.

'She's doing fine. I only wish... well... that both were a bit keener to see me.' He looked reflective.

Wishful thinking thought Jenny as Robin carried on.

'Sometimes I think they take after their mother more than

me. The only reason Simon's staying with me is that he needs some money for tools, and I said that I'll pay him if he does a bit around the shop.'

Jenny inwardly cringed. Simon had stayed before for the same reason. As yet he'd never done anything much to earn payment.

'That would be nice for you if he did do a bit,' she said, the smile she gave cracked and barely hid her true feelings.

Robin bent his head as he trained his eyes on her. 'I know what you're thinking. He's glad to take my money but not so glad to see me.' He shrugged. 'That's how it seems.'

He looked genuinely saddened.

Jenny reached up and caressed his cheek. 'Here's one that's glad to see you.'

At first, he only smiled at her, then, in the shade of the shop away from prying eyes, he kissed her. 'Sorry I can't take you out tonight. I thought it best to stay in whilst he's here.'

Robin had been estranged from his wife for some time but still saw his children – mostly when Doreen wanted to have fun with her friends – mainly male friends. From what was rumoured, she had more than one.

Jenny rubbed his arms, partly to ease the ache of arduous work, partly to ease the heartache she knew he suffered.

It pleased her to resurrect the warm smile she was used to.

'Do what you must do, Robin. He's your boy and every boy needs a father to look up to.'

Robin pulled a face. 'I do everything I can, but he's still a sulky little sod.'

Jenny stroked his face. 'He's growing up. They go through funny moods. My girls are sometimes like that.' *But not as often*, she thought to herself.

Deep inside, she harboured the suspicion that Doreen

primed Simon before he left her less-than-motherly breast. She had a vicious tongue and seemed to enjoy making life as difficult as possible for the husband she no longer wanted.

Jenny cupped Robin's dear face in both hands, noting the lines of worry beneath his eyes, and kissed his lips.

'Sorry I can't be with you tonight, but with Simon here...'

She waved a hand dismissively. 'Don't worry about me. Tilly is off out with friends from work tonight and Gloria is going to a first-aid class in Broad Plain Community Centre.' She laughed. 'I left them a Woolton pie for their supper. Hopefully they've left some for me.'

'And after that?'

'I'll be fine by myself. It gives me time to catch up with Thelma.'

In her heart, she would have preferred to be with Robin, but Simon's presence prevented that. An evening gossiping with Thelma would provide comfortable consolation.

7

The sun was hanging on after a warm day, painting the sky with strips of gold against shades of mauve and salmon pink.

As she'd hoped, Jenny's girls had left her enough pie for supper. After washing her portion down with a cup of tea, she trotted across the road to Thelma, who lived opposite her at number twelve in the horseshoe shape circlet of houses that was Coronation Close.

They'd become firm friends from the very start of Jenny moving out of the centre of Bristol, where crumbling tenements had snuggled close to each other in the medieval heart of the city. A lot of them had gone now, pummelled into dust with the first air raid of the war. There had been other raids since, the heaviest finishing in April of that year when a huge bomb nicknamed Satan had dropped in Beckington Road but failed to explode.

As usual, she went round the side of the house to the back door which opened directly into the kitchen. 'Anyone home?' Her voice echoed through the house.

'Where else would I be?' answered Thelma.

Jenny laughed. 'Bertrams Modes?'

Thelma took turns with other staff taking Saturday afternoon off from the upmarket dress shop. Not that she'd been idle. A pile of material sat on the dining table and more on top of the ancient treadle sewing machine, which trundled into action beneath the pedalling of Thelma's foot, the sound of the needle going up and down comforting. A domestic scene, one that stayed the same in peace or war.

'Make do and mend. I reckon that phrase was made with me in mind.'

Jenny agreed with her. 'How's the family?'

The family was Thelma's son, George, his Italian wife Maria and their little girl, Francesca, plus her two daughters, Mary and Alice.

'Fine. Maria said she'd be around later. The last note I had from George, he'd arrived in South America. Shouldn't have mentioned the place, of course – hush-hush and all that – but he did mention the tin of corned beef we had for supper one night before he left.'

'And corned beef means South America.'

'Good job I was good at geography at school and knew where Fray Bentos came from.'

Jenny laughed. 'You are clever.'

Thelma grinned. 'I've still got six tins of corned beef in the larder. Amazes me how much my George gets in his kitbag when he comes home on leave.'

'Shouldn't be too long before he's home.'

'A month at the most. Can't wait to see him.' Thinking of her son turned her eyes moist with tears. 'Neither can Maria.' A smile tipped the corners of her mouth. 'Another grandchild on the way. My George don't believe in wasting time when he's on leave.'

'A grandmother twice over.'

'Another five months by my reckoning.'

'I'm so pleased for you. Must be lovely to have them close at hand, to see your grandson so often.'

Thelma was indeed lucky. She'd been over the moon when, thanks to her long-time gentleman friend and council house rent collector, Bert Throgmorton, George, his wife and child had obtained their very own council house and moved into number fifteen Redruth Road. Turn left at the end of Coronation Close and left again and there was Redruth Road. Only a house in Coronation Close itself would have been better, but Thelma had consoled herself that a young family should have a bit of room. Nobody wants their mother-in-law on the doorstep. Close by in case of need was good enough, so Redruth Road suited the job.

At present, only Maria and the child occupied the house. George was in the merchant navy, on leave as often as possible, but the time spent home was short – though long enough to make another baby.

At the sound of the garden gate slamming, they both looked towards the living-room window. It was followed by the squeaking of pushchair wheels.

'Maria.' Thelma sprang from her chair. Such was her enthusiasm to greet her daughter-in-law, she went to open the front door before Maria had chance to navigate the path around the side of the house and go to the back.

It was as though sunshine was brightening the living room when Maria came in. Being Italian, she had an unblemished skin kissed by warmer climes, eyes like chocolate buttons and glossy black hair pinned into a chignon at the base of her neck. Her arms and legs were brown. She was one of the few people they knew who didn't care that she had no stockings to wear. If she used a brown crayon to draw a seam up the back of her legs to pretend she wore stockings, they looked very real.

Toddler in arms, Maria managed to wind one arm around Thelma and kissed her on both cheeks in a very Italian way that her mother-in-law had got used to.

Jenny got the same treatment and did the same back.

Little Francesca, an adventurous soul and bubbling with energy, had insisted on walking part of the way to her grand-mother's house. That was perhaps why she toddled around the living room a bit, then yawned, gazed round with brandy brown eyes until settling her gaze on the settee.

'I think she's ready for her nap,' murmured Thelma.

The little girl wasted no time clambering onto the settee, where she pulled a rug from the sofa arm, pulled it over her and curled up to sleep.

'What a little angel,' mused Jenny.

'Most of the time,' laughed Maria, her laughter as full of sunshine as she was. 'Now I put kettle on.'

She was like a whirlwind, off into the kitchen, clattering around with kettle, teapot, cups and saucers whilst imparting the high events of the week. Most of it was about what her child had been up to, how she was mending some of George's clothes and unpicking old jumpers she'd got hold of and making one big new one.

'So, he will be warm for the winter. I have also brought pastries with me. I did what I could for sugar and fat. I added cinnamon and grated apple rind. I think it has worked.'

Maria loved cooking. Neither Thelma nor Jenny had any doubt that the outcome of her baking would be delicious.

Balanced on a large Japanned tray, tea and pastries were brought to the table. They were round, shaped like jam tarts and smelt strongly of the cinnamon and apple she had used to give them flavour.

Fats, flour and especially sugar were in short supply. Maria had a way of making something from nothing. Every bit of everything got used in her house, a way of cooking inherited from Italian peasants who used herbs and spices to stretch what they had.

'Delicious,' said Jenny after taking a bite.

'I could eat more than one,' Thelma added.

Pleased with the praise, Maria's face was wreathed in smiles. 'That is what I brought them for. To be eaten. To be enjoyed.'

Maria was blooming like a rose for whom the best was yet to come. Expectant now, a new baby in due course. Jenny felt obliged to comment.

'A few more months and another little Dawson will be in the world.'

'This is true,' said Maria, her face flushing a pretty shade of pink. 'It is like the pastries. It is in the oven. Is that what you say?'

Thelma and Jenny burst out laughing.

'Yes. We do.'

'I am thankful. I love the one I have and will love this one too.'

'Your little one is growing,' Jenny remarked. 'Your George won't recognise her when he comes home again.'

Maria sighed. 'I hope it's not too long. I miss him so much.' All signs of exuberance abated, and a sad wistfulness came to her face.

Thelma clutched her hand. 'We all miss him, darling. The sooner he's back, the better.'

Teacups were raised to toast the deepest wish in their hearts.

'Here's to George. Come on home.'

* * *

After Maria had left, Thelma retrieved half a bottle of sherry from behind a jug commemorating Queen Victoria's diamond jubilee. The royal family were of great interest to Thelma, and she'd been collecting commemorative china and pictures for some time. The jug was the oldest item she had, and although it had a chip or two around the rim, it was also her favourite. This was partly due to it being the first one she'd been given. But also, because she'd been fond of the person who'd given it to her.

'Here,' she said, offering Jenny a small tumbler of sherry. 'Help me settle my nerves.'

'Gladly.'

Jenny eyed her friend over the rim of the whisky tumbler, its glass thick and faceted, so chunky it would likely last throughout the war and way beyond. 'Do you think our PC Percy Routledge is aware that his nephew has gone AWOL again?'

Cath Lockhart was Percy's sister and John was her eldest. Twenty years of age and called up over a year ago. The problem was he'd decided he didn't like the army and much preferred home.

Thelma almost choked. 'If he doesn't, then he's thicker than I thought. Though, mind you, I saw military police, the redcaps here the other day. Cath didn't give them chance to bang on the door though. Percy would have seen them then and she's trying to stop him finding out. Hates the army. They took him back to camp. Cath's mortified. She's keeping it under wraps, hoping that Percy doesn't find out anything about it.'

After taking another sip of the dark red fluid, Jenny frowned. 'He won't be pleased when he does find out. He finds others at fault, but not his own family. That's my take on him. To my mind he hasn't got enough serious work to keep him occupied.'

'He must be a right tartar to live with. His wife scurries behind him like a whipped dog.'

Jenny drew in her chin and eyed her with quizzical interest. She'd noticed a few things but wasn't one to speak out of turn. 'You don't think he hits her, do you?'

Thelma shrugged. 'I'm not sure about that, but what I do think is that he's lord of the manor under his own roof. His word is law. The poor woman can't move without his say-so.' Thelma shuddered. 'That wouldn't suit me.'

'Me neither,' declared Jenny, accompanying the comment with her own disgusted shudder.

Thelma only nodded at Jenny's statement. There had been a time when Jenny had been subject to the dictates of her husband. Roy Crawford joining the army had finished all that. Whilst he was serving in the army, Jenny had taken greater charge of her life and therefore was ready to carry on alone once her husband was in his grave, victim of a tropical disease. 'Never mind. Let's just drink to all those lads and lassies we know that are away serving their country.'

Jenny raised her glass. 'Bless them all.'

On the outside, Thelma was as exuberant as Jenny in her toast to everyone they knew who was away from home fighting for their country. In her heart, her thoughts kept returning to George and the jug given her by his father, the love of her life, the man who had broken her heart and left her to face being unmarried and a mother.

Jenny had an urge to make Thelma laugh before she left. The events surrounding Mrs Billings, the pram and the pair of chairs did that.

'Funny old world,' Thelma declared.

Jenny responded that indeed it was.

Later, after Jenny had gone, and Thelma gazed towards the living-room window, the bottle of sherry in hand, ready to be put back behind the Victorian jug, the sombre face of an elderly woman stared imperiously at some point beyond the spout. Her ample skirts were bunched towards the ornate handle. Queen Victoria looking every inch Queen and Empress, stern and authoritative.

Perhaps it was the three sherries Thelma had consumed or perhaps what happened next was due to the sudden chill that ran over her back. Her hand trembled. She caught the bottle before it slid off the edge of the sideboard, but didn't save the jug. As though suddenly having a life of its own, it seemed in the wrong place at the right time. With a resounding crash, it hit the floor, handle, base, spout and queen all on separate pieces of broken china. Queen Victoria was no more.

Thelma groaned. 'Gone forever.'

On sudden reflection it came to her that gone too was the man who had given it to her, George's father. Gone forever.

8

Maria left number twelve Coronation Close with a spring in her step and a face wreathed in smiles. She loved her husband and their child, plus the one she was expecting, which she confidently believed to be another girl and had already christened her Olivia, after the olive trees that grew so prolifically in the country of her birth. Most men might yearn for a son, but George only concerned himself that any child of his was healthy. That was all that mattered.

She also loved her mother-in-law. If she could have had a choice of mother-in-law, she would still have chosen Thelma.

The man who lived next door to her in Redruth Road was lounging at his front gate looking as though he was waiting for someone whilst reading the newspaper which he held wide open. His head moved from side to side as his gaze skimmed across the print – small print because of the war – and poor-quality paper. Just a few pages, half of what a newspaper used to be.

On seeing her approach, he looked up and straightened. The look on his face was never cheerful, but something about it brought her happiness up short, like a train running into the buffers. Folding the newspaper in half, he brought it up in front of him so that the front page and its dense black headline faced her.

It wasn't often that he spoke to her or any of the neighbours, except to complain about children kicking a ball into his front garden or that they should be a bit quieter when they came home from the pub. He'd never been unfriendly towards her despite her Italian heritage. Some people couldn't seem to get it into their heads that not everyone agreed with what the enemy – whether Italian or German – believed in.

On this occasion he stared with an oddly wide-eyed expression, mouth turned down at the corners.

There are times when one's instinct picks up a deeper meaning behind the expression on a face and this was one of them.

Taking her courage in both hands, Maria dared ask, 'Mr Wendell, is something wrong?'

His expression remained unchanged as he fussed with the newspaper. Hands holding each corner, he held it out in front of him, arms full stretch. The big black letters shouted a headline she had hoped never to see.

HEAVY LOSSES ON SOUTH ATLANTIC CONVOY.

Taking one trembling hand from the pushchair, she took the paper from her neighbour. The warmth of June suddenly seemed to have changed into November.

'They names the ships inside,' he said in a low, gravelly voice that to some might seem to hold no emotion. But Henry Wendell did *feel* emotion; it was just that men of his generation were trained to keep a stiff upper lip, not to show emotion.

Only cissies did that. That was what the English believed. Maria had always been surprised at the English attitude. Italian men would show emotion, passionately, deeply. She thanked God that George was more like an Italian than an Englishman in this regard.

Resting the handlebar of the pushchair against her belly, Maria used both hands to open the newspaper.

'No. Just the front page.'

He was guiding her, forcing her to read the rest of the article. The wording beneath the headlines was still fuzzy. She shook her head. 'My English. I do not understand all of it.'

Henry took the paper from her and read aloud. 'Six merchant ships were sunk in the latest convoy to leave Buenos Aires carrying beef and grain...'

Maria gasped. Her fingers curled over the handle of the pushchair. 'Six.'

'Six. From Buenos Aires.' He paused as he waited for her to digest what he had said. 'Your husband?'

She nodded silently. George had been on the South American run for quite a while and had reckoned it safer than crossing the Atlantic from North America. 'We're coming up from the south,' he'd told her. 'Bigger expanse of ocean and not so close to the enemy submarine pens in France. It's them devils that do most of the sinking. Not so many make it down into the South Atlantic. That's what makes it safer.'

'Can you read me out the names of the ships,' Maria asked quietly.

Henry cleared his throat and opened the paper at the second page, the usual spot where suspected casualties and those missing action were mentioned. In the case of merchant or royal navy personnel, that mostly meant they were drifting in the sea in a lifeboat and hopefully safe.

He uttered the name of the ship she'd been dreading to hear. Cold as her blood had been before hearing the name, it turned colder now.

Camborne Castle. George's ship.

The world spun around her as he carried on and read out loud, 'A list of those missing, presumed dead, will be issued in due course once the families have been informed.'

She clasped and unclasped her hand, pointing at the newspaper. 'Can I... His mother... she will be...' She closed her eyes as if that might help her cope. But nothing would.

He pressed the newspaper into her trembling hands. 'You take it to Mrs Dawson. She'll want to know. And give her my kind regards and best wishes.' He sighed. 'There's going to be many a mother needing hope and the good wishes of others before this war is over.' He touched the brim of his cap. 'I knows you was born in a country that's our enemy now, but you married George Dawson and that makes you one of us. God bless you, Mrs Dawson.'

Murmuring her thanks, Maria took the paper and turned the pushchair round so quickly, the stout rubber wheels whined against the pavement.

She was hurrying back to Coronation Close, yet her legs didn't seem to be going fast enough – she wished she could fly, land in the living room next to the dresser that groaned with coronation china, and cry and scream that it couldn't be true. It just couldn't be true.

9

Jenny was halfway down the garden path sweeping up masses of trimmings from the privet hedge, a job she tended to leave until the end of the day. The idea was that she could have a bath after that before going to bed and pretend that the minimal water level was enough to luxuriate in. It wasn't but still felt good after snipping away at the hedges.

Thelma called to her from the other side of the road. 'There'll be no hedge left if you carry on snipping with those shears.'

'Good. I could have a wall built instead then I wouldn't have to do any trimming.'

Thelma's cheerful expression melted on seeing her daughter-in-law dashing back into Coronation Close waving a newspaper.

Thelma stood like a statue, alarm frosting her face into a tight grimace.

'What have you forgotten, my girl?' Even to her own ears her attempt at jolliness seemed false. But there it was. Hope was a shield against the very worst that could befall.

A breathless Maria thrust the newspaper at Thelma. On sensing something was up Jenny dropped her shears and came darting across the road.

Even before she said, 'My God. George's ship's gone down,' Jenny had already guessed that Maria's return had been for a serious reason.

'What about casualties?' she asked once the initial dryness had left her mouth.

Thelma's eyes scanned the article. 'There are survivors, but also casualties.'

'Do you know any of his mates that were on the ship with him?'

Thelma shook her head. 'No. Bob Norton in the next street was on a different ship. Same run though. And Nobby Clarke is royal navy.' She gave a little laugh. 'And never the twain shall meet.'

Her laugh at the small joke was too fragile to be serious. Jenny knew her friend well. She was putting on a brave face, but deep down she was worried. Seriously worried.

A grim look passed between all three women, Maria's bottom lip quivering as though she was on the verge of breaking down into floods of tears. None of them wanted to believe that George was dead.

'They don't let you know until they're sure, do they?' asked Jenny, trying her best to sound positive, the only alternative to drowning in a sea of utter devastation. Facing the loss of a beloved child – even when that child was a grown man – was never easy.

'Perhaps, but...' Thelma stopped in mid-sentence as Maria's legs buckled and she slumped to her knees. 'Maria!'

Thelma put one arm around her daughter-in-law.

'If you can bring the pushchair,' she called over her shoulder to Jenny. 'I'll get her inside.'

Assisted by Thelma, Maria made it up the garden path, into the hallway and eventually into the living room where she slumped into an armchair.

Feeling sick to her stomach, Thelma began wafting the newspaper in front of Maria's face but stopped when the headline caught her attention for the second time. It was as if the words were haunting her, daring her to hope – or to accept the worst. Throwing it to one side, she picked up a copy of *Woman* magazine and used that to fan her daughter-in-law's face. It had fewer pages, and the paper was thin, and she could stomach its headlines.

The toddler had fallen asleep in the pushchair. Jenny eyed the rosy cheeks and peaceful expression. Here was one unaware of the horrors of war. All was peace and happiness.

Thelma brought a cup of water from the kitchen.

Maria came to, her eyes big and round as she asked, 'Is George alive? When will they tell us?'

Thelma smiled hesitantly and gave her daughter-in-law's shoulder a comforting rub. 'We would have heard by now if he was one of the casualties.'

Thelma wanted it to be true. In these turbulent times, anything could happen. There was a system in place, but things often went awry. She only hoped that they would hear soon – one way or another. In the meantime, she took it as her duty to keep up Maria's spirits.

Maria pushed her silky black hair from her face. 'I will pray for him tonight. I will pray for him tomorrow. I will go to church.'

'That's right, love,' said Thelma, stroking another stray tress back from her daughter-in-law's face. 'Praying's as good as anything at times like these.'

For her part, Thelma did not go to church and seldom prayed. Tonight, might be a different matter. Anything to bring her son home.

Seeing the shock on Maria's face filled her with love. She hadn't felt that way when she'd first learned that George had fallen in love with and intended marrying an Italian girl.

George had met his bride in her home country. The shock of receiving a letter from him a few years ago saying he'd married her had taken Thelma aback. Her dearest wish had been for him to marry a girl of their own kind, preferably one who lived around the corner. Deep inside, she had harboured the fear that he wouldn't come home or, if he did, he and his new wife and any children that might come along would go back to Italy and live close to her family. Daughters tended to cling to their mothers once they had their own children. But it hadn't turned out that way, and for that Thelma was grateful.

The colour came back to Maria's face, along with a sigh of relief, a closing of her eyes, a genuflecting of her delicate hands across her breast. Without her saying a word, Thelma knew that Maria had said a heartfelt prayer, an entreaty that George would be safe. She fervently hoped it would be answered.

'I'll just make a pot of tea,' said Jenny, recognising that Thelma and her daughter-in-law might want a moment together.

'I am so afraid,' said Maria, her voice trembling.

'Our George's got a lot of common sense. He's a fighter. All we have to do now is wait,' Thelma proclaimed.

Tea tray carried before her, Jenny had overheard the tail end of the conversation.

At that moment Alice, Thelma's younger daughter, came

dashing in, her face flushed and breathless from whatever she'd been doing.

'What's for supper, Mum?' she called from the kitchen.

'Fried giblets,' barked Thelma, somewhat miffed that the important conversation had been interrupted by something so trivial as her daughter's demand for food.

Alice, thirteen years old now, poked her head around the door and pulled a face. 'In that case, I'll have bread and cheese, ta very much.'

'Only joking. There's cheese and potato pie. Won't take long to heat up in the oven. I'll do it for you.'

'It's all right. I can do it. Is this pie all for me or have I got to share with our Mary?'

'It's all yours. Mary's had hers.' Mary had been on the early shift from the factory, had dashed in, washed, changed and dashed out again.

'Out again,' laughed Alice in the same sing-song voice she'd heard her mother use.

'Are you going to tell the girls about George?' Jenny whispered.

Thelma shook her head emphatically. 'No. This war was started by adults. It's up to the adults to deal with it. I'd like my Alice to stay a child for as long as possible. As for my Mary...' She frowned. 'I've missed the boat there. She's growing up too quickly.' Thelma's eyebrows, black and thick with eyebrow pencil, dived into a deep vee. 'All these young men from all over the world, lonely, looking for fun...'

'And too good-looking for their own good.'

'Too good-looking for my Mary's good. I worry about her.'

'You worry about everybody,' remarked Maria as she tucked a blanket around the now sleeping child.

Thelma agreed that she did. 'Someone has to.'

Maria's dark eyes fixated on her mother-in-law. 'I am sorry for bringing this news.'

'Don't worry, love,' she said, giving Maria's shoulder a firm squeeze. 'We'll know more before very long.'

Jenny offered to walk Maria back home. As they walked, it occurred to Jenny that Maria had to be lonely – a foreigner in a strange land, her husband away at sea. What was worse was that there were those who went out of their way to taunt her. One day up at the shops, she'd seen some scruffy kids shouting abuse and saluting like they'd seen the Italian dictator do on the newsreels at the Broadway Picture House. Jenny had chased them away with the threat that she would tell their mothers – better still their fathers and they'd get a good thrashing.

She'd apologised to Maria, who shook her head and said, 'It does not matter. They're just children. They don't understand.'

When they got to Maria's council house, one she'd been lucky to get just before the beginning of the war, Jenny escorted her down the garden path and made sure the door was securely closed before she headed for home.

When she got there, Tilly was waiting for her in the kitchen, drinking a cup of tea and nibbling at a sandwich.

'Is that all you're having?' Jenny asked. 'I did make an apple pie from the windfalls we dried before last Christmas. Not much custard, but enough.'

The way Tilly kept her head down was uncharacteristic. Her eldest daughter had always had an open face, one easily read and incapable of keeping emotions hidden. Apprehension suddenly gripped Jenny's stomach.

She sank onto a kitchen chair, a honey-coloured pine one she'd purchased from Robin. She leaned forward, a whole host of possibilities for her daughter's demeanour flipping like playing cards in her mind. 'Is something wrong? Please tell me. I promise I won't be angry.'

Tilly pushed the sandwich she'd been eating around her plate before raising her eyes – such blue eyes – such serious eyes that could melt the hardest heart. 'I don't want you to be angry. Promise you won't be angry.'

That feeling of apprehension immediately intensified.

Determined her voice would not crack, she replied softly, 'I promise.'

Tilly drew in her lips before exclaiming. 'I've decided that as soon as I'm eighteen I'll join the Land Army.'

Jenny's jaw dropped and for a moment she couldn't find her voice. She consoled herself that the war might end between now and then so for the moment at least she had nothing to worry about.

'You must be between eighteen and forty to be a land girl,' she finally managed. It struck her suddenly that she herself was only a year over that upper age limit. Forty-one. Where had the years gone?

'I'm almost eighteen. So, I'll join in six months' time.' She reached across and took hold of her mother's hand. 'I'll be fine, Mum. I can look after myself.'

'But your job...'

Head held high, Tilly stated in no uncertain fashion that she was bored working as a filing clerk at the Royal London Life insurance office in the city centre. 'I want to do something useful. Something that counts. Please try and understand, Mum. This war is horrible, but I want to do something that makes a difference – even if it's only to plant carrots or milk a cow.'

There was such pleading on the young face, and much as

she wanted to keep her daughter safe, Jenny knew that she had to let go. She vaguely recalled an older woman telling her that your child is only on loan. Once they're ready, they will fly the nest – and you had to let them go. Anyway, her joining up was six months away. Much as she wished the war would be over by then and her daughter's plans would come unstuck, Jenny didn't think it would happen. There was too much going on – the fighting having spread to North Africa.

'If you're sure.'

'I am.'

Jenny sighed, a restive, worried look in her eyes. 'Well, at least you'll be safe on a farm.' She was thinking of George as she said it.

'Unless I get run over by a tractor or a stampede of cows.' Tilly laughed.

Feeling glad she had no sons, her mother joined her.

Once the laughter had ceased, she told Tilly about George.

Tilly made a slight moaning sound. 'Poor George.'

'Yes,' said Jenny. 'Poor George.'

The serious, senior look came to her young daughter's face. 'I feel guilty not doing anything, Mum. That's what you must understand. I have to do my bit.'

Jenny felt as though her heart had swollen to bursting point. Taking her daughter's hand in hers, she nodded and said, 'If that's what you want to do, then I won't stand in your way.'

Tilly's smile was like the sun suddenly coming out from behind a cloud. 'It's different. It will all be so different.'

Later that evening, when she was sitting alone on the back step staring at the sky, Jenny said a silent thankyou that Tilly wasn't a boy. A farm was relatively safe – very safe when compared to a battle zone. God protect George Dawson, wher-ever he was.

10

It was gone twelve at night, but Cath Lockhart, Percy Routledge's sister at number eight Coronation Close was up at the window, the curtain held slightly ajar. She hadn't been able to sleep soundly after the visit of the military police, their red caps an emblem feared by those who absconded from military duty, her son amongst them. If there'd been a choice she would have held onto him. Better a live son than a dead one. The visit had frightened her enough. On top of that she would have to face her brother, Percy which in itself would be quite an ordeal.

A voice she recognised rang out loud and clear. 'Put that light out, draw the blackout curtains properly or you're on a charge.'

'Bloody 'ell. Don't that brother of yours ever go to bed,' her husband, Bill, grumbled from the bed behind her whilst giving the pillow a good punch with his fist.

Cath bit her lip. She'd so looked forward to her brother moving into Coronation Close before the war and had been proud to say that he was a policeman. She no longer felt quite the same. He took his duties very seriously – too seriously, some might say.

Forehead resting on window frame, the breath from her sigh misting a glass pane, Cath searched for an excuse for him being the way he was, but it wasn't easy.

'I wish he would stop doing it. It's getting embarrassing what with that and the other stuff he's been doing. It's not 'is job but he's going round looking in bins in case somebody's thrown out a bone that's still got a bit of gristle on it.'

'Long as it ain't ours,' grumbled Bill. 'If I got to pay a fine there'll be 'ell to play. The Ministry of Food don't take no prisoners when they think stuff 'as been wasted. Who's he after now?'

Cath tilted her head slightly so she could see better. If there hadn't been a full moon, she wouldn't have seen anything. The streetlights were out and when there was no moon outside, there was total darkness. She could just about see an elderly neighbour in old-fashioned nightgown floating between the trees like a ghostly apparition.

'Mrs West at number four.'

Bill turned his face into the pillow. 'The poor old girl don't know what she's doing.'

Cath bit her lip. His comment made her feel sorry for old Mrs West, who had moved in with her daughter, Betty. When she'd been in her own home, the dear old soul had got into the habit of wandering around at all times of the day and night. Eventually, her daughter had made the decision that her mother could not be trusted to stay in the Victorian terraced house where she lived in Eastville, an old suburb on the eastern side of Bristol. There was the odd occasion when she still wandered around, but at least Betty and her family were there to retrieve her.

But she did daft things. She couldn't help herself, but Percy gave no quarter for any physical or mental shortfall. The law was black and white. She wished she'd accepted that more readily before he'd come to Coronation Close.

Cath's brother, PC Percy Routledge, had moved into number five some time ago before the war. At first, she'd been excited at having him so close by. Unfortunately, she'd forgotten how officious he could be towards family, friends and neighbours alike. Not that he had any friends, as such, and the way he was going wasn't likely to gain any.

It hadn't been so much of a problem before the war, but with the advent of new and sometimes trivial laws, he'd made it his patriotic duty to keep everyone in Coronation Close on the straight and narrow. Even the air-raid wardens were not such a nuisance as he was. Not a day went by when he wasn't sitting on the tail of somebody in Coronation Close, though Cath had noticed he was wary of upsetting her friend Thelma Dawson at number twelve, who was fierce when roused – not that he could find much to fault with her.

About to let the curtain go, Cath stopped herself. From here at the head of Coronation Close, she had a view beyond the green, which was shaded by three immature sycamore trees. Her house was poised slightly higher than those on either side, so she could see all the way to where Coronation Close joined the main road.

A figure ran into the close and although Percy's brass buttons turned in that direction, the running person slipped through the gate of number twelve – Thelma Dawson's house – too quickly for him.

'Mary Dawson's late coming home. She'll be for it.'

There was no response from Bill, except for a resounding snore.

She saw Percy hesitate – for the shiny buttons certainly belonged to him – obviously in two minds whether any law had been broken. In official terms, it was unlikely. In the Dawson household, it might be another story. Mary was coming home late. Thelma would not be amused.

* * *

Mary had taken off her shoes before entering Coronation Close, had closed the garden gate carefully and did the same with the front door. Although she could do with using the bathroom, she decided to leave it for now. Get to bed first, leave it for an hour and then attempt to go downstairs when she was sure her late entrance had not been noticed.

Thelma appeared at the top of the landing. Mary blinked as the single hanging lightbulb came on, her face upturned, mouth slightly open as she fought to find the right words, a believable excuse. Quite frankly, there was only one that came to mind.

Turning her head aside in a futile bid to hide her expression, she announced that the bus had been crowded. 'The conductress said there was no more room inside or on top. I had to walk.' Fancying her chances that all was well, and she'd got away with it, Mary swung her shoes to the ground. 'My shoes were hurting me. I've got blisters.'

'My arse,' exclaimed Thelma. 'I weren't born yesterday!'

Her right hand was clenched ready to administer retribution. Mary was saved by an insistent knocking at the front door.

Thelma grimaced. 'Who the bloody hell's that?'

Mary galloped up the stairs even before Thelma had reached for the switch that doused the landing light.

'I'll speak to you later. Don't think you've got away with it,' Thelma warned.

There was blackness inside and out when she opened the door to her friend Cath's brother.

'Percy. Am I showing a light?'

Her voice was crisp and had an edge to it, a warning to him that he was in for a fight if he cared to chance his luck and pick holes.

'No. I cannot see a single chink in your blackout arrangements. You're one person in Coronation Close who I can count on to obey the rules.'

Smarmy, she thought. If he wasn't Cath's brother, she'd give him short shrift.

'It's gone midnight, Percy. Say what you want to say and let me get to my bed. I need my beauty sleep.'

'Of course you do. It's just that I saw someone come up your garden path.' His chuckle was insincere and made her toes curl. Cath was a nice person. Her brother was a sly fox and not to be trusted. As for that family of his – downtrodden, under his thumb. She imagined living with him was like being in prison with no chance of remission.

'What's it to you?' Her tone of voice remained hostile.

That sickly, slightly pompous chuckle again. 'I thought it might be an intruder.'

'It wasn't. It was my Mary. Not that you didn't already guess that, Percy. But there you are, you can't help but poke yer nose in, can you?'

Before he had chance to say any more, the door was slammed in his face.

Thelma was up the stairs and into Mary's bedroom. Before the war and back further, the girls had shared a room. That was before George married Maria. Alice now slept in that room.

A petulant-looking Mary was undressed and wearing her nightdress.

Thelma was not in the mood for letting her eldest daughter get away with anything. The young just didn't seem to understand that their mothers had had the same careless and carefree attitude to love, romance and having fun when they were young. She'd fallen into trouble. She didn't want her daughter to go through the same pain of being abandoned, of being ostracised by society.

Her stance was grim, her jaw set in a straight line. 'So where have you been that took you an age to walk home?'

'In town.' Mary moved towards the bedroom door. Her eyelashes fluttered and not once did she raise her eyes to meet those of her mother. 'I need to go to the bathroom.'

Thelma ignored the plea. 'Out with soldiers, were you?'

'Mum. I need to pee.'

She raised her voice. 'Answer my question.'

Mary raised her chin defiantly, unknowingly exposing the love bite on her neck and not noticing the sudden tautness of her mother's features. 'So, what if I was? I was out enjoying myself and why not, I say? Why shouldn't I live for today. A bomb might drop on me tonight. Old people like you don't seem to realise that. You've forgotten how it is to be young. You've forgotten what it's like to have fun. All you do is work and sew and do nothing else. No wonder Bert doesn't come around here so much nowadays...'

A red mark appeared where Thelma slapped Mary's face. 'That's enough!'

Mary gasped. She covered the redness with her hand, her eyes wide with jaw-dropping surprise.

Thelma immediately regretted her action, but Mary had inadvertently hit a nerve. She was right about Bert. He hadn't been around so much as he used to be. She'd told herself he had important duties at the council offices where he worked as senior rent collector. Plus war duties. Fire watching and suchlike.

'I hate you,' Mary shouted. 'I hate you.'

She ran off down the stairs. Thelma knew she was sobbing but couldn't bring herself to make amends. Mary was at a vulnerable age, the same age she'd been when George had been conceived. The father had disappeared, and she'd been left, a single woman with a baby who she had refused to give up.

There was guilt that she'd hit her daughter, but the regret of having fallen by the wayside in her youth had made up her mind. She would not allow Mary to ruin her life as she had done.

The soldiers of the British Empire and those from Europe had arrived in droves. They were everywhere, speaking with attractive accents and bringing glamour to the dull, grey British streets. She would protect and instruct her daughter as best she could.

It was tempting to wait out on the landing for Mary to come back up from the bathroom and take the opportunity to say that she was sorry for slapping her face. Deep-seated determination to control the situation and have the last word overruled that. It was for Mary's own good, that's what Thelma told herself as she closed her bedroom door.

If only she was still a child. If only there was no war. But there it was. Mary was growing up and the war that had begun in 1939 still raged. The threat of invasion had receded somewhat, but the war wasn't over yet and its privations were biting hard. Who knew when the end of it all would be? According to the new prime minister, Winston Churchill, the country would never surrender. It was a daunting prospect, one that filled her with fear for her children's future. And her own, for that matter.

Bedroom light off, she took the opportunity to open the curtains a crack and look out. The sudden emergence of the moon from behind a bank of cloud silvered the windows of her neighbours' houses on the other side of the street. The sky glowed with its light, black turned to indigo.

Notepad and pen in hand Percy Routledge was standing in the centre of the oval-shaped green at the heart of Coronation Close turning to each house in turn and making notes.

Within weeks of him and his family moving in, the residents had learned to give him a wide berth. The man was a snitch who wouldn't hesitate to get someone in trouble for the slightest reason, whether they were guilty of a misdemeanour or not.

Thelma had voiced her reservations about Percy to her friend Jenny Crawford in number two. She stated her firm belief that his behaviour would one day get him in trouble. 'If he had a whip, he'd crack it. Mark my words. One day he'll be laying down the law and spying on the wrong person. He'll get his comeuppance – and not soon enough in my opinion.'

11

'Lie down. Go to sleep.'

Albert Routledge had wet the bed again. His mother had swiftly swapped the wet bedding for fresh.

Her little boy did as he was told. Like her, he wanted to be asleep when his father came home. Sleep brought oblivion from their constrained life.

Margaret sped downstairs without turning on the landing light. She knew those stairs by heart. Once downstairs, she pushed the wet bedding into the galvanised boiler in the corner of the kitchen. It was where all the laundry was done.

Once that was done, she dashed back up the stairs. Before going back to her own bed, she looked in on Albert. He hadn't been well of late, not that wetting the bed had much to do with that. He just hadn't grown out of the habit. But he would. That's what she told herself. That's also what she'd told Percy. Not that he'd taken much notice.

'No drinks after midday.'

That was his cure. And a spell in the coalhouse under the stairs when the lad dared to say that he was thirsty.

He'd been thirsty a lot of late. And his cheeks were red. Percy refused to accept that he might be falling ill. Unlike Percy, she didn't believe that the boy was just being difficult.

It was hard to sleep when such worries troubled her – and there were plenty of them. Alone for now in the marital bed – a blissful event because it meant she could sprawl out, have the light on if she wanted, read or sing to herself – she tried to divert her thoughts to other things, silly girlish things like wishing she could curl her hair, but she had no curlers. Strips of rag torn from an old pillowcase would do the job, but she dared not do that either. Percy wouldn't like it. She wondered if she dared do it tonight before he got back. The trouble was she had no idea what time he would get back.

She thought of what he would say if he caught her.

'A woman must be grateful with what God has given her. No curls. Curls are born of vanity.'

She'd released her hair from its austere bun and dared to smear a little Vaseline on her lips. 'Because they're chapped,' she'd said when he'd accosted her about the shininess.

He'd accepted that.

Before they'd married, she'd dared curl her hair and wear lipstick. That stopped not long after they were married. Once, she'd dared smear her lips with lipstick. He'd noticed and instantly demanded she go back into the house and take it off.

'Only harlots wear lipstick,' he'd growled when she'd dared to protest.

That same evening, he'd confiscated every vestige of make-up and thrown it into the big metal bin meant purely for the ashes from the fireplace.

'And don't dare buy any more. Do you understand?'

The tip of his nose had pressed against hers. His features

had been a night-time caricature of his daytime, ordinary, bland, boring face.

She'd taken a step back. He'd stepped forward. She'd repeated her action, and he'd repeated his until she was standing with her back pressed hard against the wall, nowhere else to go.

She shuddered at the thought of his thumb rubbing the last vestige of lipstick smeared across her mouth.

'I'm sorry,' she'd said, her voice trembling. 'I will try to please you. You know that.'

The hardness of his forehead had purposely banged against 'I don't want you to please me. I want you to obey me. Just as you promised on our wedding day.'

She'd dared to open her mouth and say, 'I like to look nice for you...'

Something in him had snapped without warning. He'd grabbed a handful of her hair and dragged her across the room to the mirror that formed the centre panel of the wardrobe and thrust her against it. He'd held her there by her hair, pulling it back from her face and twisting it at the nape of her neck.

'This is how I want you to wear your hair,' he'd said. 'In a respectable manner, as befits my wife. No curls. No make-up. See?' He'd banged her forehead against the mirror, brought her back and asked her again. 'See? That is how I want you to look. Not tawdry. Not attracting the looks of other men. And no women friends.'

'Your sister...'

'No women friends. No cups of tea with my down-at-heel sister. You're my wife. You vowed to love, honour and obey me – until death do us part.'

She'd dared not disobey. Neither did the children. They were all under his iron-fisted rule that only showed within his house, within his own family. The outside world would never know – unless a miracle occurred.

On hearing the clang of the garden gate followed by heavy footsteps, she pulled the bedclothes over her and pretended to be asleep and prayed that a miracle would indeed occur – even if it was death.

12

It was hard for Mary Dawson to know quite how to respond to the news that her brother was missing. She felt guilty about living her life when goodness knows where George might be. The possibility that she might never see him again weighed heavily on her mind, and yet she was enjoying her life. War had brought added excitement that she didn't want to miss out on. Still, she felt she had to offer some small sympathy and anyway showing she cared would help heal the fracas when she'd come in late. The slap across her face was still fresh in her mind.

'Mum. I won't go out tonight if you need me here. I can't bear you looking so glum.'

'Glum? When have I ever let anything make me glum? Anyway, we don't know how George is yet. No news is good news, as they say.'

Mary knew her mother was putting on a brave face, but even so, it was hard to know what to do, how to react.

'I'll stay in with you. If you want me to.'

Thelma shook her head. 'Eat your tea. And go out and enjoy yourself. Our George will turn up, mark my words.'

Why not, she thought. Life seems so short nowadays. We're living daily with the fear that we might not be here tomorrow.

With a mixture of relief and guilt, Mary gobbled down her tea. It had been a long day at work and being worried about her missing brother had declined the stodge on offer in the factory canteen.

Stomach full, she swooped on the bathroom before anyone else could, clutching a single bath cube she'd bought in a sale in Woolworths, one that had perhaps fallen out of a packet and was being sold off cheaply. The silvery wrapper had seemed to wink at her. She closed her eyes as she held it to her nose and breathed in the perfume described on the wrapper as lily of the valley. The very thought of immersing herself in a tub of scented water made her feel special and in a hurry to strip off her work clothes, put on some clean underwear and that pretty dress of blue silk with pink rosebuds on the cuffs her mother had cut down from something that might at one time have had a bustle under its rear.

Giggling at the very thought of wearing a cushion on her bum soon disappeared once the bathroom door was locked. She grimaced at the black line her mother had scrawled on the cold enamel bath, having imagined herself immersed in soapy suds up to her neck. Not allowed of course. Five inches was about it. That's what the black measuring line was all about. Still, a girl could dream. Dare she break the rules?

A warning came from outside the bathroom door. 'Don't drown yourself in water. Stick to the rules.'

'I will,' she shouted back. Not for the first time, she wondered whether her mother could see through the door or through her skull into her brain. It certainly seemed like it at times.

Sighing and thinking about the night to come took Mary's mind off such trivialities. The gas jets of the bulky geyser that heated the water spluttered and popped before the water pounded through the pipes into the bath.

Seeing little steam, she plunged the tips of her fingers into the rusty-coloured surface to check for warmth and grimaced. It wasn't cold, but she would have preferred it to be a bit better than tepid. 'Bloody war.'

Shivering, she watched as the water rose in the bath until eventually it reached the black line. As the bath cube released the faint smell of lily of the valley, she couldn't resist dipping her toes in, then her foot, followed by her whole body.

Once immersed, she thought of the night to come. Thankfully, her mother had not pressed her further on why she'd come home late the other night, where she was going tonight and who she was going with. For that she was grateful. She'd never liked being questioned and now she was older she figured she was enough of an adult to make her own decisions and live her life as she pleased.

She'd hung the blue dress on the back of the door and eyed it, imagining how it would swirl in a light breeze – or a jitterbug – the dance taught her by one of the stream of Canadians she'd taken a fancy to. They'd been just fun, but her new beau she thought a bit more than that. *Now how can I describe him*, she thought to herself. *Exotic? Yes*, she decided lying back in the last warmth of the water which was swiftly turning cold.

She'd seen the look in her mother's eyes when she'd first mentioned him. Wary. Worried.

Never mind. It was a fine night, and the blue dress flattered her gleaming red hair and the dancing brightness of her eyes.

Once she'd dried off, she headed for the mirror above the fireplace in the living room, face powder, lipstick and mascara in hand. She spit on the hard block of mascara, which was contained in a small plastic compact, applied it, stood back and beamed at the result. It did seem that it had lengthened and blackened her eyelashes.

Pouting at her reflection, she said, 'Sweetie, you're absolutely gorgeous.' In her mind it was him saying it, her latest handsome Canadian serviceman who was over here to protect the mother country from the threatening foe. 'Mwa!' Her red lipstick left an imprint on the mirror when she kissed it.

'Not too much lipstick, young lady.'

The sudden intervention made her jump.

After grabbing her pale pink crocheted handbag and slipping her feet into her white leather sandals, Mary made a dash for the door, though not swiftly enough to escape hearing her mother reminding her not to be late.

'I'll not have you out till all hours and have Cath's brother sneaking in here to tell on you,' came the strident voice as Mary slammed the door closed.

No, Mary thought rolling her eyes. Please not that again. Cath's brother, PC Routledge, had taken her by surprise the other night. Perhaps if he hadn't been loitering, her mother might not have been alerted. My, but older people could be such party poopers at times!

The incident when she'd been out of sight overhearing Percy's conversation with the man in the trench coat didn't seem as interesting now as it had then. All she recalled was his name – Quentin Appleyard. An odd name. She thought it sounded as though it had been lifted from a cheap novel. Oh well. Who cared! Her mother would probably tell her off for being nosy, so best not to say anything.

She dashed down the garden path and didn't stop for breath until she got to the bus stop, where several people in the queue of about ten people smiled in welcome, said hello or eyed her admiringly.

Brenda Andrews from the next street, a girl of ample proportion and cheeks that almost matched the colour of her lipstick, commented on her dress. 'Must have cost you a fair packet.'

'Nineteen shillings and sixpence,' Mary replied in a lofty manner.

There was no way she was going to admit that her mother had made it from something she'd bought at a jumble sale. Such events were more popular now than they'd ever been, what with all the shortages, but the secret was that her mother had a good eye for quality and design, plus a trusty treadle sewing machine.

The floaty blue dress had been floor length – obviously expensive when new. 'There's enough material here for half a dozen pairs of camiknickers and even two or three full-length petticoats. Full length means I don't need to use elastic.'

Mary grinned at the memory. Her mother hoarded elastic, along with buttons, thread and bits of old lace cut from yet more dresses from an earlier age.

I'm lucky to have a mother who can sew. Wish I could do it. She couldn't. Only a few darns and mends – especially of stockings, which were in as short supply as elastic.

'How's your workmate, Pauline? I 'ear she's getting engaged.'

'She is. Jeff has finally gone and popped the question.'

It had all happened just as Pauline had wished it to happen. Two days later, she'd admitted the wedding had been brought forward. 'A bit earlier than planned, but under the circumstances...'

The circumstances were easy to guess at. Pauline was in the family way. A wedding was in the offing whether Jeff or Pauline wanted it or not. Pauline would definitely want it.

'I'm working up to six months,' Pauline had told her. 'We need to get some money together. His aunt has a couple of rooms to rent and won't mind there being a baby.'

A couple of rooms. Mary's brow creased at the thought of it. Two rooms in a dingy house shared with an aged aunt. Hardly heaven.

The bus was packed, but she managed to get the last seat downstairs. Thankfully, the woman sitting next to her looked to be a non-smoker.

'I'm off to see me daughter,' she said, without prompting from Mary.

'That's nice.'

'She's 'aving 'er third kiddie. Already got two.' She shook her head and tutted. 'Don't know what 'er old man's going to say when he gets back. He's in Singapore.'

'That's nice.'

She knew nothing of Singapore but liked the way it rolled off the tongue. It sounded exotic.

The woman shook her head again. 'My Bertha's always been careless. They've already got two girls.'

'Well, I expect he'll be dead excited if the next one's a boy.'

More head shaking. 'He would if the baby was his, but it ain't. He's been away too long for the figures to add up.'

Two more stops and the woman got off the bus, leaving Mary relieved that she didn't have to hear more or make comment, though she had the old adage ready, the only thing she could think of to say. *It's all down to the war.*

She settled herself down and thought pleasant thoughts. She was out for an evening of fun – with Beau. *Beau*. What a lovely name, the first letters of the word beautiful.

She enjoyed having the seat to herself and became aware of looks of appreciation from the young men on board. Some tipped her the wink, anticipation written all over their faces.

Calm and collected now the woman was gone, she smoothed the skirt of her dress and was happy that not too many people were smoking. People smoked upstairs as well as down, and she didn't want the fabric contaminated with the smell of cigarette smoke. Neither did she want it to smother the smell of the perfume she'd dabbed behind her ears.

She was meeting Beau in The Bear and Rugged Staff, one of the old pubs still left standing close to Castle Street and St Peter's Church. Nothing else mattered.

13

Mary's heart seemed to be doing somersaults as she alighted from the bus and tripped her way up the cobbled lane to where two pubs, The Bear and Rugged Staff, and its neighbour, The Catherine Wheel, still stood following the enemy bombing of the previous year. Everything else – shops, pubs, hotels and businesses in the area – had been flattened. All that remained were these two pubs and the external structure of St Peter's Church, plus a few shells of buildings down towards the river.

A vivid sunset streaked the sky, giving enough light to find her way over the cobbles to where Beau was waiting for her.

He was leaning against the window ledge of the pub but stood to attention at the sight of her, which made her feel rather special.

After looking her up and down with obvious appraisal, it was him who spoke first. 'Wow!'

She felt herself blushing but recovered quickly, hiding her nervousness with a spikiness she didn't really feel. 'Is that all you can say, Beau Blackbird. *Wow*?' She knew she sounded a bit offhand, but that was the way she was. Her knees were like jelly and a whole cloud of butterflies were doing whirligigs in her stomach.

He snatched his cap from his head and stood there fiddling with it with a broad smile on his nutbrown face. 'I mean it. You leave me speechless. You look like the dog's dinner?'

Mary's face crumpled. 'What? I look like a dog's dinner?' She folded her arms and turned petulantly aside. 'If that's the best you can do, I think you should stay speechless!'

He looked confused, twirling his headgear with both hands as he thought of what to say next. She didn't want him to know how much he fascinated her, how much he made her heart thunder like a freight train.

'The guys said it was the right thing to say. An English compliment. That's what they said.' He looked perplexed. 'Were they having me on?'

Mary glowered. Inside, she felt like a queen. 'They were pulling your leg.'

Now it was her date who blushed and took on a cringing look. 'It ain't a compliment, is it?'

She shook her head and said grimly, 'No. It most certainly is not.'

'Sorry. The guys, they're great pals most of the time. Not this time though. I apologise again.' He pointed at the entrance to the pub. 'Can I buy you a drink?' He jingled the coins in his pocket. 'I need to make it up to you. The sky's the limit, baby. What would you like? Oh. I remember. You only drink shandy, don't you.'

'Not tonight,' she said in a resolute fashion. 'Tonight, I fancy a port and lemon.'

'Oh.' His face dropped at first. A port and lemon drink was more expensive than half a shandy. 'I deserved that.' He offered her his arm but paused with one foot on the step before the pub doors. 'You're a sight for sore eyes. Does that work?'

Smiling and feeling quite chuffed with herself, she told him that it did.

After two drinks, they left the pub. The light from the setting sun was no more, but the sky was clear, and the moon had risen.

Arm in arm, they strolled through a street that had been lined with shops before the bombing of the twentieth of November. Solitary walls, all that remained of grand buildings, stood sentinel over piles of rubble, a forest of weeds and deep hollows that had once been cellars where merchandise had been stored for the busy shops of Castle Street and Mary Le Port Street. There was nothing but ruins to either side of them and there was an impenetrable gloom thanks to the remaining warehouses on both sides of the river.

At one point whilst passing through a black shadow where neither sun nor moon could go, she stumbled, which necessitated him getting out his flashlight.

'There's some kind of path here. Where does it lead?'

'Down to the river.'

Like an oversized firefly, the beam flashed over the rough path that Mary believed led through the strewn rubble and down to the river. Arched windows like empty eye sockets, the shadow thrown by the carcass of St Peter's Church fell over them, backlit by a full moon.

Because of the blackout there was no other light except for the torch beam bouncing on its way and the gossamer gleam of moonlight shining from a clear sky.

A frisson of excitement shot through her. They were descending into darkness, into a place where nice girls shouldn't be going, not alone with a man not much more than a stranger. The truth was, she liked being with him. Going for a drink at the pub was all well and good, but she felt excited at the prospect of being alone with him. Was she bad for wanting that?

Quite frankly, she didn't really care. Her young body tingled in anticipation. She felt grown up and thought she looked grown up, but these feelings and tingling she didn't yet understand.

She'd met Beau at a dance in St Barnabas church hall where they'd served fish paste sandwiches, watery lemonade and bottles of Tizer which had tasted as though it had been watered down like the lemonade. It had no bubbles. Beau and several of his Canadian friends had sneaked in hip flasks of Scotch, a good deal of which had found its way into the lemonade. Things had progressed very quickly from thereon. This was the fourth time she'd met this homesick young man with slicked-back black hair, a square jaw and a light bronze complexion. He was tall and his shoulders were broad. She believed the muscles of his arms, when not covered by a sleeve, would be extraordinary. As yet, she hadn't had the opportunity to find out. His mates had always been around, laughing, drinking and making jokes – some about their officers, some about what they got up to. Because of this their physicality had been confined to caresses and kisses at the bus stop. She'd thought him a gentleman to wait with her until the bus came.

The moon disappeared and rain began to fall, not heavily but enough to sprinkle her hair.

'We're going to get wet.'

'No, we won't.'

The wandering beam of the torch filtered into a doorway, where it picked out the bare brick walls of the bombed outbuilding which appeared to have retained its roof.

His free hand clasping hers, Beau peered into the black void. 'This looks a good place. If the rain gets heavier, we'll be warm and dry in here.'

Still holding her hand, he stepped forward, rubble, stones and broken glass crunching beneath his feet.

'Be careful where you step. There's debris all over the ground.'

Once inside, some of her courage left her. She was beginning to get the collywobbles, all her bravado left behind, and just a little excited at the prospect of being totally alone with him. It was an unexpected feeling and made her have second thoughts.

He was easy to be with when they were in a pub, or a dance hall surrounded by other people. Tonight, they were alone, mooning around in the shadow of a bombed outbuilding in Wine Street. Shoppers had once thronged this area in the centre of Bristol, where bright lights had shone from shop windows, some until midnight, and Victorian streetlights had stood sentinel equidistant along the flagstone pavements. Thanks to the enforced blackout, all was darkness now, those streetlights that had survived dark skeletons against the night sky. No lights, of course. The darkness was almost absolute and not helped by the remains of taller buildings which threw rectangles of dense blackness over the sad scenes of desecration.

Mary was wearing her best shoes and was mindful that the heels could so easily be scuffed and scratched on the uneven ground. She knew she was being a bit reckless going with him into the darkness but couldn't help herself. What was it the girls at work said? *Live for today. Tomorrow might never come.*

Their words stayed with her as she perched on a window ledge, her back against a glassless window frame. The faint light of the torch and the silvery searching of the moon was enough to enable her to see him. Beau had such a strong look about him. She'd read descriptions of men like him in the tatty romantic novels that were pre-war offerings passed from one workmate to another at the tobacco factory.

Twirling a tress of auburn hair between finger and thumb, a coy expression on her clear complexion, she sucked in her breath as he came closer.

'Mary,' he whispered, his hands reaching for her waist. The fragile light filtering in from outside picked out the details of his features. His breath was warm on her face, his lips inches from hers.

From the few dates she'd had with him, she knew Beau to be a good kisser – so good in fact that she'd been dreaming of him every night since. In her dreams, she'd tingled at the warmth of his flesh against hers, falling into his arms, tipping her head back like the film stars did at the pictures whilst his mouth ran up and down her throat, causing her to moan in ecstasy. In the films, the hero and heroine appeared to submit to their passion, helpless to resist, the heroine's long-painted fingernails tangling in his hair. Him whispering that he loved her and that she was the most beautiful woman he'd ever seen.

She sighed inwardly. Whatever happened after that was left to the imagination of the audience – and she had imagination in bucketfuls.

Tonight, she imagined she was that film star – Claudette Colbert or Jean Harlow – losing themselves in the arms of Clark Gable or Cary Grant, submission glowing in their eyes.

The fiction melted and the reality took over. Desire was more powerful than the warnings about not giving in and the stark truth that he might love her tonight but once he'd had his way there might not be a tomorrow. And she would be left with the aftermath. But, somehow, she didn't care.

She allowed his hands to wander a bit further than they should. But fear of possible consequences resurfaced without warning. She wasn't going to fall as easily as that! She attempted to nip this in the bud.

'Steady on.' She swiped away his exploring hand. 'We ain't known each other for that long.'

'It seems like a lifetime.' His breath tickled her ear and was warm. 'I feel as though I've known you forever.'

'And so, says all of us,' she pronounced in a moment of denial whilst giving his hand another push.

He jerked back. 'What do you mean? All of us? How many boyfriends have you had?'

'Enough,' she said, her manner pert and accompanied with a toss of her head, a distracted look meant to make him feel as if he really was one of many – which wasn't true. 'You're not the only fish in the sea, you know.'

'But I want to be,' he said, both arms gently but firmly dragging her towards him. Once their bodies were flat against each other, his big rough hands cupped her face. 'I think you're the girl for me, Mary. In fact, I'm sure that you are.'

Inwardly, she moaned. She wanted him, but if she gave in, if anything happened... She imagined her mother's face – and what she would say. She gave him another push.

'Your hands are rough.' Her tone was petulant.

She sensed his disappointment, the careless way he took his warm hands off her and leaned away. 'I can't help having rough hands. I do a rough job; in fact, I work hard back home. But I'm just an ordinary Joe. I ain't no guy in a smart suit working in an office. If you want one of them, look elsewhere. There's a few in my unit used to be insurance clerks.'

Hearing the stinging tone of his voice, Mary felt a bit guilty that she'd tendered such a biting comment. She'd liked the warmth of his hands and although she'd pretended a liberty had been taken, she wanted them back. Some back-pedalling was in order.

'What kind of work did you do back in Canada?' Her voice had softened. Now it was her that got closer to him.

'I'm a lumberjack. I cut down trees.'

'Big trees?' She knew the answer, had seen films and pictures in books of logs being floated downstream in mighty rivers and two big men – lumberjacks – using a two-man saw to cut down tall trees that seemed almost to scrape the sky. But she wanted to hear him say it and thus regain their intimacy.

'Very big trees.' A faraway, awestruck tone came to his voice. 'My, you should see them, so tall they look as though they're touching the sky. After a long winter, it's great to get out in the forest and start logging. The forest is filled with sound.' He shook his head, lost in the vision only he could see. 'The sound of leaves rustling, fallen trees hitting the ground. And bears, elk, moose and wolves.'

The eloquence with which he described the surroundings he had known was impressive and made her want to know more.

She ran her fingers down his arm and thrilled to feel it so hard and muscular. She finally nestled her hand into one of those warm, rough hands, so big that it could hold both of hers.

'Is Canada very big?' She was pretty sure that it was but wanted to continue showing an interest in him so that he'd forget her sharp words.

'Vast. There's prairies, mountains, big rivers, lakes and forests.'

She tried to imagine what it was like, to see all these features through his eyes.

'What's the name of the place you come from?'

'Brooklyn Falls. A little town in British Columbia. That's in the far west, in case you didn't know. The town is small, but the state of BC is big. It could swallow Great Britain whole.'

She didn't want to admit that she didn't know, but instead of saying so, went on to another question that was nothing to do with logging. 'What about your mates. Are they from all over Canada?'

'Yep. All over. But we're all good buddies although we haven't long been thrown together. Couldn't be without them now. Don't ever want to be without them again, in fact. My, but we have some good times together. I'd miss them if they weren't around.'

'In that case, are you all right being alone with me,' she asked teasingly. 'Not frightened to be with me without yer mates around, are you?' She gave him a quick nudge with her elbow so he might know that she was only teasing.

'Of course I'm not,' he responded hotly.

'I didn't mean it.'

His voice softened. 'I wanted to be with you.' His hands travelled to her hips, fingers following her curves. He seemed suddenly to make a quick decision and gave her a tug that slammed their bodies together. The top of her head just about reached his chin, which made her feel safe. 'You're beautiful. The most beautiful girl I've ever met.'

So, there it was. That line from the movies – as the Canadians called them.

'Am I supposed to be flattered?' She was flattered. Of course she was, but she wasn't going to let him know that. She wanted to fall all over him, but she'd learned that appearing to fall hard wasn't the best thing to do. One of her mates at the factory had told her that men were best kept dangling on a hook.

'Keep them keen. Keep teasing. Keep them wondering what you really think of them. A bit of mystery goes a long way. Might take you all the way to the altar.'

She smiled into his chest as he kissed the top of her head and ran his fingers through her hair. She felt his lower region harden against her, which both thrilled and frightened her.

They stood there for a moment, neither saying anything, just clinging to each other, at home with private thoughts.

When it seemed as though they'd be turned into wood, so tight was their closeness, he suddenly said, 'Hey, honey. I've had a thought.'

'Mary. My name's Mary. I'm not sure I like being called honey.' The previous tone of defensive petulance was back, her way of drawing back from where she feared to go. A shield against what might or could happen.

'Why?' He sounded puzzled.

'Because you've probably called all your other girlfriends' honey. I don't want to be one of them.'

'Sure. Mary, Mary, quite contrary...' Now it was him who was teasing.

She flipped a hand at his shoulder insignia. 'Who do you think you're calling contrary? Mind how you go.'

His arms tightened around her and he turned slightly so that the moonlight caught the way he was gazing into her eyes. That look was so intense that she almost gave in and repeated all the most romantic lines she'd ever read or seen on the silver screen.

Those doe brown eyes of his, the bronze tint to his skin and the blackness of his hair reminded her of Clark Gable.

Her legs turned to jelly. *I think I'm in love.*

She held the words back, but it wasn't easy. A tingling sensation had spread from the touch of his lips and his hands all the way down to her toes. Yes, her toes were tingling – and much more in-between.

'Honey,' he said softly before realising his mistake. 'Mary.' By the light of the moon, she saw the look in her eyes. It was that look which might melt her resolve. The tingling had certainly increased. 'You and me are made for each other. How about we get married?'

She couldn't help bursting out laughing.

His dark eyebrows beetled over his deep brown eyes. 'What's so funny?' Not for the first time that night, he looked hurt.

'Us getting married. You say some pretty stupid things, Beau Blackbird. Whyever, would I want to marry you?' Even to her own ears, she sounded unnecessarily strident; yet another barrier to this extraordinary night when her resistance was close to breaking down. It was all she had left to keep these feelings – and him – at bay.

A shadow seemed to flit across his eyes and cloud his face. 'Mary. Let's talk seriously. I don't know when the call will come, but at some point, I'll be leaving England and sent to fight over-seas. I'm not scared – well, not that much, but it would be nice to know that there's someone waiting for me. Someone to write to me. Someone who'll keep the home fires burning until I come back – if I come back.'

His voice was only just shy of a whisper and there was a sad look in his eyes. Both made Mary feel guilty that she'd acted so offhandedly, had teased and cajoled in equal measure. Suddenly, her soldier was no longer the man the uniform made him out to be a hardened warrior who would give the enemy a bloody nose. He was not much more than a boy and, as such, the very thought of him fighting a lethal enemy was frightening.

Her resolve to hold him off was melting as swiftly as winter snow beneath a summer sun. There was true affection as well as sympathy in the way she eyed him without sharp comment or sarcastic witticism. He looked so vulnerable, a young man thousands of miles from home and in desperate need of love and affection.

She took a deep breath, at the same time smoothing the material of her blouse flat over her stomach. The truth had to be told.

'Right,' she said purposefully. 'Pin back your ears. Yours isn't the only proposal I've had, and I could receive a lot more by the time I'm twenty-one. That's the age I can marry without needing my mum's permission.' The statement about having received a few marriage proposals was a lie. It was the last barrier she could construct between him and her and what their closeness could lead to.

He looked so taken aback, she felt the need to modify what she said next.

'I'm sorry, Beau. But I had to tell you the truth – about needing permission to marry.'

The moonlight betrayed the glum look on his face before a quarter-smile lifted one side of his mouth. 'But you'll think about it?'

She laughed. 'If I was going to get married, you'd be top of my list.' She smiled playfully and tickled his chin with her index finger.

His face brightened. 'Fancy some chocolate?' Out from his pocket it came, a whole bar of chocolate that was part of the Canadian army's standard supplies.

Mary's eyes lit up as she reached for it. 'Lovely!'

'Oh no.' He purposely held it up above his head beyond her reach. Now it was him with the playful look, his dark eyes dancing. 'You've got to give me a kiss first.'

Mary pouted and shook her head reprovingly. 'You've got a nerve!'

The petulant look was meant to convey reluctance, but as every young man knew, stockings, cigarettes and chocolate were a sure way to a girl's heart – and more besides.

Face wreathed in smiles, she entwined her arms around his neck, even though she knew it might be her downfall. 'Okay. A kiss.'

His lips were soft as velvet and the tip of his tongue penetrated gently between her teeth. He kissed her long and deep before they broke, but by then it was too late. She wanted the chocolate, but she also wanted more of him, this warmth, this close physical contact.

Moonlight silvered the broken beams, the cracked stone and the patch of weeds that had taken hold between mounds of rubble and covered the ground beneath them. More kisses followed and then they were reaching for the thick carpet of greenery that dared live between broken bricks and beams.

Mary loved chocolate more than cigarettes or stockings. But more than that, she was beginning to realise that she also loved Beau Blackbird. Despite the warnings she'd received about not being led astray, she just couldn't help herself. Her guard was down, and his wandering hand had travelled up from her knee to the gap of flesh above her stocking top.

It was the point of no return. She was lost and didn't care that she was.

14

Nothing much changed in the Routledge household from day to day or night to night. Percy Routledge often opted to do night duty rather than day duty. He liked the feeling that he was observing a world which could not observe him. Darkness was the cloak that made him special and, in a strange way, a greater upholder of the law. Simply because he could see whilst not being seen by people who used the darkness to break the law, whereas he hid behind it in order to catch them out. Like that silly old woman, Mrs West, who would continually break the blackout rules.

Today was day duty, and although he did his best to concentrate on his beat, the incident on the bus when he'd met Quentin Appleyard had fired him up with the hope of gaining a place in a service where darkness reigned supreme – the secret service where observation of those who would do the country wrong was paramount.

'Are you going out again, dear?' Margaret asked.

'Yes,' Percy responded gruffly. He wasn't going to tell her about Quentin Appleyard, the man he'd rescued from a gang of stupid women who'd thought him a fifth columnist, a spy for Adolf Hitler. He swelled with pride at the thought that Quentin – obviously a very important man – had sworn him to secrecy about his top-secret work at the aerodrome. What was more, Quentin had identified him as an observant man who was wasted in his current position but perhaps would like to take on more clandestine operations.

Percy prided himself on being a good judge of people. Quentin's speech was eloquent, his vowels well rounded, his aitches never dropped, in fact he'd called himself the Honourable Quentin Appleyard, son of a baron, or duke or some such thing. Percy couldn't recall which, but it didn't matter. They all impressed him equally.

He'd always thought himself too good to remain a constable and this opportunity to show his mettle was like a dream come true.

'You can count on me,' he'd gushed. If it had sounded as though he might drop down and lick the man's shiny shoes, he didn't care. Percy Routledge was going places. He was going to become a man of considerable importance, known to the War Office, of use to them in their struggles against all enemies.

Margaret hovered like a bird caught in a net. 'Would you like your tweed jacket or—'

'Oh, for goodness' sake! My black suit jacket of course.'

I'm going out at night. In certain circumstances I have no wish to be seen. That's what he thought but did not say. This was men's work. Women had no part in it.

He felt no guilt when he saw her face reddening. He knew she hated it when he was grumpy or angry. Still, she should think herself lucky. He laid down strict rules but did not throw punches like some men, but he did go into lengthy silences or throw a look of condemnation at her or the children. The latter

slunk away from him. His wife remained her usual uncom-
plaining self. A martyr, he thought. Totally submissive to his
patriarchal role.

'I was expecting you to be at home tonight seeing as you've
been on earlies...'

'The country needs every man to do his duty. Just like Lord
Nelson said at the Battle of Trafalgar.'

'Trafalgar?'

'Yes. The naval battle.'

Margaret looked confused. 'Was it in the paper? I don't
recall reading about it.'

Percy fixed her with a piercing look. 'Of course it wasn't,' he
snapped, looking at her as though she was the stupidest person
in the world. 'It happened over a century ago.' His tone was
contemptuous. Besides being meek and mild, Margaret was not
as well read as he was. At times, it was downright embarrassing, although her ignorance and innocence was the reason he'd
married her. Somebody who attracted looks of admiration or
preferred dancing to housework wouldn't have done. Yes,
Margaret had proved to be exactly what he wanted. Her world
revolved around him and the children, of which they had three:
two boys and one girl. Howard, who was fourteen and expected
to get a scholarship at the grammar school; Judith who was
three years younger than him; and young Albert, who had
been five years old when the family had first arrived in Coronation Close. He was now eight, had a shock of blond hair that
verged on white and fell in ringlets, just like Little Boy Blue on
the Pears Soap billboard advert, profligate on hoardings on the
sides of buildings or behind the platforms at railway stations.

Margaret was tying her fingers in knots and fidgeting as she
carefully considered what to say next. He guessed she wasn't
going to ask him outright what he was up to. She'd presume it

was something to do with the church committee and wasn't to know that he'd fallen out with them ages ago. Too much molly-coddling of those who had no work and no inclination to get any.

'Right. Right. Oh. Shall I leave you out some supper? I've got beef dripping. A nice slice of bread and a sprinkling of salt should make it go down a treat.'

She wrung her hands, face stiff with neediness as she awaited his response, smiling a weak plaintive smile, living in hope that he might show her some affection, utter a word of endearment. But he didn't.

Pulling back the cuff of his shirt, he eyed his watch out of admiration rather than a need to check the time. 'No point. I don't know what time I'll be back. And don't wait up.'

Margaret hesitated before daring to ask if he could tell her where he was going.

'Are you... are you... going somewhere nice?'

It wasn't usual for his wife to question him about his where-abouts and caused him to throw her a scathing look.

'Well, I'm not going to the pub if that's what you're implying!'

She cowered away from the impact of his sharp tone. 'No. Of course not.'

She was loitering. Wouldn't leave him alone. He guessed there was something she wanted to say.

She wrung her hands together tightly enough for her knuckles to make a soft clicking sound.

Fired up with his plans for the evening, he spun round to face her, raised a finger and wagged it in front of her face. 'Don't say it! Our Albert doesn't need a doctor. It's just a bit of a cold.'

'But he's been like it for three or four days...'

'Three or four days...' he squeaked, jerking his head from side to side as he mimicked her high-pitched voice.

Percy was of the old school. He firmly believed that back in the Garden of Eden, Adam had been put on this earth to rule the lower orders – and that included the descendants of Eve.

For her part, Margaret was frantic. She genuinely feared for her child's condition. Just for once, she dared raise her head and speak out.

'He's been coughing and spluttering and hasn't eaten a thing for days.'

'Give him soup.'

'I tried that. He can't swallow.'

'He hates school. That's what it is. He should be more like our Howard – once he gets that scholarship, there'll be no stopping him. The world will be his oyster. It's my dream to see that both our boys aim high and be all they can be.'

'And our Judith.'

'Girls don't matter.'

'I think they do.' Margaret bit her lip.

Her response brought a lowering of his eyebrows. 'Margaret. Do not contradict me. I know what I'm talking about. Spare the rod and spoil the child.'

'She's a good girl. You must know that.'

Her attempt at placating his overblown ego fell on deaf ears. Percy was adamant. 'Mark my words...'

There were many times Percy had browbeaten his wife into submission, insisting she agree with his point of view. Agreeing was something she did as an obedient wife and loving mother. Keeping the peace and maintaining a veneer of respectability was the only way she could cope. But this evening a seed of resentment was growing inside her. She feared for Albert's health and desperately wanted to call for the doctor. She dared intercept. 'He's sick...'

He stopped putting across his opinion and looked at her as though not quite recognising the shy little mouse he'd trained to do his will. Ultimately, he was the master here, the one who laid the rules and owned the right opinion. It was imperative that he always stood on the higher ground, the one that put a man above a woman. He knew best. Perhaps she'd forgotten that.

Without warning, he grabbed a handful of her hair tightly enough to pull her head backwards so she could barely move. 'Now listen to me, Margaret,' he spat, saliva wetting his lips. 'I'm not forking out money for a doctor who'll say the same as me.'

Flinging her aside, he adjusted his tie for what must have been the third time.

Margaret eyed him nervously from beneath a fringe of tousled hair. Wherever he was going he wanted to look his best. But why? she wondered. Some wives would suspect a man smartening himself up and going out at night to be meeting another woman. A bit on the side, as they said in Coronation Close. She only wished it were true. Her most cherished dream was that he might run off with another woman. She wouldn't mind at all. She daydreamed of living alone, just her and the children. What a wonderful life that would be.

At times, she wished he would go to the pub like Bill, his sister Cath's husband. But he wasn't like Bill, who was adored by his wife even though he worked on the docks and came home smelling of sweat and dirt. In times past, she had told herself that Percy was a fine figure of a man, a serving police officer who had been promoted a while back but then got demoted. The reason was never that clear but had something to do with overreacting to a minor misdemeanour, which had in turn resulted in an accusation of wrongful arrest. He'd been silent for days after his demotion, staring into space, brow furrowed, and jaw so tense it had seemed to her he was in danger of breaking it.

Since then, he had determined he was going to throw himself into his job in order to regain his previous status – and more besides.

He'd tried explaining all this to his wife. 'Believe you me, Margaret. There are traitors among us. It's my job to maintain vigil, watch for those who are not what they seem and cater to those who put their trust in me to do keep the King's realm safe.'

She hadn't understood a word he was on about or what he was up to. The only thing she did know was that he prowled the streets at night, spying on their neighbours, reporting any who dared to break one of the many wartime rules.

His eyes rose to the ceiling in response to a slight bump from upstairs.

'Better go and tell our offspring to get to sleep. Otherwise, they'll have me to answer to.'

She headed with him out into the hallway, where he peeled off to the front door.

'Turn the light off before I open the door.'

Don't come back. That was what she wanted to say. Stay out all night, and in his absence, she would go to the telephone box and ring for a doctor.

She thought of the few shillings she kept in a biscuit tin in the kitchen. It might just be enough to pay for a doctor. If she didn't tell him, he wouldn't know. Best get him out of the door first before she found the courage to disobey and do what was in her mind.

His hand was on the Yale door lock. 'Did you hear what I said about turning that light off?' he snapped.

'Yes, Percy.'

'Good. And remember to pull the blackout curtain across it before you turn the light back on.'

'Yes, Percy.'

He swept out into an evening fast turning to night, the brim of his trilby hat pulled low over his eyes, his footsteps beating a tattoo, a man in black who lived in his own little world and had no idea he wasn't even a big fish in a small pond. He was about to find out exactly how small he was. Nothing more than a minnow.

15

Percy Routledge was certain he could do excellent work for the intelligence services. He read spy books; he obeyed orders without question, though also used his own initiative. The man from the bus had hinted at a fruitful career and assured him he could be of use in the cloak-and-dagger side of national security. At least, that was what he believed. That's what Quentin had meant when he'd insisted he must keep what he'd told him to himself.

'I can definitely use you and be assured, I never make a promise I can't keep,' Quintin had added. 'I'll be in touch.'

But he hadn't. Percy could understand that to some extent. The man was involved in state secrets – that's how he saw it. And anyway, he'd noticed the address on his new friend's identity card on Broad Walk which was part of his beat and had kept an eye on the place.

According to the details he'd given, the Honourable Quentin Appleyard was lodged in one of the red-brick and grey stone Edwardian houses skirting the Wells Road at the top of Broad Walk.

A few days ago, he'd knocked on the door and asked the landlady if he was in. She'd told him he'd only stayed for one day and had not left a forwarding address.

Percy had felt badly let down. The man was a liar. He'd found it hard to believe, but then he'd read enough derring-do novels to know that his type was like will-o'-the-wisp, here today gone tomorrow, reporting for duty to wherever they were needed.

Perhaps things would have gone on in the same old rut if it hadn't been for the report of a theft of chickens from a farmhouse at the very end of Knowle West on Airport Road. Theft of food, specifically poultry, was a widespread problem.

The farmhouse had remained isolated from the new housing estate that had encroached on its surrounding fields on one side and the airport on the other.

The farmer was a gruff man, who waved the arrival of a police constable aside, saying he had better things to do. The details of the theft were left to his wife.

She took Percy out to the henhouse, clucking in a similar manner to her hens, pointing at the gap in the fence big enough for someone to burrow under.

'You need to get that mended,' he said to her. 'Any idea what time this occurred?'

With an officious flourish of hands, he brought out pencil and notebook, licking the end of the pencil before writing the date in the top left-hand corner.

'I didn't hear a thing.'

Percy put on his most solicitous of raised eyebrows, his questions fast and clear. 'Nobody heard anything. Not your husband? Did he not hear anything? No squawking of fowl? No cock crowing?' Percy didn't have a clue about animals and certainly not about chickens. He wasn't to know that cocks only crowed in the morning.

'No. But I ain't asked me lodger. He comes in late. On night shift at the airport. I'll go and knock on his door.'

Ten minutes and she was back.

'Mr Appleyard says he didn't notice anything amiss when he got back from his shift.'

'Mr Appleyard?' A sudden suspicion had invaded Percy's thoughts. 'Mr Quentin Appleyard?'

Excitement surged in Percy's chest as he scribbled the name down. It had to be the same Quentin Appleyard. It was not a common name, but he wanted to believe that it was the Quentin Appleyard, the Honourable Quentin Appleyard that he so wanted to emanate.

'Yes.' He caught the farmer's wife looking at him queerly.

'Ah!' said Percy in a resolute manner, his brain working overtime. 'I take it Mr Appleyard occupies one room with you?' he asked.

'Yes. That's where he sleeps, but he's also got a workshop in the loft above the barn. But he's not the sort to steal chickens.' She shook her head forlornly. 'No. Not 'im. Not at all.' She pointed to a stone building with a tin roof that looked in danger of being blown away in a good south-westerly wind. 'Spends time up there during the day when he's not at the airport.'

He wanted to say it was a wonder Quentin Appleyard found time to sleep if he was working at the airport but also working in the hayloft.

After assuring the woman that he would report the incident of the stolen chickens and that the police force would keep their eyes open, he bid her good day.

All the way back down the lane, he burned with anger. If

Quentin Appleyard – if that was indeed his real name – thought he was going to get away with letting him down, he had another think coming.

Suspicion about the man he'd hoped to work closely with did not constitute reason to report him to the authorities. He needed evidence and he'd be blowed if he was going to hand over what he knew to some faceless wonder from outside his own sphere of operation. This was a job for PC Percy Routledge!

First on the agenda was to get sight of the suspect and making a positive identification before taking the matter further – and that shouldn't be too difficult. It had to come after phoning in at the police box at the bottom of Leinster Avenue. He'd report the incident about the chickens and that he had a statement. He would also call in the case of the stolen bicycle, the smashed window at the back of the Inns Court Tavern, the possible theft of petrol from the butcher's van and the stealing of women's underwear from a washing line in Clonmel Road.

Daily duty completed; he headed back down to the farm-house towards Airport Road. He'd spotted a dilapidated shed that might once have been a pigsty on the opposite side of the lane to the farmhouse. Weeds grew from its foundations and a vigorous growth of ivy scrambled over its pan-tile roof. Slender branches of elder saplings tickled its roof like silken fingers, giving it shade and camouflage.

There was a hedge bordering a dried-up stream on the same side of the lane as the pigsty. Keen not to be seen, Percy took off his helmet and, tucking it beneath his arm, bent low enough to be out of sight but able to pop up and scrutinise what was going on opposite.

A sudden movement made him look down. The tail of a

tabby cat curled around his leg, the tip of the tail almost at knee level.

He grimaced and with the side of his boot nudged it away. He might have kicked it more forcibly but didn't want it to yowl loudly and give him away.

The cat retreated to a few feet away, where it sat down and stared at him with amber, almond-shaped eyes before it began to wash itself.

Percy hissed at it to go away, but it took no notice.

Hearing a sound from the farm, he got down as low as he could, peering through a screen of elder leaves. That was when he saw Quentin Appleyard striding across the farmyard to the hayloft.

What was he doing in there? Something secret? Percy would certainly like to know more and wasn't leaving until he had reminded Quentin Appleyard about his promise to get him into the secret service.

Mrs Cooper appeared, took in a line of washing, then went back into the house.

Still keeping low, Percy stepped out, crossed over the lane and skirted the edge of the farmyard, heading for the hayloft. He stopped outside, looked all around him, then moved towards the building.

One half of the barn door was open and inside it was cool. A few remaining chickens that should have been in the henhouse had found their way out and were now pecking at scattered seeds fallen from the bales of hay piled up to the rough wooden beams.

A set of rickety-looking wooden stairs climbed upwards disappearing behind a wall of hay and straw bales. Rickety or not, Percy was determined to confront Quentin, ask him why he hadn't been in touch and not told him that he had moved from the address given on his identity card.

With that in mind, he set a stair creaking with the weight of one foot as he called, 'Mr Appleyard? Police Constable Routledge here. I know you're up there.'

He'd got to only the third stair when the man he wished to speak to appeared at the top of the stairs. At first, he wore a startled look, but this was swiftly replaced by a narrowing of his eyes and a locking of his jaw, which in turn became an oddly welcoming smile.

'Ah,' he said as he came down the stairs. 'I was meaning to get in touch with you, Percy.'

Suspicion that he'd been led up the garden path vanished simply because his new friend had remembered his name. Percy. Not Constable Routledge. He'd actually remembered his name. The fact filled him with self-importance.

'Quentin.' Percy extended his hand. Quentin shook it. 'I did call in on you at your last lodgings but was told you'd moved. It was pure coincidence that I visited here. The farmer's wife complained that someone had stolen her chickens. You didn't hear anything, I suppose?'

Quentin shook his head. 'I don't think I was here. There was a flap on. Can't say what it was of course, but take it from me, there are times when our feet don't touch the ground.'

'I can imagine,' Percy replied, feeling that he'd been taken into the confidence of a man who was in the thrust of this war.

'Let's go outside, shall we?'

Percy appreciated the friendly arm around his shoulders as the two of them made their way outside.

Clouds tumbled across the sky, sometimes obscuring the sunshine which seemed to be competing with the breeze to make the day warm, the wind to cool it down again. Long grass whipped around their legs as they moved away from the barn and back towards the pigsty. Bees and butterflies flew up from flowering nettles. They stopped in the shade of a giant buddleia, Quentin with his hands in the pockets of his well-cut flannel trousers, looking thoughtful.

'I must insist you say nothing of my whereabouts, my very existence in fact.' His look was dark, almost threatening.

Percy frowned. 'I won't, but you were seen by the women on the bus. I can't guarantee that they won't gab.'

Quentin threw back his head and laughed. 'Now who's going to believe a crowd of old women. Besides, they only encountered me on the bus. They have no idea where I live.' His expression darkened. 'The only one who knows where I live is you. And you can keep a secret, can't you, Percy?'

Percy was in half a mind to respond that not all of them were old. There was Mary Dawson for a start, a sharp little madam who had queried his French. But Quentin was right. It was a one-off incident that the women would have forgotten about by now.

'It shouldn't be a problem, although one of them did speak a bit of French.' He laughed. 'She said that you were lying about speaking it, but as you said, just a bunch of women.'

Percy didn't see the hard look return to Quentin's eyes. He only heard the mocking laughter. It rankled. He was disappointed.

'So, what's the chance of me being taken on by your mob,' asked Percy, forthright in his approach to a job he really thought he could do standing on his head.

Quentin looked around him, his expression serious and his eyes searching beyond Percy to the foliage between them and the road. 'I take it you came alone.'

'Of course. I'm on duty.' Percy pulled back his cuff and

looked at the face of his expensive watch. 'It's nearly time for me to call in at the police box. Three o'clock. I've called in once to make my report – nothing very exciting. Now I have to call in again or they'll be sending out a search party.'

He laughed at his own statement, and, after a short reluctance, Quentin did the same before suggesting that Percy come back later.

'When it's dark, then we can talk about you joining the secret service – if you want to, that is.'

Percy almost swallowed his tongue. 'I'm dead keen. Dead keen!'

Quentin's gaze searched the empty fields and the leaves of the shivering trees. Not a soul in sight. He suddenly relaxed, smiled and slapped Percy's shoulder. 'Tonight, I'll outline what to expect if you become one of us.'

'I'm your man! I'll be here at seven.'

'I won't be. I'll be here once it gets dark. And tell no one where you're off to. Is that clear?'

Percy shook his head avidly, his heart beating in double time, his blood racing with excitement. 'Mum's the word.' He made a zipping motion across his mouth.

He marched off with a spring in his step, convinced that he was going places, that he would be party to greater things than checking his neighbours pig bins or whether they'd let a chink of light through their blackout curtains. Quentin had hinted at more serious stuff when they'd first met. And that was exactly what Percy wanted. Involvement in the greater scheme of things.

* * *

The man who called himself Quentin Appleyard slunk back into the shadow of the tangled trees and bushes and watched Percy until he was out of sight.

His expression set like cement; he cursed himself that the women on the bus had not reacted as he'd thought they would. The weaker, gentler sex had turned on him like a pack of wolves. Luckily, the police constable had been easily persuaded that he had contacts at the airport, that he worked there, that he was involved in security. Percy Routledge had been mightily impressed. Quentin thought he'd escaped him by changing his address, but obviously had not.

So, what was he to do next?

On thinking it over, he decided that Percy was the weakest link in the chain and, as with any link, it needed knocking out to return the strand to its former strength.

Tonight, when it was dark would be the best time to despatch Percy Routledge. Much as Quentin disliked the task he had no choice. He had a job to do. Three weeks of taking notes and watching the comings and goings at the airport, the only true civilian airport left in the country. He'd made notes on the people he'd seen flying in and out, everyone from film stars to military commanders, royalty and high-ranking politicians. Most of the flights went to Lisbon, capital of a neutral country. He could not allow a pathetic little policeman to upset his plans. The Third Reich depended on him.

'Heil Hitler,' he said softly so that only the bees, the birds and the butterflies could hear.

16

————

Back at number five Coronation Close, Margaret Routledge carried out her husband's instructions in her usual methodical manner; one, turn off the light; two, draw the blackout curtain back across, let him out of the door; three, turn the hall-way/landing light back on. The atmosphere seemed lighter once he was gone.

'Has Father gone out now?'

A small voice carried down the stairs from the boxroom at the back of the house.

'Yes, Judith.'

One of her boys whimpered from one of the single beds in the other room.

'Our Albert's wet the bed again. All over. And he's making funny noises.'

'I'm coming.'

She took two stairs at a time. Margaret had once thought she'd loved her husband, but not in the same way or to the same extent as she did her children. Their health mattered very much to her. She wanted them to live a long life. Along with many other parents, she'd considered sending them to the country before the bombs started to fall. Percy would have none of it.

God will protect the righteous.

She couldn't imagine the Germans having a way to tell the righteous and wicked apart, but Percy would call her stupid if she opened her mouth, so, as usual, she'd swallowed her conclusion because Percy would glare at her and tell her that it wasn't her job to think, that she didn't, in fact, have an intelligent thought in her head. In Percy's opinion, most women didn't, and the more he told her this, the more she believed it true.

Sitting on the side of the bed, she placed her hand on Albert's brow. It was hot and his glorious curls, usually as soft and white as a swan, were slick with sweat and stuck to his skull.

Albert was soaked from head to toe, but she could tell that this was one occasion when he had not wet the bed. Praying inside and promising God she would not flinch from going to church so long as Albert recovered, she ran her fingers through his wet hair. His brow was hot with fever, in fact his whole body felt hot to her searching fingertips.

Everything to do with Percy and where he'd gone fled from her mind.

'Are you thirsty, my darling?'

She thought she saw a slight nod.

'I'll get you a glass of water.'

She dashed downstairs and drew a glass of water for her poorly child and dashed just as quickly back up again, taking care not to spill a drop.

'Here you are, darling. Drink some water.'

Cupping the nape of her son's neck, she raised his head

from the pillow so he could better drink without spilling. As she did so, her fingertips brushed a swelling in his neck. His eyes were closed now and his breath struggled up into his throat and out of his mouth in deep, gut-wrenching gasps.

'Drink, my darling,' she said as fear became a dull ache in her stomach and felt like a metal ingot on her tongue. 'Drink.'

Much as she cajoled, her lovely boy lay there, rosy-cheeked, the water she'd so desperately tried to give him trickling down his chin.

Margaret tried again to pour a measure of water between her son's dry lips. Yet again it trickled out.

She glanced across at Howard, her elder son who slept in the other single bed. 'How are you, Howard? All right, are you?'

He grunted something. She supposed he was half asleep, but the fear for her younger son also extended to him. He was too quiet. Too still. Was he ill too? Had he died without her noticing?

Irrational as it was, she couldn't drive the fear from her head. She reached across, touched her son's bare arm. On feeling only coolness, she breathed a sigh of relief. The gentle movement of his body and the sighing breath told her this son at least was well but fast asleep. Understandable really. Howard loved sport, would play football or cricket in any weather. His father egged him on, proudly standing at the side of the pitch, truly believing that his son could win a match on his own.

As for her younger son...

Fear became like an iron fist clamping tighter and tighter around her heart.

'Darling?'

Her little boy, his curls damply flat on the pillow made no response. Eyelids finely traced with blue veins were tightly closed over his blue eyes. His breath came in short, thick wheezes and a thick slime seeped from his nostrils, which she wiped aside with a large white handkerchief.

Finding herself unable to rouse him, panic took hold. Frantically, she searched the room as though her eyes might alight on the help she so badly needed. There was nobody there. Of course there wasn't. But there should be. A silent scream echoed in her mind. Where was Percy? Why wasn't he here?

The little head flopped as she laid it gently back on the pillow.

Her own mouth and lips were dry as she grappled with what she should do next.

An ambulance! She had to call for an ambulance. But she was all fingers and thumbs using a phone.

Cath! She had to get Cath, her sister-in-law.

There was no time to inform her other children where she was going. This was too urgent.

At the bottom of the stairs, Margaret hesitated, thinking she really should take off her slippers and put on her shoes.

'Don't you ever dare go out of this house in your slippers,' Percy had said to her. 'I don't want you becoming slovenly like my sister.'

Cath Lockhart was often to be seen out on the Close, her oversize slippers flip-flopping along the pavement.

Inside her head, a thought screamed, *But he isn't here!*

Neither did she bother to turn off the hall light as she almost fell out of the door. Not that it mattered. None of the air-raid wardens bothered to patrol Coronation Close because they knew PC Percy Routledge was more stringent than they were.

Dark as it was, Margaret ran as she'd never run before, heading for Cath's house at the top of Coronation Close. Running recklessly and blinded by panic, she stubbed her toe against something, which sent both her and her slippers flying, lost in the darkness.

Out of sheer desperation, she shouted out for help, her hands and knees grazed, perhaps bleeding, but she didn't care.

'Help,' she shouted, but she was too far from Cath's house for her sister-in-law to hear her.

A thin voice came out of the darkness. 'Please. Are you my mother? Can you take me home?'

The voice was plaintive, weak and high-pitched.

Getting back onto her feet, Margaret's eyes searched the darkness beneath the trees for the source of the ghostly voice. Suddenly, there was a flash of white, a pale face, a long string of plaited grey hair, barely discernible in the blackout darkness, but shining like silver thanks to the wide beam from the torch she was carrying.

Margaret's first urge was to shout, 'Put that light out. The enemy can see that at twenty thousand feet.' That's what Percy would have said.

Blow the torch. Blow everything. Staggering like a drunken sailor, she headed towards the figure and called out. 'Hello. Hello. Who is that?'

Nightdress billowing around her scrawny form, the elderly Mrs West approached her, arms outstretched ready to embrace. 'You know who it is. Your little girl, Emmaline...' The frail, elderly voice was full of sorrow.

The sound of a door opening, light illegally falling out into the blackout, gave a little more to the proceedings. Another voice rent the air, followed by the sound of running feet.

'Mother. What are you doing out there. Come on 'ome right now!'

The moment Margaret heard Betty's voice she knew for

sure that she had not seen a ghost. Mrs West was wandering again.

Betty gathered her mother in with softly reassuring words and a gentle but firm grip of her arms.

'Now come on 'ome, you silly old thing.'

Betty's mother stalled. Old and confused, she looked into her daughter's face and said, 'I'm looking for my mum. Do you know where she's gone?'

'Let's get a cup of hot cocoa inside you.'

'I need my mum.'

'You'd better get back into bed. Your mum won't be pleased if she finds you out and about, now will she.'

The old head nodded. 'I'd better get to bed.'

Margaret was touched by how gentle the daughter was towards her mother. She hadn't shouted at her that she was living in the past or to pull herself together as Percy did. She was gentle, caring.

Margaret's overwhelming need suddenly broke through. 'I need an ambulance for my little boy...'

'What's all this noise about? Who's calling for an ambulance?'

A figure came across the grass and beneath the trees from the other side of Coronation Close.

Desperate to get help, Margaret ran towards whoever it was, slipping on the dew-laden grass. She fell into the arms of Jenny Crawford. She noticed she was warmly wrapped in a dark-red dressing gown and smelt of fresh bread and lily of the valley talcum powder.

Even in the fragile light thrown by a crescent moon, she could see that her expressive eyes were full of tenderness. 'Mrs Routledge. Margaret. What's wrong?'

'My little boy's very sick. I need help.' There was panic in her voice and her knees were going weak. 'If someone could get my sister-in-law to call for an ambulance...'

Roused from yet another sleepless night, Cath Lockhart came from the other direction. 'Margaret? Is that you making all this noise?'

Margaret turned away from Jenny to Cath. 'Albert is sick. He needs a doctor.'

'What's the matter with him?'

'He's dying. I'm sure he's dying,' she cried, her voice veering on hysteria. Wetness glistened on her face as the tears streamed from her eyes.

'Does Percy know?' asked Cath.

'He's out.'

She didn't go into further detail. All she wanted was help for her little boy.

'Before we phone, I think we should take a look, so we can describe it to the doctor,' Cath suggested.

Jenny agreed. She was already thinking forward, one of them phoning for an ambulance and one sitting with Margaret and the boy until it came.

She suggested this to Cath as they hurried across the road.

Jenny had never had much to do with Margaret Routledge except for a quick hello. She always seemed to be in a hurry. Either that or disinclined to speak to people she didn't know that well. Percy's wife wasn't the sort to call in for a cup of tea – even at her own sister-in-law Cath's place.

Once the door was closed against the blackout, Margaret turned the light on. Jenny and Cath followed. Nothing in the Routledge household was out of place. Not a speck of dust anywhere and the smell of polish hung heavily in the air.

Like the rest of the house, upstairs was spick and span.

The amber glow of a single bedside lamp turned the boy's

face yellow, but it was not that which made Jenny inhale a deep breath. She was leaning over the sallow face, seeing the closed eyes, the parched lips and closed eyes. Worse than that, she could hear the wheezing breath and see the shallow rise and fall of her chest.

'Is he hot?' asked Cath.

Jenny touched the boy's forehead. She nodded. Their eyes met.

'His neck's swollen. All down here. Like a tree trunk it is.' Margaret's bottom lip trembled as her fingers indicated what she was talking about – not that she really needed to. The boy's neck lacked definition due to it being considerably enlarged.

Jenny trailed her fingers over the hard swelling. Cath did the same, alarm written all over her face.

The two neighbours exchanged worried looks. The boy had a temperature and trouble breathing. As for the swelling... worried looks became knowing looks. They'd both come to the same conclusion. Both knew this was a dire emergency.

'I'll phone the ambulance,' said Jenny. She turned to Margaret. 'Cath will stay with you whilst I go. I won't be long.'

The cooler air outside did nothing to clear Jenny's head of her concern for the child. One look was all it had taken to realise how serious this was. From experience, she guessed the boy had contracted diphtheria.

The phone box stood at the end of Coronation Close and Leinster Avenue. As she ran, a sudden thought hit her. Pennies! She needed pennies for the phone box. And here she was wearing her dressing gown. She dug her hands into the pockets of her dressing gown and found only fluff and a used handkerchief. Muttering a few well-chosen expletives, she came to a halt because the dash for the phone would be in vain, or so she thought, until it came to her that calls to the emergency number, 999, were free.

The operator answered almost immediately. 'Police, fire brigade or ambulance.'

'Ambulance.'

'Who is the patient and what is the problem?'

Jenny rubbed her furrowed brow with her fingers, determined to say the right thing, the thing that would bring the ambulance speeding to Coronation Close and thence to the hospital.

'The patient is a little boy.' She swallowed the shakiness of her voice, forced herself to speak calmly and clearly. She pressed on. 'He's having trouble breathing, has a high temperature and the glands in his neck are swollen.'

'Any spots? Rashes?'

'I don't think so, but I do believe he has diphtheria.'

'Are you a nurse or doctor?'

Did she detect a slight disdain in the operator's voice? She held her own voice firm. 'No. I'm just a mother. I've seen it before.'

Diphtheria was a disease feared more than whooping cough, more than scarlet fever and certainly more than measles or chicken pox. But there was a method of prevention.

'We'll get an ambulance to you as quickly as possible. Just keep the patient hydrated and kept warm.'

The phone cut quickly. Perhaps a sign that everything else would be done just as quickly.

She'd left the door on the latch. The stairs inside Margaret Routledge's house seemed unduly steep. Should Jenny tell Margaret what she suspected? *Of course you should*, she told herself. She had her two vaccinated. Surely Margaret had had her children vaccinated too.

As Jenny reached the landing, voices in the bedroom that had been subdued rose.

'You don't know where he's gone?'

'No. He wouldn't say.'

Jenny's appearance at the bedroom door brought their conversation to a halt.

Margaret's eyes widened in a face whiter than pale. 'Is the ambulance coming?'

Jenny nodded mutely.

Cath studied her as though trying to pull out the look on her face. 'What is it?'

Jenny caught hold of her elbow and tugged her out onto the landing and whispered so that Margaret could not hear. At present, she was totally engrossed in mopping her son's sweaty brow, smoothing the wet curls back from his face.

'They asked me what I thought it was, and I told them.'

'What is it you're saying?' Margaret's voice verged on the hysterical.

Jenny took a deep breath before she said, 'I think it's diphtheria.'

The older boy stirred in his bed. He grumbled about not being able to sleep and needed the bathroom.

Jenny accompanied him out onto the landing and suggested that when he came back up, he went to his parents' bed. 'Seeing as your brother's ill and your dad's not home.'

Once he'd gone downstairs to the bathroom, Jenny entered the bedroom and closed the door. None of this was going to be easy.

'Can I ask you a question, Margaret. I'm sure you would have done it...'

'Done what?'

Even Cath looked puzzled. 'Spit it out.'

'Have you had your children vaccinated for diphtheria?'

Jenny could not have foreseen Margaret's face getting any paler as she shook her head, eyes like dark pools, as though she was looking inwards and realising a terrible truth. She finally uttered, 'No. Percy doesn't believe in it.'

'Doesn't believe in it?' Cath shook her head forlornly before exclaiming, 'My brother's a right turnip at times.'

At any other time, Jenny would have laughed. But the repercussions of Percy's denial filled her with disbelief – and foreboding.

The jangling bells of an ambulance sounded from some way out on the main road.

By the time it had turned into Coronation Close and pulled up outside, it must have awakened all the neighbours.

With great care, Margaret and her sister-in-law Cath wrapped Albert up in a blanket. His eyes were still closed, his chest heaving as he fought for breath.

A rasping, snuffling sound accompanied them as Cath, strong and determined, carried him downstairs.

Jenny shone the torch down the garden path just in front of Cath's flapping slippers.

The night was strangely quiet, except for the sound of the bell sitting in its own little tower on the front of the ambulance.

Nothing else, she thought. Something's missing that was sounding only a moment ago.

Jenny froze as she realised that the sound she could no longer hear was the most important sound of all. She could no longer hear the ongoing fight for breath from the bundled-up child.

The ambulance crew were opening the back doors of the ambulance, pulling out a stretcher. The driver was a woman, one of many who had taken over the job in order to release a man to fight for his country – or drive an ambulance in a battle zone. Her male companion took the sleeping child from Cath's arms.

'Let me have him love.'

Jenny held back, her skin taut over her high cheekbones, fearing the worst but hoping against hope that she was wrong.

The moment the man exchanged a glance with his colleague, and she saw his features sag, she wound her right arm around Margaret's trembling shoulders. Her left hand clutched the icy fingers.

'What is it?' demanded Cath. Her expression was usually animated, full of life. Tonight, it was static, as though flesh had become marble. She repeated the question. 'What is it?'

The man seemed loath to answer and when he did, it came out quick but quietly.

'Sorry, love. He's gone.'

Suddenly the night seemed blacker.

17

Jenny sat with Margaret, hardly noticing when the grey light of dawn crept into the room and steadily became morning.

Cath had gone back to her own house to ensure that her husband, who worked at the docks, was up and on his way to work. The man was dog-tired what with all the battle-scarred shipping coming into the port of Bristol.

'I want to make sure the alarm clock went off on time,' she'd said before she left, leaving Jenny to deal with things alone. She looked devastated and Jenny understood why. They all had children, and it was only natural to feel empathy with a grieving mother, her heart broken in two, memories of giving birth, baby growing into toddler, toddler growing into small child, larger child, imaginings of its future. All those dreams that would now come to nothing.

An hour or so later Thelma came over to find out what was going on. Without anyone asking, she made them tea and told them not to hesitate if there was anything they needed.

Mary was helping herself to bread and marge when she got back.

'That was a racket last night,' she muttered. 'Woke me up.'

'Once you got home.'

'I wasn't late.'

Thelma conceded that she had not been late.

'Out with that Canadian lad?'

Was it her imagination or was that pale pink diffusing her daughter's face?

'Yes.' Her eyelashes flickered. 'He's very nice. I'll bring him home if you like.'

'Give it a bit of time,' said Thelma. 'Early days, eh?'

'Of course it is,' Mary replied somewhat hotly.

It surprised her when her mother enfolded her in her arms. The truth was the death of young Albert had made her treasure her children all the more.

'I don't want anything to happen to you, Mary. Or to our Alice. I would die if it did.'

'Mum. You're crushing me.'

When Thelma let go, Mary spotted the moistness in her eyes.

'What is it? What's wrong?'

Brushing the wetness from her eyes with the end of a tea towel, Thelma told her that young Albert Routledge was dead. 'Diphtheria.'

'Oh no! That's horrible. His poor mother... father too, I suppose. I don't like Mr Routledge, but all the same...'

'His mother's devastated. Not sure his father knows yet. No sign of him.'

'Not even chasing Mrs West across the green?' Her tone was scathing.

In response to that tone, a thoughtful crease furrowed Thelma's brow. 'No. Apparently, he was on days yesterday but went out last night. His wife doesn't know where, and from what I know he doesn't have any friends – male or female.'

Mary paused in her chewing of the hunk of bread and marge. 'That's not strictly true. He's got a new friend.'

Thelma's eyebrows, outlined in dark pencil, rose in surprise. 'How do you know?'

'I heard him talking to that bloke who was asking questions on the bus. You must have heard about it.'

'I did. The passengers apprehended him. Brave lot.'

'Led by me,' said Mary with a proud toss of her head.

Thelma's jaw dropped. 'You?'

'Yes. Then I hid between the telephone box and the police box. PC Routledge had quite a chinwag with the bloke from the bus.'

Intrigued by what her daughter was saying, Thelma pressed her down into a kitchen chair. 'Tell me what they said.'

Mary shrugged. 'Something about the airport. I still thought it was all a bit suspicious, but Percy seemed all right with it. Fascinated in fact. I've never seen him fascinated with anyone – or even friendly. But he was with this bloke.'

'What else did he say?'

Mary's brow creased in concentration. 'Let's start from the beginning,' she said somewhat loftily, proud that she'd had the leading part to play. 'On the bus he told us he was from the Channel Islands and that's why he spoke English with a foreign accent. Said he spoke French. But I don't think he was from there.'

'And him and Percy. What were they talking about?'

Mary swallowed the mouthful of bread and looked up at the ceiling as though the answer was floating around up there above her head.

'He seemed to be making Percy an offer. Something about a

job – or at least I think it was. And talk about being in touch. Percy seemed over the moon. Personally, I wouldn't trust the bloke. As I've already told you, he said on the bus that he had a foreign accent because he comes from the Channel Islands and speaks French.' She frowned and shook her head as though she was an old woman not a girl of seventeen. 'Beau speaks French,' she said brightly. 'Some people in Canada do.'

'Oh, do they now,' said Thelma. She folded her arms and looked disapprovingly at her daughter – not that the look lasted long.

'Mum. He's nice. I know you'll like him. Honest you will.'

Thelma eyed her daughter with something approaching pride. That glorious red hair, that silky white skin. She could hardly believe that she was her daughter. She was perfect. Beautiful in fact. And hopefully they'd have many more years together. Not like poor Margaret Routledge and her youngest son. What a terrible tragedy. She wanted to see her children grow up. She also wanted to see George striding down the garden path, kitbag thrown nonchalantly over his shoulder and whistling as though he hadn't a care in the world.

Thelma sighed and shook her head – a sure sign of surrender. 'Then you'd better invite the young man.'

* * *

There was sadness in the Crawford household when Jenny informed her daughters of the tragedy of the night before.

'I need to get back over there and give the poor woman my support. Can you cope with getting your own breakfasts?'

Of course they could.

After gulping back half a cup of tea and wrapping a cardigan around herself against the early-morning chill, Jenny returned to number five Coronation Close. The front door had been left on the catch. She paused in the hallway. It had been chilly enough outside and inside wasn't much better. There was a pristine emptiness about the house, even in the narrow hallway. In her own house, several coats and hats hung on hooks, bulging against the front door when it was open. Boots, shoes, umbrellas and shopping bags jostled for space beneath them. Here there was nothing. Empty coat hooks and a bare floor beneath.

Entering the living room, she found Margaret was wielding a dustpan and brush, flicking at specks Jenny failed to detect.

'Percy hates dirt,' was her excuse when she felt Jenny's eyes upon her.

It was easy to feel uncomfortable. Things about the house and Margaret's behaviour were downright odd, including Margaret's grief. She didn't cry. When she wasn't picking up invisible specks or using the dustpan and brush, she just sat there unblinking, staring at nothing, pale as alabaster.

Moved to show empathy and give solace, Jenny covered Margaret's hand with her own and felt icy fingers. It was as though the blood had ceased to flow or if anything did flow, it was no longer blood but iced water.

She sought words of solace. At the end of the day, small comments were like stepping stones, one at a time back to reality.

'Do you know when your husband is coming home?' she asked softly.

At first, Margaret seemed not to have heard.

Jenny gently squeezed the freezing fingers.

Margaret started.

Jenny repeated the question. 'Do you know when Percy is coming home?'

A pair of wide staring eyes looked at her, not compre-
hending at first and then almost with horror. Her mouth
spread wide exposing her teeth in an angry snarl. 'He should
have said yes. He should have. He was wrong not to. I'll never
forgive him. Never.'

Jenny was taken aback. Margaret usually spoke softly, not
sharp like this.

Not quite clear, but devastating if she was understanding
this properly, Jenny asked again.

'I'm sorry. I don't know what you mean. Do you mean Percy
should have said yes to Albert having the vaccination, but he
didn't? Is that what you mean?'

Margaret nodded vigorously. 'Yes.'

'Vaccination. There was a special clinic at the school. For
diphtheria. I wanted our children to be vaccinated. Percy said
he didn't believe in it.'

Jenny was shocked. The vaccine against the deadly
disease had been available for some time. Before its intro-
duction, deaths had been around seven thousand a year.
They were now rarer, single figures in fact. This explanation was enough for Jenny to have her girls done. The
wonders of modern medicine. Sadly, not everyone accepted
it as fact.

Pushing her own views aside, Jenny concentrated on the
job in hand. 'When did you last see your husband?'

Margaret sucked in her lips and blew her nose. 'Last night.
About eight o'clock.'

'A policeman's work is never done,' Jenny said somewhat
glibly and then wished she'd kept her mouth shut. It sounded
thoughtless, unsympathetic, but she was finding Margaret's
stillness and silence slightly odd. All she could think was that
the bereaved mother was digesting everything. Or maybe she

was wishing against all odds for the clock to turn back, for this never to have happened.

'It's his fault,' she blurted.

To Jenny's surprise and without more prompting, Margaret began to explain.

'He worked the day shift yesterday.'

'And the nightshift? That's a lot of hours if he was.'

'He wasn't.' Her tone of voice was cold and abrupt.

Feet thudded down the stairs. The children were up.

Two round-eyed children, Judith the daughter and Howard, the older son, hesitantly entered the room, peering around as though checking it was safe to enter.

'I'll get you toast and butter,' Margaret exclaimed and got to her feet.

'Butter?'

The children looked surprised, and to Jenny's eyes, excited at the prospect. She felt obliged to make comment.

'Do you like butter?'

'Dad doesn't let us have toast and butter. We're only allowed dripping,' explained Howard. He sounded nervous.

'Your father's not here,' said Jenny, a clattering of plates, cups and saucers sounded from the kitchen. It seemed as though Margaret was keeping herself busy.

'Isn't he?'

Was it her imagination or did Howard sound as if he welcomed the fact?

Silently, Judith joined her mother in the kitchen. Holding her head at an angle, Jenny saw mother and daughter hug each other and bury their heads on one another's shoulders. Mother and daughter sharing grief but also something else. Was she seeing a sense of relief in their action? Relishing the fact that he was absent even in such a terrible moment?

Howard remained looking at her.

Jenny felt she had to say something.

'Your brother's gone to heaven,' she offered.

He nodded. 'I know.'

His matter-of-fact manner surprised her. She wanted to ask him if he was upset, but somehow couldn't get the words out.

He spoke before she did. 'What about my dad? Has he gone to heaven too?'

To Jenny's amazement, he sounded almost relieved, the same reaction she'd thought she'd seen in his mother and sister.

Putting on a brave and as understanding a smile as possible, she shook her head. 'I think he's at work.'

He looked crestfallen.

The children ate their toast and drank their tea in silence, melted butter running down their faces, the simple breakfast disappearing in minutes as though it was a luxury feast to be relished.

The two of them were obviously saddened by their brother's demise, yet there seemed to be something else going on here. Their father wasn't around to support them, to provide a united front in the face of adversity, yet it didn't seem to concern them.

'You can go now,' Margaret said to her. 'I'll wait another hour before going along to the funeral parlour to make arrangements. We'll use Mr Langley,' she said, her eyes filling with tears. 'He's a Methodist.'

'Shouldn't your husband have been home by now? I mean, wouldn't he want a say in the matter?'

'He's not here. I am.'

Jenny was surprised at her blunt manner. She presumed it was because she was used to him being absent due to the nature of his work. But surely if he had been on duty, he might have heard by now and come home. News travelled fast in Knowle West.

Margaret pushed back a lock of hair that had fallen onto her forehead. The poor woman tried to smile, though it was not a happy smile. There was a bitterness to it that Jenny found hard to understand.

'He should have been. Perhaps he's left me.' She laughed hysterically.

Jenny sought some idea of what she could do to help and decided that Percy should be here.

'I have to go into Bedminster. Would you like me to go into the police station and ask if they can get a message to Percy?'

Margaret nodded. 'Yes. It's very remiss of him.'

It surprised Jenny that she spoke in such a clipped manner. Following the sudden death of her little boy, her demeanour had become more abrupt.

'I'll call in later then.'

'Yes. You can let yourself out.'

'Are you going to be all right, Margaret?' Jenny said softly, her hand resting gently on her neighbour's shoulder. 'Only I've got to see my girls off.' Her girls were quite capable of looking after themselves, and although she felt guilty even mentioning her own children, she was eager to get away from Margaret's strangeness. Yes, she was sad about poor little Albert, but Margaret's behaviour unnerved her. Jenny just didn't know what to make of it.

The sound of scuffling slippers preceded Cath's return.

'Cath.'

Jenny got up from the two-seater settee where she'd been sitting next to Margaret.

In a soft voice meant to be shared just between them, she exclaimed how glad she was to see her.

'She's bearing up.'

'Good.'

'Do you mind if I go?'

'You go,' Cath whispered back.

'I've promised to go to the police station and ask if they can get word to your brother.'

'Oh, thank you,' returned Cath. 'I'll keep an eye on her.'

On Jenny's return home, Tilly and Gloria looked up and asked, 'How's Mrs Routledge?'

'Sad.' It was all she could think of to say as she sank into a chair. 'I could do with a cup of tea.'

The teacup rattled in its saucer before Jenny steadied her hand and took the first sip, aware that the girls were standing in front of her awaiting an explanation.

One more sip of tea and she told them all that she knew about Albert Routledge. Inwardly, she thanked God that she'd had both girls vaccinated despite the old wives' tales that it was against natural law or some such thing.

'Poor thing,' whispered Gloria.

Tilly brushed a tear from the corner of one eye.

Jenny shook herself out of her torpor and reminded Tilly of the time and if she didn't hurry, she would miss her bus.

Bus fare in pocket, an umbrella was snatched from the coat rack in the hallway. Before she was out of the door, Jenny grabbed her and wrapped her in a hug.

'I love you, darling. Keep safe.'

The hug persisted until Tilly reminded her mother that she had a bus to catch so could she please let go.

'Take care. See you this evening.'

Like a young colt, legs kicking behind her whilst the

umbrella was swiftly opened to cope with the early shower, Tilly headed for her job in the insurance office in Bristol city centre.

When it came to her turn, Gloria wiped off the kisses and, when Jenny patted her on the head, reminded her mother that she was no longer a little kid.

Despite that, Jenny grabbed and kissed her again and watched her until she'd turned the corner of Coronation Close and disappeared. Such was the effect of the death of a child.

From the living-room window and alone in the house, Jenny looked across the green to the houses opposite. Her fingers fondled the pearl buttons on the pale blue short-sleeved blouse she was wearing. Thelma had made it from a length of silk. Robin had said she looked pretty in it, that it matched her eyes. She wasn't sure about that, but it was a lovely compliment and made her feel almost young again. Like her, he loved his kids. He too would understand how Margaret was feeling.

She and Robin had been young together. They were getting older, both with kids and responsibilities. He'd become a big part of her life, but today she was glad not to be working at his shop. The larder was looking bare, and she needed to go shopping in Bedminster. Before that, she would call in at Bedminster police station.

18

Bedminster police station had a grey stone edifice and the look of a small castle. Sandbags were piled either side of the main entrance making the interior seem dark as a cave.

When Jenny stepped inside, she felt as though the grim building was swallowing her whole. Wall-mounted gas lights spluttered weak flames. Above her head, conical lampshades hung from long wire flex. Only half of them had bulbs that worked, hence the gas lights. Even the police station made an effort to conserve supplies.

The floor was flag stoned, the walls the colour of mud to the height of the dado rail and sludgy green above. Her first impression of a cave was a correct one.

A police sergeant, wearing a uniform that looked too big for him, coughed and spluttered into a handkerchief before asking if he could help her.

'I'm looking for Police Constable Routledge. Percy Routledge.'

'Oh yes. Why him, missus?'

'There's been a tragedy. He needs to get home to his wife. Can you give him a message please?'

The man behind the high desk had a ruddy face and a head of white bristly hair. She guessed he had been recalled from retirement to cover for younger men who had chosen to join up. The expression that creased his wrinkled face was one of puzzlement. 'I'm sorry?'

She repeated what she'd already said.

More coughing ensued. He lit up a cigarette, taking in great gulps of it and expelling a cloud of smoke that hung like a stratified halo above his head. A few more coughs.

Jenny was getting impatient. 'Is he here? His little boy...' She couldn't bring herself to say that Albert was dead.

'Bad, is it?'

'Very bad.'

He read something in the look on her face and shuffled back from the counter.

'Hang on a minute.'

He opened a door behind him and shouted out if anyone had seen PC Routledge. Another man wearing a police uniform came out looking slightly put out and not a little concerned.

'He's not here.' He turned his attention to Jenny. 'We thought he might be taken poorly when he didn't turn in for his shift this morning.'

Now it was Jenny who looked surprised. She shook her head. 'You must be wrong. He went out last night and hasn't come home.'

The two men looked nonplussed.

'Well, this is a right mystery,' said the man who'd come out from the back. Threads of sandy-coloured hair was combed over his freckled skull.

Jenny stroked the creases on her forehead as she tried to work this out. She'd been up most of the night, she was tired, but even so, she was certain that Margaret had said that he'd gone out last night.

'This is so terrible,' she said, shaking her head. 'I must tell you what's happened in case you see him first.'

She told them that his youngest son had died suddenly last night from diphtheria.

Both men were sympathetic.

The snowy-haired man shook his head. 'What a shock that's going to be when he hears about it. Terrible thing to happen.'

And something that could have been avoided. She held back the urge to yell it out.

'If he comes in, we'll tell him, but, in the meantime, you might find that he might have returned home by now.'

'Thank you for coming in,' said the bald man.

The one with the white hair lit up a second cigarette, even though half of the previous one smouldered in a tin ashtray. Another spasm of coughing broke out before she'd even exited the gloomy interior and gained the daylight outside.

Jenny left the police station feeling even more tired and confused than when she'd gone in.

Shopping, queuing and a few words with other women waiting to get what they could to feed their families helped lift her mood, although not entirely. If she was feeling this way, how must Margaret be feeling. Her reaction to losing her child had been difficult to comprehend. No wailing or gnashing of teeth, just a sudden cold detachment, as though something had snapped deep inside.

Rain lashed the bus windows all the way home but had gone off by the time Jenny got back to Coronation Close.

Rosellia, who was of Spanish extraction and lived in number one, was leaning over her garden gate, hands clasped together as though in prayer. 'The little boy,' she said in broken English. 'So sad. I pray for him.'

'That's all any of us can do,' sighed Jenny. She asked if she knew whether Percy Routledge had returned home. Leaning on her garden gate was a distinct vantage point, especially seeing as her house was the first on the left when entering the close.

Rosellia shook her head. 'No. Cath, she is over there with Mrs Routledge.'

Jenny nodded. 'That's good.'

Rosellia nodded in agreement.

In one way it was good because it meant that Margaret was not alone. In another way, it was not good. Where was Percy when his wife and family needed his support? He was the one who should be here. Where was the man who spied on his neighbours and harboured a holier-than-thou attitude second to none?

19

Six days had passed since little Albert Routledge had died and his father had gone missing. The former was a tragedy. The latter a mystery that was talked about from one end of the estate to the other.

There was genuine sorrow for the passing of the little boy, sad-eyed neighbours watching the white coffin surrounded by flowers in a black hearse. As was usual for neighbourhood funerals, someone had gone door to door collecting donations towards flowers for the funeral and money for the boy's mother.

There was conjecture about why Percy had not reappeared. Even the hardest man would at least attend his young son's funeral. But there was no sign of the boy's father. Rumours abounded that he'd taken a trip into town and fallen into one of the craters left by enemy bombing. It was easy enough to do in the blackout. Other less believable rumours were that he had run away with another woman, joined the services, or had an accident of some kind. Conjecture was the order of the day, a puzzle that would in time be sorted.

The police did a cursory search, half a dozen constables asking questions from door to door. No trace was found, so, like the neighbours, the police took the view that he had disappeared for personal reasons.

The harsh fact was that nobody had cared much for Percy. His not being around any longer was a mystery but, due to his rubbing up people the wrong way, not a source of despair. The little boy and his distraught mother attracted sympathy.

Once the funeral was over, the curtains in living-room windows pulled back to let in daylight. Black-bordered funeral cards were removed and the resilient residents of Coronation Close got on with life. Tragedy was a familiar and lifelong companion to the likes of the solid working-class people who lived in Coronation Close.

In their drab world of shortages, it was easy to get downhearted. In this regard, Jenny made a conscious effort to rise above the doom and gloom that could so easily dampen the most vibrant of spirits. Never had the wartime slogan 'keep calm and carry on' been such an apt rallying cry.

The wake at the Routledge house was for relatives, friends from the church and the methodist minister who had conducted the service. Tea and biscuits only. The neighbours were not invited.

Jenny let a respectable hour pass, then made her way across the road to her friend Thelma.

It was with overwhelming relief that she shouted, 'Yoo-hoo! It's me.'

She pushed open the back door of number twelve Coronation Close, went through the kitchen and stopped in her tracks.

She wasn't sure what she'd expected to see; perhaps Thelma in tears or at least her brow creased with worry. Funerals were sad events when thoughts of one's own loved ones were recalled. There had still been no word of George, so Jenny had no intention of mentioning him. Quite frankly she was concerned as to how Thelma was bearing up after the night they'd had. Would the death of young Albert cause her to dwell on her missing son?

Jenny's fears were greatly relieved.

Thelma flashed a smile. 'Wasn't expecting you. Glad you came though.'

'Sad days need to be compensated by good friendship.'

Jenny cast her gaze around the familiar living room, glad to see that nothing had changed. The world would go on as it had done. Normality persisted in Thelma's display of coronation china on the dresser, the pictures of the royal family cut from magazines and newspapers and mounted in picture frames. The cosy atmosphere of busyness and homeliness was unchanged.

Thelma was sitting at her oak dining table with a pile of items of mainly white clothing in front of her. The lid of the treadle sewing machine had been removed, the machine made ready for action. The light coming through the living-room window picked out the gold lettering of the manufacturer 'Singer', the pale pink and green mother-of-pearl decoration.

Jenny eyed the pile of material. 'Goodness. What have you got there today?'

Thelma plunged a pair of scissors into the legs of a voluminous pair of old-fashioned knickers and held them up for Jenny to inspect. 'Knickers.' Thelma plucked another pair from the pile and held them up. They were huge. Bloomers, of a sickly pink colour and of a sort no longer worn unless of advanced years. 'I bought these years ago at a jumble sale. Can't recall where, but they certainly seemed to corner the market in old ladies' unmentionables. Just look at the amount of elastic in the legs alone – loads – and tons more in the waist, besides a row of buttons at the side. Talk about harvest festivals. All is safely gathered in.' She laughed and demonstrated just how much elastic she was likely to harvest by inserting and spreading a hand inside one leg.

Jenny laughed and spread her own slim hands around her waist, still trim despite heading towards forty and having had two children. 'Enough to go around my waist at least once. Twice depending on how tight I wanted it. Nice bit of silk too, though I'm not keen on the colour.'

Thelma agreed with her. 'Flesh colour is taking things a bit far. Looks the same colour as tinned salmon to me.'

'What a lovely thought,' Jenny said somewhat dreamily.

'I'm not taking the elastic out of silk knickers. It's the old-style fleecy-lined cotton bloomers I'm after. I can use the material to make a liberty bodice for my Alice. I would do the same for Mary, but the little minx reckons she's too old for wearing them.' Thelma sighed. 'That girl is growing up too fast. Caught her using my lipstick and my nail varnish. Told her it's got to last me a long time.' She looked up at Jenny tellingly. 'Judging by the way things are going, it might have to last until the end of the war. I take it you heard about the riot outside Woolworths. Who'd ever have thought fights could break out over a bottle of nail varnish!'

The war was responsible for a lot of shortages. Scarcity of knicker elastic had been unforeseen and was caused by the rationing of rubber – the most important constituent of tyres for military transport, aircraft, gaskets for engines, factory and mining conveyor belts, as well as industrial machinery. Nail varnish and lipstick were viewed by the powers that be as necessary to have women look as good as possible, their conclusion being that pretty women kept up the morale of the fighting man.

Jenny pulled out a chair and sat down to hold the end of a piece of material while Thelma sliced it along with her very sharp scissors. Conversation replaced their silently held thoughts. Neither wanted to mention the death of Albert Routledge. The whereabouts of his father was a different matter.

'Heard anything about Percy Routledge? Has he been found?'

Jenny shook her head. 'No. It's all a bit strange. The same old rumours keep going. He may have had an accident in the blackout. Unless he ran off with another woman.'

'Not likely,' said Thelma, shaking her head.

She snipped somewhat aggressively at the strong seam of an old-fashioned cotton nightgown which looked as though Queen Victoria might have worn it – it was certainly voluminous in the extreme and of that age. There was a ripping sound. Using both hands Thelma had torn along from the initial cut. The two edges were jagged.

'Blast. I didn't mean to do that.'

It was hard to tell whether Thelma was angry with the fabric or the subject of men. She certainly had lifelong experience of both. She asked Jenny to hold one end whilst she used the scissors to recut in a straight line.

Deciding not to ask what had made her so uncharacteristically impatient, Jenny decided to keep the conversation centred on the disappearance of Percy Routledge.

'Nearly a week and still no sign of him. If he was alive, he'd have heard about his little boy by now and I believe he would be here. Any loving parent would be.'

'It's a strange kettle of fish and that's for sure.'

Thelma was glad of Jenny's company. She wanted her to stay a while so went out of her way to lighten the mood that she lived with every day since George went missing in action. This was the Thelma that had survived an assault some years back and, although hurt and anguished, she had bounced back, determined not to let anything or anyone dampen her fire. Worrying about her son, her job and Mary growing away from her was bad enough.

'Seen anything of Bert?' Jenny asked.

Thelma plunged the scissors into another piece of material as though the fleecy cotton had upset her in some way. 'No. I saw him in East Street the other day. He looked in a hurry. Just a wave. That's all I got.' Her jaw tightened. Her red well-defined lips set in a grim line.

Jenny suggested that he must be very busy. 'Holding down a job, doing fire watching and such like, plus sorting out his mother's affairs.'

There was reluctance – or was it disbelief? – in Thelma's response. Either way, Jenny knew that Thelma was missing her manfriend. Bert was not exactly Prince Charming but dependable. He was like a handbag, handy to have around.

It was somewhat telling when the topic of Thelma's conversation went back to elastic – or rather the lack of it.

'I reckon old Hitler is cracking jokes about our knickers falling around our ankles. Hopes it stops us helping with the war effort. But there it is. Keeping our underwear in place is not top priority to those in charge of the army, navy and air force.' She threw Jenny a mischievous look. 'Not priority for some women with their men away fighting; letting the side down along with her knickers!'

'Including a certain woman we both know,' Jenny said acidly. Doreen Hubert, Robin's estranged wife, had a reputation that had spread far and wide. Jenny grimaced at the thought of her.

Thelma raised one eyebrow. Knowing how Jenny felt about Robin, her look was both knowing and sympathetic. 'Ah yes. Doreen. Trust her to drop them for the war effort – with or without elastic!'

Jenny's laugh was brittle, but her humour did tend to be subdued when it came to Doreen and the way she treated Robin. They were separated and that should have calmed things down, but Doreen liked to put the knife in. She used their two children as weapons and also to spy on Robin, and her – Jenny – as a matter of fact. All last weekend she'd felt like an insect under a microscope, Simon's eyes on her as though he was taking note. 'I expect she's primed him to report back and tell her everything we got up to.'

Robin had told her she was imagining things. She held back saying that he was like an ostrich, head in the sand to what was really happening. But Simon was his son. He was bound to think the best of him. Don't we all think that of all our children?

Anyway, she was more than glad when the weekend had ended, and Robin had taken his son back to where he lived with his mother.

Although Robin was quite happy to have a quiet life separate from her, Doreen took great pleasure in taunting him, threatening him that she would move away and take the children with her. Not that Jenny thought she would and anyway Simon and Susan had left school. Robin had insisted that they were both quite bright and could have got a scholarship enabling them to stay on for an extra year beyond the customary fourteen years of age. Their mother would have none of it.

'She wanted them to bring in a wage. Said she couldn't go on keeping them forever. Not that it's her money keeping them,' he'd added grimly. 'Working three nights a week in a pub bar don't go too far.'

Doreen sponged off Robin like a leech on a feeding spree. There was always something she needed: the rent money, money for new shoes for either of their offspring, money for the electricity and the gas meter. Robin paid it all. Doreen's priority was nights out and spending the clothing ration on herself.

Although Robin seemed loath to face it, Jenny had long ago ascertained that his estranged wife was a leech who wasn't averse to blackmail or lying to get what she wanted. She'd also heard rumours that she was on the game, one of the many women who took advantage of the huge influx of foreign servicemen crowding the pubs, nightclubs and dance halls.

Even though she was past the first flower of youth, Doreen was out having a high old time with the glut of men in uniform camped all around the city. The pubs were full of them every night and in Jenny's opinion was one of the reasons she'd got the job as a barmaid. It certainly wasn't because she enjoyed working. She was one of those who had married because she didn't want to work.

Jenny clamped her lips tightly together so none of this would tumble out – although she knew Thelma's opinion of Doreen Hubert. In the meantime, she and Robin guarded their relationship. Someday they would marry, of that she was sure. It was just a question of when.

She noticed that Thelma had gone quiet, even a little introverted, as though deep in unspoken thoughts. She felt an urge to get her to snap out of it.

'All this material. You're going to make enough new undies

and whatnot from this lot to fill a shop,' Jenny exclaimed brightly.

Thelma barely responded, her busy fingers pulling out another old-fashioned item of clothing, the scissors close by ready for action.

Jenny understood. Still bruised from having received no news about her son, Thelma did her best to rise above her low spirits and overall hid it well. Jenny had been a close friend for a few years. It was inevitable that she picked up on her low vibes.

Thelma was aware of how she must be appearing to her dearest friend. It just wasn't like her. *I won't stay down*, she told herself. *I won't be beaten by anything!*

Rousing herself into a false aura of cheerfulness, she picked up a jam jar and gave it a shake. 'If I don't have enough elastic, there's always my button collection. One button and a button-hole work well on camiknickers. Leave the bloomers to them that like to keep their nether regions warm as toast. We're made of sterner stuff than that.'

Jenny laughed with her, but Thelma saw the questioning look in the kind eyes she'd first encountered before there'd been any war, in the days when Jenny had moved into number two Coronation Close.

Thelma forced a smile. 'Now how about you pop out into the kitchen and make us a cup of tea?'

'I knew I'd come here for a reason,' Jenny said cheerfully. 'Let's get that kettle on.'

'There's some broken biscuits in the tin. Put a few on a tea plate, will you?'

Whilst the sound of water pouring from the tap into the kettle came from the kitchen, Thelma sat quite still, her thoughts arcing from one concern to another. Each thought was like one of those painted horses on a roundabout, forever going round in circles, stopping for a moment before setting off again – and going nowhere.

The new worry was that her job at Bertrams didn't seem as safe as it used to be. The building housing the upmarket women's fashion store had not been bombed, but there was not so much stock as there used to be, most that was available confined to utility items, boxy pleats and a far cry from what had been on offer before the war.

She'd seen Mr Bertram standing at the top of the stairs that led from the shop floor to his office, a deep furrow across his brow. It was almost as though he was counting how many customers were milling around, although milling might be the wrong word. Customers were getting scarcer.

Jenny came in with two teacups carefully balanced in each hand.

'I poured boiling water on the leaves left in the pot and let it brew a while. I hope it's strong enough.'

'It should be fine. The leaves in the pot have only been used once.'

Once was a luxury. Thanks to rationing, it was quite normal to use tea leaves at least three times.

'Here you are. There's nothing like a good cup of tea.' Her cheerfulness persisting, Jenny pushed the cup and saucer towards her friend.

Thelma took a sip. 'Not bad. I think I might get a third brew from these leaves.'

'Waste not, want not.'

Thelma sighed. 'Oh, for the days when we used the tea leaves just the once.'

'They'll come again,' said Jenny, sounding as though she had total confidence that they would. She certainly hoped so.

After relishing a sip or two of tea, Thelma too showed determination to keep to the trivial and began to explain the minute details of the underwear she was making.

'I've got bits of old lace trim to hide the joins,' she said, pushing the tea to one side.

She held up a strip of mauve lace she'd cut off an ancient sunshade that had seen many a Victorian summer and pinned it to the silky fabric that would make a very pretty petticoat or pair of camiknickers.

Jenny agreed that it worked. 'It looks lovely. I'd wear them.'

Thelma sipped and put down her cup again. 'I'm not good company. Sorry. I've got too much on my mind.'

'Of course you have. I don't suppose...'

'I've heard nothing.'

'No news is good news.'

It was a trite thing to say, and Jenny could have bitten her tongue the moment it was out of her mouth. George was missing at sea. Being on convoy duty, his ship had been prey to U-boats, the enemy submarines that hunted in packs, their aim to send both merchant ships and their accompanying protection to the bottom of the sea. Not knowing for sure was a huge burden for a mother to face and Jenny felt both sorry and awkward, although she did her best to reach out, to show sympathy without stirring up Thelma's worse fears. She went as far as asking how George's wife, Maria, was coping with one small child and another on the way.

'She's a brick,' proclaimed Thelma and sounded genuinely impressed.

Jenny knew that, as someone born in Italy, Maria wasn't having it easy. Some people made nasty comments even though they could see she had a child. Those who knew she was married to George Dawson tended to be friendly just in case Thelma found out and gave them a piece of her mind.

Best, Jenny thought, to divert Thelma's thoughts with triviality, though goodness knows anything to do with the war was far from being trivial. In fact, she hated the war with a vengeance. It had been at its worse the year before – 1940 – and earlier this year, when the Luftwaffe had bombed Bristol on several occasions, the sky a bright red glow over the old heart of the city.

'I wonder what Castle Street and Wine Street will look like after the war. They're bound to rebuild it,' Jenny remarked.

Thelma agreed, just a straight one-word agreement. Jenny carried on with reminiscences of how things used to be – and hopefully would be again.

'It used to be so lovely shopping there. Even window shopping. I could never afford anything.'

Again, the muted response.

Jenny made a few more comments, mentioning how it was the last time she'd gone into the city centre. Out of a sense of nostalgia, she had only visited the Castle Street area once since the last bombing raid. The old heart of the city had been razed to the ground, leaving gaping holes where cellars used to be, lone chimney stacks standing forlorn and sentinel like soldiers on guard amongst the rubble and ruins.

Her voice drifted on along with her thoughts. 'I can shop in Bedminster if I have to, though I've registered with the Co-op on Melvin Square.'

Rationing ensured that everyone got their fair share so that nobody would starve. To receive rations, you had to designate a shop where you would purchase your food.

Thelma finally contributed to the conversation. 'I'm fine with the Co-op. I could go to George Inman in East Street,

Bedminster, but Melvin Square is more convenient. I can send Alice there if need be. Inconvenient at times, but it must be done what with...' She paused. 'Things being the way they are.'

'How's Mary getting on at the tobacco factory?'

'Fine.' Thelma shook her head. 'Thinks herself a grown woman. Getting to be a cheeky minx too. And she has a boyfriend. A Canadian. I've said she can bring him home. Not sure when that will be. Who knows, she might have swapped him for another without telling me.'

Jenny laughed.

Thelma shook herself from her downhearted stupor as she sought diversion. 'I suppose we were like that at one time.'

'I suppose we were.'

And we were foolish, thought Jenny. *Thought we were in love, fooled by youthful inexperience.*

'We were tempted,' Thelma said as though reading her thoughts.

Jenny agreed. 'Fell in and out of love at the drop of a hat, mostly with boys we'd known most of our lives.'

Thelma grimaced. 'At least we weren't tempted by all these young men in uniforms. I worry about Mary. She's wilful and no matter me laying down the law and telling her to be careful, it goes in one ear and out the other.'

'You don't think...' Jenny said slowly.

'I do the thinking, but Mary doesn't think. She lives for the moment.'

They both fell to silence as they contemplated what this meant. Jenny most certainly understood. She'd feel the same if it was one of her daughters. As it was, her girl Tilly was level-headed, and Mary was... She concluded that Mary liked a good time. Liked young fellas in uniform too. Another worry for her dear friend Thelma who suddenly interrupted her flow of thought.

'Must show you this,' she said, reaching into the bottom cupboard of the fitted dresser that occupied one wall of the room, her skirt tight against her broad behind. Out came her latest sewing project. 'What do you think of my new bolero?' She was all smiles as she held up a rust-coloured bolero that would look stupendous with a fitted black or navy-blue dress.

Jenny fingered the material. 'It's lovely. Am I mistaken or is that chenille?'

Thelma beamed with pride. 'Spot on. It used to be a table-cloth. I never used it so altered it to suit. A nice little jacket.'

Jenny laughed. 'You are clever. Your Mary always looks so smart. She's lucky to have you making her clothes.'

'She's lucky that I don't lock the front door and stop her from going out,' Thelma said grimly. 'She pushes her luck at times, getting home late and full of excuses. Mind you...' Her dark eyebrows met in a deep vee above her powdered nose. Indoors or out Thelma wore make-up.

Jenny pressed her to continue. 'Go on.'

'You know that bus incident...'

'You mean when a man was apprehended by the passengers.'

'I do.'

'Well, Mary, being a sneaky little thing...' Thelma laughed. 'Well, they didn't know she was there, but Percy was talking to the man – not as though he was going to arrest him – but as a friend. She reckons Percy was angling for a position with wher-ever it was the foreign bloke worked. And my Mary was convinced he was foreign, though not convinced that he was French. Because of her new boyfriend being French Canadian,' she added in response to Jenny's questioning look. 'She reckoned Percy was hanging onto the bloke's every word.'

Jenny's eyebrows rose. 'Was he indeed. Perhaps that's where he is. Perhaps he's gone off with the stranger from the bus.'

Thelma shrugged. 'I suppose it's possible.'

'Should you tell the police? Or Margaret?'

'No.' Thelma shook her head, a look of consternation on her face. 'Not yet anyway, I mean, poor Margaret has enough to cope with at present. Let her get over Albert's death first, then I'll think about it.'

Jenny agreed with her.

'I know Cath's a friend, but I do wish her brother would join up rather than hassling his neighbours.'

'Perhaps that's why he's disappeared. Ashamed he wasn't in the army and joined up without telling anyone.'

Jenny's brow furrowed when she recalled the night Albert Routledge had died. 'You know, Margaret's behaviour was very odd. I never saw her shed a tear on the night her son died. She had an air of devastation, yes, but she didn't cry. It was as though she was contemplating the whole thing or suddenly seeing things from an unfamiliar perspective – facing something.'

'What do you mean?'

Jenny shook her head. 'Oh, I don't know.' She shook her head, her hair falling forward around her face. Reliving that evening in her mind, she sought and found the moment when the woman's persona had altered. 'It was after I mentioned my girls having had their inoculations. She said that Percy didn't believe in having them.'

Fabric loose in her hands, Thelma sat back in her chair. 'Each to their own. He won't be the only one who doesn't believe in it, but on the other hand...'

Their eyes met in mutual understanding. 'Could it be that she's blaming him for Albert's death?'

'And it's suddenly come to her in a rush. What a terrible thing. The poor woman.'

'So she doesn't care that he's gone missing either,' Jenny suggested.

'Possibly. I wonder if he crept back, found out about Albert and couldn't bring himself to face the music, her blaming him for their little boy's death.'

'It's at least thoughtless, at the most a mystery, although he could have had an accident. Did you hear about people falling into bombsites in Wine Street? You know those deep cellars that used to be under buildings and are now gaping holes. The blackout's to blame, of course.'

'Plus, a drop too much beer,' Thelma added with a grin.

'That's what might have happened to Percy – the falling into a hole, I mean. Not sure about drinking. I don't think he did.'

'No. Percy is – or was – a church-going man. Methodists don't hold with drink.'

'Another cuppa?' asked Jenny.

Thelma drained her cup and said that she would like another.

'At least you've got Bert.'

'You could say he's been absent without leave of late. He's taken on fire watch at the council house and does a few shifts at the air-raid posts when he can fit it in. The last time we went out – only for a drink at the pub – he fell asleep over half a shandy – nearly drowned in it in fact, but... I do fancy a night out.'

'Never mind a night out, I could do with a day out,' said Jenny, 'seeing as the weather is nice. What do you think?'

Thelma took two seconds to agree. 'Sunday?'

'Sunday is fine with me.'

They parted, each harbouring their own thoughts. Jenny thought about Robin and where their relationship was going; Thelma thought about her son and whether the baby her daughter-in-law was expecting would grow up without a father.

'Please God,' she muttered. 'Send him home. Please send him home.'

20

Maria Dawson tugged her home-knitted cardigan around herself as she stood in the queue outside the Co-op. One hand gripped her ration books, all ten fingers curled over the handlebar of the pushchair.

Women with tired faces had been waiting here since nine that morning and the queue had quickly grown from half a dozen to a string of women stretching along the front of the shops, each jealous of keeping their place in the queue. Not that anyone really knew what they were queueing for, but news had gone round that there might be a bit more offal than there had been last week.

Joints, chops, poultry and sausages were rationed, but offal – that was hearts, lungs, liver and pigs' tails and trotters – was not. People who had never eaten liver, kidneys, heart and lights – the latter, cow's lungs and light as a feather – were doing what they could with what they could get. Stuffed hearts had become a staple replacement for a rib of beef for Sunday roast, made tastier with a bunch of sage dried over the cooker and onions grown in the garden.

At least there were plenty of carrots, potatoes and other root vegetables, though housewives were told to make them stretch further simply by cooking them in their skins. *More fibre and more nutrition when cooked in their skins. Waste not, want not.*

Gardens where flowers had once grown were turned over to the growing of vegetables – cabbages, sprouts, broccoli – anything edible, in fact.

With her daughter in the pram, a shopping bag over her arm and grimly holding onto her ration book, Maria stood patiently, aware that several people who knew who she was – and what she was – were eyeing her suspiciously. After all, she was Italian and looked Italian. A whisper of her origins from a single person who knew, quickly spread along the queue.

Since the beginning of the war and Italy's part in it, Maria had kept her head down and not responded to some of the snidey remarks she'd received. Putting on a cheery face with Thelma had become routine rather than admit to the abusive comments people hurled at her. She hadn't wanted her mother-in-law to worry and kept telling herself that soon the war would be over, and everyone would be nice again. At present, there was no sign of the war being over and no sign of people being nice again. However, it was only some people who were nasty towards her.

So far, her day had been rosy – until she'd joined the queue. Maria looked over her shoulder and saw two women who always gave her dirty looks and made some comment about her being a dirty Iti, a foreign enemy who should be locked up.

It was too much to hope that she wasn't noticed by the two women. She had seen their expressions clear enough. Faces chapped with weather and the passing of the years, mean and sour, out to bait someone who they considered weaker and different from them. One had a cigarette drooping from the corner of her mouth. Both displayed a sunray of wrinkles around their mean lips and there was no warmth in eyes grown weary from a dull, hopeless life.

Discretion being the better part of valour, she faced resolutely forward. The moment would pass. That's what she told herself.

The queue moved forward two abreast. She hadn't realised who she was standing next to until she spoke.

'Hello, Maria. I thought that was you.'

The young woman who'd greeted her so warmly she recognised as being Clara, the daughter of Mr Wendell from next door, the man who had told her about the ships that had been sunk in convoy.

Having a friend in the queue helped ease her discomfort.

'Yes. I need a few things.'

'Well, let's hope there's something left by the time we get to the front of the queue.'

Maria laughed with her. Clara Wendell – she didn't know her married name – was expecting her first child. Judging by the size of her belly, she was fast approaching her term.

The queue shuffled forward.

'Such a shame that Mrs Routledge lost her little boy to diphtheria,' Clara remarked. 'I saw the funeral. That white coffin. It seemed so small.' She shook her head.

Maria agreed with her. 'Yes. It is very sad.'

'Has the father turned up yet? I hear he was missing and, seeing as your mother-in-law lives round there, thought you might have heard something.'

Maria shook her head as they shuffled a few more steps forward. Sometimes she might queue for hours. Today didn't seem quite so bad. Before long, they would at least gain the black and white tiled floor immediately before the shop door.

'It's very strange,' said Clara, shaking her head.

Facing steadfastly ahead, Maria failed to see the two women – she vaguely recalled their names: Violet Shepherd and Rose Anderson – exchange knowing looks and pinched smiles, a prequel to their intention to stir things. Yet she felt it, like a sudden shiver on a hot day when thunder hangs in the air.

'I think foreigners should have half the rations of us. Especially those who are our enemies. Don't you, Rose?' Violet said it loud enough to turn heads.

Her bosom buddy responded just as loudly. 'Too right, Vi. Bombing our convoys they are. Foreigners all of them. Germans and *Italians*. All in cahoots, strutting around in their black uniforms. Trying to bomb us out of existence, they are, skewering babies on their bayonets, so I 'eard.'

'It ain't right. Ain't right at all. I think the lot of them, those still in this country, should be left to starve. Don't give them any rations. Push 'em out of the queue, that's what I say. Don't give 'em anything.'

Maria felt her legs turn to jelly as a low muttering spread amongst the women waiting patiently for food to feed their families.

'All blokes between the ages of seventeen and seventy were arrested ages ago,' Rose went on.

'But not women.'

'Can't see why not. They're enemies too, ain't they?'

Maria's complexion, born of a race who lived mostly in sunshine, turned pink with embarrassment, and fear was like an icicle being trailed down her spine. Scared and frightened for both her and her child, she considered heading for home and coming back another day. Then she thought of George. He had been one of those serving on a merchant ship in a convoy carrying food for his country. His country didn't mean just his countrymen of the same blood as him, it meant everybody and that included his wife and child.

Suddenly Clara Wendell touched her arm. 'Don't listen to them, Maria.' Her voice was gentle and reassuring.

Maria turned and smiled into her clear blue eyes. Maria admired those eyes and the blonde hair that complemented them so well. Clara was a person she'd quite like as a friend.

'Thank you.' Her voice was barely above a whisper.

'No need to thank me. I'm only doing what's right.' Clara's voice had been soft and gentle but now suddenly turned strident and loud.

At first Maria startled until she saw Clara jerk her head in the direction of the two women in the queue behind them.

'Any word of your husband?' Clara's voice remained loud. She obviously had every intention of letting everyone know Maria's circumstances.

'No.'

'I read in the newspaper about his ship. If it weren't for the likes of him, we'd all be starving to death. Let's hope that he is alive,' she added even more loudly.

Murmurs of sympathy rumbled through the women around them.

Clara smiled and patted Maria's arm again. 'Let's hope he's all right and will come home to you and your little one. And so say all of us, don't we, girls?'

More murmurs of agreement drifted around them like a fine, warm blanket.

Although Maria hadn't exchanged many words with Clara before today, she felt this was someone who she could trust.

The little she'd heard about her in Redruth Road – mostly from her father, Mr Wendell – was that Clara had been bombed out of London and had come home to live with her parents for good. Clara's father was not the most approachable of men, although he had shown her moments of kindness.

'I don't suffer fools gladly,' he'd said to her one day.

On reflection, Maria realised that she was one of the few people he did speak to. He rarely responded when somebody wished him good day but threw most of his neighbours a glowering look, as though he had no patience for any of them. Except for Maria. For some reason, he'd taken a liking to her.

Mrs Wendell, his wife, rarely ventured away from her front garden but could be seen weeding, planting edible crops, hanging washing on the line or cleaning her windows, sweeping her front path and scrubbing the front step as though her very life depended on it. Rarely did she look in the direction of passers-by or share a friendly word. All in all, they seemed a couple well matched.

Clara, who seemed at times to glow like gold, what with her blue eyes and honey-blonde hair, seemed more outgoing, although this was the first time Maria had had occasion to exchange a word with her. This, she decided, was one of those moments when it was down to her to offer the hand of friendship. She asked her when her baby was due.

Clara's eyes sparkled when she patted her stomach. 'Two months' time. I see you're in the family way too. When's yours expected?'

Maria smiled contentedly. 'Another four months.'

A wide smile lit up Clara's face as the thought came to her that they had something very important in common. 'Next summer we can take our newborns out together. I'll be glad of some company. You too, I shouldn't wonder,' she said. Maria guessed she'd heard nasty comments even in the street where they lived but was too polite and too kind to mention it.

'That would be nice. Are you hoping for a girl or a boy?'

Clara laughed. 'Boy or girl, I don't care what it is as long as it's healthy.' She sighed, at the same time rubbing her bump with affectionate longing. 'There was a moment when I thought it was lost.' Her eyes took on a sorrowful sadness. 'I was buried under the rubble in London during a bombing raid. It took them two hours to get me out.' She bit her lip as though reliving the memory. 'I really was worried I might lose it. I still am, just in case I suffered anything that might have injured my baby.'

Maria felt a great upsurge in spirit, enough to encourage someone else in whatever was to come. She hadn't made many friends of her own age since she'd arrived in this country and those few she had made now seemed awkward in her presence. Now there was Clara. She was so grateful she gave her arm a squeeze. One good turn at reassurance surely deserved another. And she so wanted a friend. 'You'll be fine.'

Behind them in the queue, Rose and Violet, who had decided that Clara's raised voice was just a flash in the pan, prepared themselves for further onslaught. Like the two aged-old boilers that they were, they craned their scraggy necks, their pinprick eyes narrow with menace.

'Foreigners should go to the back of the queue. Especially Musos.'

Maria knew the word they were using referred to Mussolini, Il Duce, the Italian dictator who had allied himself with Adolf Hitler and the insult was directed at her. It didn't matter to them that she was married to an Englishman and had lived in the country for three years or more, that he served in the merchant navy, or had done until she'd received the news that he was lost at sea. There were murmurings around her from those she feared might agree with these two women's vicious comments.

'Gives them council houses and all, we does... them Musos.'

Maria and Clara's eyes met in mutual understanding before the latter's deep blue eyes flashed with fire.

'I'm not having this.' Clara's voice rang out like the bell in the University Tower at the top of Park Street – before the war, of course. No bells rang out now, not until the war was over and the bells of victory were rung. That was the big moment they were waiting for, but for now there was Clara.

At first, Maria interpreted the way Clara's eyes seemed to change shape as sympathy before realising it was mixed with mischief.

Clara gave Maria's arm a reassuring squeeze. 'Leave it with me,' she whispered, then up went her head and outpoured her voice. 'Your married name's Dawson, so I hear. Very English that. My married name would have been Kowalski. Ivan was Polish. He was shot down over the south coast. We'd planned to get married two days after the date he got shot down. Broke my heart, it did. He was a brave man, bravest man I ever met. Didn't shirk his duty, not like some I've heard of round here whose idea of doing their bit is shouting patriotic platitudes – as if that's going to win anything. My Ivan was a foreigner. He gave his life for his country and for this one.'

'No quarrel with Poles. They're on our side,' grumbled a more subdued Rose.

Clara threw her a scathing look. 'Is your husband away fighting?' She purposely increased the volume of her voice so that everybody could hear.

A scornful voice piped up. 'Her husband? That's a laugh. He don't even go to work half the time, let alone go away fighting.'

Someone else joined in. 'Directs the war from 'is armchair. Reads the paper and thinks he knows all about it. Don't go square-bashing though. Not up to putting his size tens on the parade ground rather than the fire grate. Lazy good-for-nothing.'

Chuckles of derision ran through the crowd.

'And Vi's husband's in 'Orfield Prison,' somebody added. 'Light-Fingered Len they call 'im. If it ain't nailed down, he'll pinch it.'

'Horfield Prison is as safe a place as any,' somebody laughed. 'I expect he prefers it there. Not going to call the likes of 'im up, are they?'

As the queue shuffled forward, the two women seemed isolated, looking as though they'd been physically slapped in the face. Faced with strong opposition, the corners of their mouths were downturned, their bravado quashed, their attempt at bullying at an end.

'You should be ashamed of yourself,' shouted Clara. 'Your husbands have done nothing to win this war, whereas this poor girl, baby in pram and expecting another, has received the dreadful news that her husband is missing. How do you think she feels about that?'

'So sorry for you, luv,' said a woman close by, smiling at Maria. 'Let's hope yer husband comes home to you.'

Maria managed to mutter her thanks. Tears pricked at her eyes. She could endure any of this if only she could be sure that George was still alive.

Another comment was directed at Clara. 'Best of luck with your baby. Shame you couldn't get married.'

There had long been condemnation for those who had babies outside of marriage, but nowadays the extreme circumstances of war had gone some way to softening attitudes. War had divided many passionate relationships, and the consequences were left behind.

'It will have no father, but it will be loved,' declared Clara with proud defiance. 'And you're right, he was brave. He fought the Nazis when they invaded Poland and continued the fight when he arrived here. Not all foreigners are enemies. And some, like my friend Maria here, have no choice. Her heart is with her husband.'

The woman standing behind them patted Maria's shoulder. 'I'm sorry about your husband, Maria.' She deliberately turned round and addressed those at the front of the queue and then those at the back. 'Here's to Maria's husband George, bringing us the food we need to keep us going. Let's clap him home.'

'Hear, hear.'

The same token went up and about, travelling around the crowd in a never-ending crescendo, work-worn hands brought together to clap George Dawson home.

The tears that had glistened in Maria's eyes now trickled down her cheeks. 'Thank you,' she said, gazing round at them all with a grateful expression on her face. 'Thank you. All of you.'

When she dared glance further back in the queue, the two women who had bullied her were looking awkward, their heads bowed.

The clapping died out, but a renewed atmosphere of camaraderie remained.

'That's telling them,' declared Clara, a self-satisfied expression on her face.

The woman who'd instigated the clapping chuckled. 'Not 'alf.' She nodded towards Vi and Rose. 'They knows yer mother-in-law and should know that she's not one to tangle with if you don't want a smack around the chops and a piece of her mind.'

Maria had always found Thelma Dawson even-tempered, strong but willing to concede if she was in the wrong. Those who knew her understood she loved her family above all else; threaten them at your peril.

The queue of women moved steadily forward. A few offered for Maria and Clara to jump ahead of them.

'Though goodness knows what we're queuing for. Anyone any idea?' one woman asked.

'Some kind of mince,' another said. 'More gristle than meat, if last week's supply was anything to go by,' she added with a laugh.

It was agreed that no matter the quality, mince would be a change from offal.

'I'm sick and tired of liver and onions.'

'I'm sick and tired of pigs' kidneys. Lambs' kidneys are not bad, but pigs' kidneys... And as for pigs' tails... Though the fat comes in handy for making pastry...'

'I'd love a nice bit of chicken breast,' someone piped up.

'A steak.'

'You ain't never 'ad steak.'

'No, but I can dream.'

Laced with good-humoured laughter, the comments went round. There was silence from behind them, although Clara chanced a look.

She nudged Maria's arm. 'Well, that's them two shut up. Their faces look as though they've collided with a frying pan.'

The queue sidled forward and, to everyone's great joy, there was indeed a large tray of mincemeat on the counter next to a tray of chitlings – boiled intestines from sheep and pigs. Tripe, boiled long enough to turn grey cow stomachs white, was also available. All in all, today was a veritable feast.

A host of stout bodies pushed forward, hands outstretched, offering their ration books and putting in their orders.

Shopping done; Maria and Clara walked back to Redruth Road together. They talked husbands, babies and what Clara's life had been like in London.

'I miss London, though not the bombing. Worse than here, it was. It was Ivan that made it all seem better.' The dreamy look in her eyes was countered by sadness. 'Still, we all have to move on.'

'Will you stay in Bristol?'

Clara shrugged. 'My mum and dad want me to stay, but it all depends on how well I pick up the reins and carry on.'

'That might be all you can do when your baby comes.'

Maria looked at her new friend with admiration, although sensed she was not a woman who conformed to the status quo. Being an ordinary housewife was enough for some women, but not all. How would it sit with Clara once she had a baby and no husband? It was hard to tell.

'Tell you what. How about we go to the pictures.' She leaned over to tickle Maria's little girl under the chin. 'My parents will look after this little mite.'

'My mother-in-law would look after her,' said Maria. She hadn't been out with another female for some time. One of the factors stopping her had been the stares she'd received on account of her dusky looks and her accent. Clara made her feel much more confident. How good it felt to have a friend.

'No need to bother your mother-in-law. My parents haven't had babies and young children in the house for years. They need to get in some practice.' She gave Maria a gentle nudge. 'I'll be needing them to do the same for me.'

By the time they got back to their respective dwellings in Redruth Road, they'd made a date for the pictures.

'We could even have a drink perhaps,' Clara added gaily. 'There must be something we could celebrate.'

Maria sighed. 'There's one thing above all others I want to celebrate and that's George coming home.'

Clara's expression saddened. 'Oh, Maria, I'm so sorry. I wasn't thinking. Though, as they say, no news is good news.'

Maria sighed. 'I should have heard something by now one way or the other, but... nothing.'

'It would have come by now if he wasn't coming back.' Clara sounded upbeat. 'Telegrams are reliable, and you haven't had one.' She smiled. 'Give it a bit longer and you'll see him coming through the front gate looking tired and battered but still in one piece.'

Clara's jolly face and positive comment was so uplifting that Maria dared to hope it was so. Her face brightened.

'Do you think so?'

'Yes. It's a topsy-turvy world and full of surprises.'

Maria eyed her stoically. 'You seem so happy despite losing your fiancé.'

Clara shrugged. 'Life is not a bowl of cherries. Things happen, but life must go on.'

Maria suddenly had an urge to dash into the house and see if anything had arrived. Telegraph boys didn't stick to the same hours as the postman, so there was a chance.

She bid a hasty farewell.

'Thursday's best for me,' Clara shouted.

Maria looked at her vaguely.

Clara confirmed what she was talking about. 'For the pictures. Matinee okay for you?'

'Yes. Yes. Of course.'

She bumped the pushchair through the archway that divided her mid-terrace council house from her neighbour. Round the back, she pushed open the gate and made her way to the kitchen door.

Once that was unlocked, feminine intuition took over and sent her running from the back of the house to the front, tugging back the living-room door and out into the hallway.

That's when her excess of hope came crashing down to earth. The coconut fibre doormat set just beneath the letterbox was just that – a coconut fibre doormat. Nothing else.

Her new friend's optimism had given her false hope, hope that was now dashed, broken like a Venetian glass fallen onto hard ground. For the first time for a long while, Maria yearned to be home in Italy with her family and friends around her, not here where she was an enemy alien and viewed by the more narrow-minded with suspicion. Despite Clara's willingness to be friendly, she suddenly felt that she would always be an alien in this country, always different and never quite accepted.

The threatening tears came in a flood. Her heart was broken. Nothing was going right. All she could hope if she was ever to settle in this country was for George to be by her side. And that was all it was. Just hope.

21

Sunday kept its promise of fine weather. The day was clear, the sun was shining, and even though high wire fences had sprouted amongst the trees surrounding the airport, they couldn't have picked a better spot for a picnic.

'We picked the right day, that's for sure,' said Jenny, bouncing along as though she was twenty-five not forty-five. Her daughters, fourteen-year-old Tilly and eleven-year-old Gloria, trailed behind carrying a battered wicker suitcase that served as a picnic basket. It was ancient and if it wasn't for the leather straps holding it together, the lid would be flapping open, leaving a trail of debris behind them.

'*Off to see the wizard*,' sang Gloria, skipping in time to the much-loved song that she'd memorised from the film pre-war.

They chattered merrily, glad to be away from Coronation Close, which wasn't that far away, but any excursion was a big adventure nowadays. Every opportunity was taken to alleviate the dark clouds of war and the memories of those terrible days of the blitz when Bristol had taken its share of enemy bombing.

Thelma held up a brown paper bag that looked to be smeared with grease. 'I managed to get some stale tea cakes from Carwardines. A bit of butter and jam and you won't notice that they're two days old, will you, Alice?' The last comment was directed at her youngest daughter, Alice, who, in response, laughed and licked her lips.

'Can't wait. Specially seeing as I won't 'ave to share with our Mary.'

Thelma's strained smile helped suppress what she was really feeling. Mary had declared she had other plans so wouldn't be coming to the picnic. Not that she was the only one who had disappointed Thelma, who had been counting on Bert, but he hadn't been in touch all week, so it was just her, Jenny and their three daughters.

Thelma confided that Mary's other plans probably concerned a young man. It was hard to let go, but as she said to Jenny, 'I'll still be worrying about her when she's married with kids.'

And in the meantime, you're worrying about George, thought Jenny, but stayed silent. Still no news. Not mentioning it was a way to cope – hardly ideal, but these were worrying times. Every day, survival was a worry; queuing for food, wondering when the next bombing raid might come, patching up clothes, and hunting down the luxury items that helped lift their spirits.

The original idea had been that the picnic was just for them. News of their plan and Alice blabbing that they had loads of stale cakes had travelled fast around Coronation Close. Trailing behind them at a safe distance was a gabbling, gawking gang of scruffy kids, some from Coronation Close, and some from the next street. None of them were in their Sunday best purely because they didn't possess clothes that could be described as such.

'Whatever were you thinking of inviting them,' muttered Thelma. She shot her daughter an accusing look.

Alice adopted a lofty raising of her chin. 'They're my friends.'

They'd climbed the stile and beat their way along a hard-baked clay path. Jenny spotted a dip in the field where a hollow of long grasses was shaded from the sun by a sycamore thick with summer foliage, though not as tall as it was in the years before the war. To ensure safe landings by the aircraft flying in and out, the tops of the trees had been lopped, so they were now only about two-thirds of their original height. Every year, and for as long as the war continued, their growth would be controlled to suit the war effort.

The feathery seed heads of long grass flicked at Jenny's skirt as, carefully avoiding looking towards the airport, she sought the best place for them to have their picnic. From the very first, even before the war had begun, Jenny had chosen to take in as little as possible of what was happening. She hated war. All she cared about were her two daughters being safe and sound.

And then there was Robin.

She'd invited him along, but he'd cried off. 'I've got some stocktaking to do.'

Stocktaking meant he was going over what he might sell to meet the weekly payment he had to make to Doreen. Jenny felt for him, although at times thought he'd made a rod for his own back. Doreen could play him like a penny whistle.

All thoughts of Robin pushed away, she jerked her chin at a promising hollow of soft green grass. 'That looks a good spot.'

Thelma agreed.

Half of the hollow was shaded from the more intense sunshine by the tree and the long grasses. The other half was bathed in bright sunshine.

Jenny took off her shoes so she could totter more easily down the sloping sides and into the hollow with her bare toes. She kept what stockings she still had for special occasions.

Thelma followed suit, laughing as her hot feet met the cool grass.

She'd brought a large blanket, which she spread out on the grass. Jenny helped her lay it flat before adding a white cotton tablecloth over that before they all sat down; the adults using the incline behind them as backrests, the girls flaking out on the higher ground.

The motley gang of boys who had followed them perched in the half of the hollow where the sun shone more relentlessly, bantering and poking at each other, pretending that they were engrossed with their own company and not at all interested in the food that was being unpacked. Pilchard sandwiches, fish-paste sandwiches, cheese and pickle sandwiches were placed on the tablecloth, along with bread pudding that Jenny had made the day before from bread they'd both saved. The sultanas were a bit old, Christmas the year before, and she hadn't had enough lard but had skimmed off the fat from a bowl of beef dripping. There hadn't been much sugar either, but a dollop of stewed apple mixed with the last scrapings from a long-hoarded pot of jam had to do.

Jenny threw Thelma an amused look and nodded at the boys. 'Their mouths must be watering. I bet it's an age since they sank their teeth into a currant bun or a teacake.'

'They might be unlucky. It's a fishpaste sandwich or noth-ing.' Thelma said it loudly.

The boys heard. Their faces dropped.

'I know you don't mean that,' Jenny said.

'Perhaps I don't.'

Several fishpaste sandwiches wrapped in newspaper were handed out to eager hands.

'Go on. It's all you're getting,' Thelma snapped, waving them away. 'Get it down you.'

The boys settled themselves, their grubby knees forming a resting place for their sandwiches.

Thelma's austere front didn't last for long. 'They must be boiling over there, and I did put a lot of salt in those sandwiches. Anything to make it go further. Do you think we can share something to drink? Have we got enough.'

They'd both saved up some sherbet crystals from the sweet ration, tipped them into empty Tizer bottles and topped them up with water. Adding water didn't just dissipate the bubbles, it made it go further.

She and Jenny had estimated that two bottles between them should be enough – if they were careful.

Thelma had them all take a swig from one of the bottles before handing it to Alice for passing on to the boys.

'Go on. Give what's left to them toerags over there before they trip over their tongues. But tell them that's all there is. If they want to cool down, tell them to go over to the fence and stretch out beneath the trees. It's too hot to be lying in the sun.'

The boys were delighted.

'Scruffy lot, ain't they,' said Gloria when she got back.

'They're happy. That's all that counts.'

Just as she was about to say there wasn't a cloud in the sky, a dark shadow drifted overhead and covered them in shadow. The sudden shadow was accompanied by an odd squeaky sound.

All faces turned upwards, including Jenny's.

'Oh, my word,' she said, recognising the silver carcass of a barrage balloon; the squeaky sound being due to its scraping the tops of the trees.

'It's a blimp,' shouted one of the boys, springing to his feet.

'It's got loose,' shouted another.

Fuelled by excitement, all the boys were on their feet gazing upwards, jaws agape at the sight of the huge monster floating like a silvery giant bumble bee above their heads.

Other shouts came from further away, the words indistinguishable but frantic. It seemed they came from the other side of the newly erected fence around the airfield. Security had increased from that before the war. Pre-war Bristol Airport had accommodated leisure flights to Gloucester or across the River Severn into Wales. Nowadays, it seemed crammed with aircraft, all of which were painted in camouflage colours, the faded decals of BOAC – the British Overseas Aircraft Company – and others faintly noticeable beneath the wartime colours. Another barely discernible company marking was KLM, which they'd learned were aeroplanes of the Dutch aircraft company. The latter had escaped Holland with their pilots rather than have them fall into enemy hands. It was also rumoured that Queen Wilhelmina of the Netherlands had flown in on one such flight, a fact not confirmed until the *Bristol Evening Post* made it front-page news. Everyone had been excited when they'd read that. It was as though their little airport had grown in status – if not in size.

Trailing its mooring wires behind it, the blimp sailed over their heads.

With round-eyed wonder and like all small boys, they quickly organised themselves into an adventurous gang, keen to get involved with this momentous occasion.

'Let's capture it!'

Like a pack of hounds out to catch the fox, they ran to the wire fence. Above them, the mooring lines followed the bulbous bag they were attached to, skittering through the tops of the trees, sending twigs and leaves flying in all directions. One of the lines, looking less robust than the others, tangled along the top of the fence.

There came the sound of raised voices and thrashing of long grass from the other side of the fence.

'Who bloody used rope instead of wire?'

Expletive-ridden threats swore revenge on whoever had made the mistake.

Face turned skyward, hand shielding her eyes, Jenny laughed to see the barrage balloon trying at freedom, until the distance between them and it narrowed.

'We'd better get out of the way, Thelma. It's coming towards us.'

When the trailing rope, perhaps indeed the reason the balloon had got loose, dangled over the field side of the fence, half a dozen keen young hands made a grab for it. They looked like a pack of puppies attacking a wild beast, one that they'd run from if it had happened to have had teeth or tusks.

A thickset lad made a grab for the trailing mooring line.

His mates encouraged him. 'Go on, 'Arold. Go on, go on.'

It looked as though they'd chosen the right man for the job. The young Harold's size was undiminished by food rationing. His thick fingers grabbed at the rope, his chunky arms reached out, his chubby hands grabbed and held the rope.

His companions let out a whoop of triumph. Unfortunately, their initial excitement had clouded their judgement of the situation. Although it was only a trailing rope, not one of the heavier, stronger wires, the balloon had a wilful mind of its own. Harold, a big lad but still only a boy, was doing his utmost to hang onto the balloon. This included him wrapping the mooring line around his wrist and being daft enough to knot it.

Men were clambering over the fence just minutes away but weren't fast enough to stop the young lad being jerked off his feet. A sudden draught of wind took the balloon that bit higher, high enough to leave Harold dangling, his grey socks and dirty knees at Thelma and Jenny's eye level.

'Oh my,' shouted Jenny. 'Somebody help us.'

She was still down in the ditch and trying to reach for one of Harold's feet.

Thelma was higher up the bank. She lunged for his legs.

'Hang on, Harold!' she shouted.

All they heard in response was a muted, 'Help. Help me.'

Half a dozen men from the aerodrome had clambered over the fence and were now running through the long grass.

The balloon lifted upwards. Thelma looked from the boy to the rope to the men surging towards them. They wouldn't get there in time. Harold was going up too fast. The poor boy would be like the soldiers in that song. As he rose ever higher, he would be over the hills and faraway.

The other boys were milling around, arms waving but not doing very much.

Thelma thought quickly. 'I'll be right with you, Harold. Just hang on.'

'I am 'anging on. Get me down. Get me down!'

A bit more weight added to his body and his rising into the atmosphere might be contained. *And that*, thought Thelma, *is exactly what I can give him.*

Taking a deep breath, she bent low, then using all the strength she could muster, took a giant leap into the air, like she used to when she was young, in the days when she could clear the whole length of a chalked hopscotch game in one gigantic leap.

Her outstretched arms hit and encircled Harold's grubby legs, her head bumped into his midriff. He yelped when her arms wrapped roughly around him. Her weight dragged him down – along with his baggy knee-length trousers.

'I'm losing me kacks!' he shouted and sounded terrified at the prospect.

His belly was bare against her face, and although it was hard not to laugh, she held on. If she let him go, or even diverted to pulling his trousers up, he'd be floating upwards again. She was stuck. He was stuck.

She muttered a few well-chosen expletives under her breath. Her toes were only barely keeping contact with the ground, her body stretched in the effort to hold onto boy and his trousers.

She felt a tugging sensation. The balloon was big and strong – and heading skywards. Her toes lost contact with the ground. She looked downwards. What was the chance of jumping without breaking something?

The barrage balloon threw a black shadow that moved like a stranded whale over the gullies, brambles and tangled shrubs. At one point, she thought she spotted a dead animal, something black and half hidden in the brambles. Before she had a chance to properly identify the creature, the balloon baulked off to one side, then jumped up and down again. Her legs dangled. Harold was moaning or crying. She couldn't tell which.

'Hang on,' somebody shouted. The male voice was close at hand. A pair of strong arms encircled her hips. Fingers spread out over her belly.

She gasped. 'Hey. Watch where you're putting your hands!'

She felt her face reddening as his hands moved and his arms followed, winding around her at waist level.

A male face, a male smell became more prevalent as she felt herself being pulled back down to earth. Not for a very long time had she had a man so close to her – so intimate – and it fuelled her indignation. What a bloody liberty!

With the help of the other men, the blimp was brought to earth. The hands moved, her feet touched the ground, and the roughness of his face was next to hers.

'What do you think you're doing,' she exclaimed sharply. She felt an early growth of bristles when she turned her face sideways, felt them rasping against the softness of her cheek. His warm breath smelt of tobacco. The lips that brushed her face suggested a kiss was imminent. None came.

He said, 'I am rescuing a damsel in distress!'

One big square hand reached around her and grabbed the boy by one trouser leg.

'I have him now.'

All around her, men were grabbing the mooring wires of the blundering barrage balloon. It stopped floating upwards and came to rest against the trees, like a horse that's been rampant for hours and is now totally out of breath.

She found both herself and young Harold returned to the ground, the grass cool beneath her feet as they staggered apart.

'God almighty,' she said, breathless from her ordeal and busily pushing her hair back into place. 'I thought for a moment there that I was on my way to heaven and St Peter was waiting for me at the pearly gates.'

A pair of twinkling blue eyes in a square-jawed face flickered with humour.

'Well, my name is Peter, but I am not a saint. And you are not an angel?' He winked cheekily as Thelma tidied her hair and clothes; her skirt having wriggled up to stocking-top level. Her stockings were not her best ones, a couple of ladders in each. But that was Thelma. There was no way she was going without stockings.

'No. I'm not an angel,' she snapped back in as cheeky a tone as he'd used. 'If God had meant me to fly, I would have sprouted wings by now.'

22

Thelma felt that her eyes were swimming in her head. Or the world was. Or both were. What had she just done? A woman of her age floating four feet or more from the ground.

She suddenly became aware that Jenny was there and saying something. At first, she couldn't make out what. Jenny repeated the same words several times before they sank in.

'Are you all right, Thelma?'

'I am now.'

Thelma attempted to tidy up the last bits of hair that had escaped her chignon and were sticking to her face. In the past, her hair had bounced around her shoulders in soft waves and was only pinned up for a special occasion. Nowadays, having a hairdo was not only expensive but hair dressing salons were few and far between. As for shampoo or hair lotions, they were in short supply, along with make-up and stockings. Fortunately, Thelma was a dab hand with a sewing needle and Jenny was convinced her friend could make a ballgown from a tablecloth if she had to.

The men who'd secured the barrage balloon were looking

over at them as though appraising them. They wouldn't be the first to think of chatting up lonely women whose husbands were possibly away fighting or had become widows thanks to the horror that had engulfed the free world.

The broad-shouldered man with the square chin who had brought Thelma and Harold down to earth joined them.

Harold and his mates stood a little way off, Harold taking the chance to crow about his airborne antics, telling them that, of course, he hadn't been scared.

'I'm going to be a fighter pilot when I'm older,' he crowed.

'If the war should last so long,' Thelma shouted.

The man who had introduced himself as Peter rejoined them.

'I hope your young lad is not hurt.' He looked tellingly over to where, still with his mates, a fully recovered Harold was holding forth whilst sharing stale cakes with the girls.

'He's not my lad,' Thelma explained, somewhat indignantly. 'This was a private picnic. Him and his mates just tagged along because my daughter told them that we had cakes. Stale, but any cake is a good cake nowadays.'

'It might have been better if you had laid your picnic further away from the fence. Civilians get in the way of men engaged in official business.' He continued to smile even when he spoke in an officious manner.

Thelma took umbrage. 'Seems to me a good job we were here. The boys snagged your blimp before you did.'

Put in his place, the man swiped the corner of his mouth with his thumb. 'Sorry. And it's not my blimp. It's theirs.' He jerked his chin at the men who were dragging the barrage balloon backwards to where it should have been secured in the first place.

'Men in uniform,' Thelma said, not looking the slightest bit impressed. 'They're everywhere. I suppose you're in charge of them.'

'Not exactly. They are British ground crew. I am a pilot. I am from the Netherlands. My name is Peter van Luntzen. I take flights out of here. I cannot say where of course,' he stated in a clear voice, each word carefully pronounced.

'I guessed from your accent that you were foreign,' Thelma said.

He winced only briefly at the intended slur, the smile remaining as he offered his hand to shake. 'Nice to meet you.'

She ignored the proffered hand and eyed him stonily.

If he was feeling insulted, he hid it well.

Embarrassed and surprised by her friend's attitude, Jenny interceded. 'Nice to meet you. I'm Jenny Crawford. This is Thelma Dawson,' she added, nodding her head at Thelma. She held out her hand to be shaken and mustered a friendly smile. 'As Thelma's already said, we only came for a picnic and didn't expect the added entertainment, Mr van Luntzen, although the uninvited company certainly enjoyed it.'

'So, I noticed, and my name is Peter. Please. No formalities. We are friends, not enemies. Call me Peter.'

Jenny's first impression was of a confident man, one who was trying to do his best to fit into a place that was not his home. He had a weather-beaten face alleviated only by the lighter-coloured wrinkles radiating from the corners of his eyes when he smiled. A happy man, she thought, or one determined to rise above any dire circumstance.

In her estimation, he was just over thirty years of age, and although his uniform was of good quality and the requisite blue of all fliers she'd so far seen, it had a tired look about it, as did his shirt collar and cuffs. Both looked a bit tatty around the edges. Unlike the RAF, perhaps he might not have access to new shirts and detachable collars churned out by workshops paid to clothe members of the armed forces.

He turned his astonishing blue eyes to Thelma. 'Thelma. Please forgive me for being so familiar with my hands, but it was an emergency.'

'As long as it's a one-off.'

Thelma's voice was uncharacteristically clipped. Was that a blush Jenny could see on her friend's face?

Peter eyed Thelma and throughout he kept smiling.

'Time we were going,' Thelma said brusquely. After refastening her shoes, she took the first step out of the long grass and back to the well-worn path back to Novers' Lane and the red-brick houses where they lived.

Peter's smile never faltered. 'It was nice meeting you.'

'You too,' said Jenny, following behind Thelma, who was striding on, shepherding their daughters and the ragamuffins before her. 'Have to go. See if we can rustle up something for tea when we get home.'

'Have a merry meal.'

'We'll try, though war rations are far from exciting.'

'Please. If there is anything you need. I know how hard it is...'

'We can manage,' shouted Thelma.

Peter's attention went back to her – like a moth to a flame, thought Jenny.

He ran to catch up with her. 'Please, Thelma. I fly all over the place. I pick things up from all over. Perhaps there might be something that you need? If your husband wouldn't mind me dropping something in, that is?'

'I don't have a husband.'

'Ah. I see.'

He was presuming she was a widow, which she always

passed herself off as. Pretending to be married was a protective barrier she couldn't easily shrug off. And anyway, she had Bert.

Consequently, she sought another subject to fill the gap and suddenly remembered the dead animal she'd thought she'd seen.

'I don't know what it was,' she said after describing the sighting. 'It's half in and out of those brambles,' she said, pointing in the general direction she'd seen it.

'Probably a cow that was frightened by aeroplanes, ran into a ditch and broke its leg.' He frowned. 'Though we have not had any farmer reporting an incident.' He grinned. 'They usually do. Even when it is only one that has strayed, they try to claim half a dozen. The Air Ministry's compensation is very generous.'

It was hard not to smile. She had to concede that he was right. Given half the chance, farmers turned tragic incidents to their advantage.

She didn't quite know why she stalked off. Perhaps it was merely because she wanted the conversation over, but if that was the case, what was the reason?

Peter turned his attention to Jenny. 'Your friend does not seem very happy with me.'

Jenny smiled and shrugged her shoulders. 'I'm sorry. Thelma's had a few worries of late.'

'I should not have mentioned her husband?' He said it somewhat dolefully.

Jenny shook her head. 'No. It isn't that. Her son is in the merchant marine. He's missing in action.'

Was that surprise or a hopeful look that crossed his face? It was difficult to tell. On the other hand, it was somewhat intriguing. She wondered whether Thelma had noticed. It wouldn't hurt to mention it.

She followed Thelma. When she looked behind them, he was still there standing like an immovable object, the long grass of the field waving around his legs.

'I will call and let you know about the dead cow,' he yelled. 'If it has not been there too long, it could be good enough to eat. Where do I find you?'

Whatever Thelma's behaviour towards the Dutchman, there was no way Jenny was going to pass up the chance of a joint of beef – even if it was well matured. All the better, in fact.

'Coronation Close,' she shouted back. 'Number two.'

Once she'd caught up with Thelma, she adopted an air of jollity, which she hoped might lift Thelma's spirits. 'I'm hoping there's a cake left for me.'

The answer became abundantly clear on taking in the sight of her daughters and the rag-taggle gang of boys who were licking away cake crumbs from around their mouths.

Thelma confirmed that they'd ate the lot. 'You're too late.'

'Oh well,' Jenny said with a sigh. 'Bread and dripping will have to do.'

Thelma only grunted.

Jenny took in her friend's tight expression. Her skin was taut over her high cheekbones and a slight dent between her arched eyebrows was a sure giveaway that she was thinking deeply.

Jenny finally plucked up the courage to ask her what was wrong.

'Hmm!' Thelma muttered grumpily. 'Life. War. Circumstances.'

'Life and the war I can understand. What do you mean by circumstances?'

Thelma scratched around for the right response. 'My son's

missing, Bert hasn't called in for a while, my daughter's in love with a man in uniform, and I might be losing my job...'

'You don't know that for sure.'

She shook her head dolefully. 'Things aren't as busy as they should be.'

Jenny kept her shrewd look trained on Thelma. 'I don't know what to say. I understand about George though. Of course you're upset. Worrying about George is enough to make anyone feel down, but I can't help feeling that he's all right. I don't know why...'

There was both disdain and disbelief in Thelma's expression when she tossed her head. 'Remind me to put your name forward as a fortune-teller at the vicarage spring garden party.' Thelma's eyes slid sidelong. Jenny met her look. 'I'm beginning to worry that me and Bert are finished.'

'Really?' Jenny's eyebrows shot up. 'He asked you to marry him.'

'When his mother was gone... well, she's gone, and we're still not spliced.'

Jenny recalled the promise. 'Perhaps he's waiting for the war to finish.'

'Well, he could let me know.'

Jenny had to agree that she was right. The war was causing havoc, destroying relationships as well as buildings and people's lives.

'How about Robin? How is he?'

The question took Jenny off guard. 'He's fine.' Impish dimples attended her smile. 'He'd be even better if Doreen joined up.'

Thelma laughed. 'Don't count on that happening. She likes uniforms that one, but only on blokes and then only if they stand her a port and lemon at the pub or treat her like a lady – which she isn't – and never will be!'

Jenny smiled a little sadly. They both knew what Doreen was like, the way she treated Robin, the way she acted as though she was a single girl not a married woman. Still, she wouldn't go into that for now.

'Tell you what. How about we go to the pictures. *Brief Encounter* is on again.'

'I've seen it twice. Had an air raid both times.'

Jenny laughed at the memory. 'At least they gave us the option of going to the shelter or staying to see it through.'

'We stayed,' Thelma said with a chuckle, then added, 'I wouldn't mind seeing it again without interruption.'

'Third time lucky.'

* * *

A few days later in the field where the barrage balloon had attempted to escape, Peter van Luntzen along with two soldiers with rifles over their shoulders, finally got round to searching for the cow Thelma had thought she'd seen.

The undergrowth was thick, and the brambles were wild and tangled. Using their rifles to brush aside the thorny growth, they made their way along a narrow path that was severely overgrown and had obviously not been used in years.

'Is this where you saw it?' one of the soldiers asked, who was fighting off a bramble that was clawing viciously at his trouser leg.

'I didn't,' replied Peter. 'The woman who had hold of the balloon cord saw it.'

It occurred to him that the creature – whatever it was – had not been noticeable on the ground but only from above and therefore a pure fluke that it had been seen at all. Like Jenny he could well imagine the glee from those likely to gain from a piece of the unfortunate animal.

He urged the soldiers on. 'Over there,' he said, pointing in the general direction Thelma had indicated.

The soldiers, whose usual job was to guard the aerodrome, had no option but to obey orders.

One of them, slightly ahead of his comrade, came to a sudden halt.

'Blimey!'

He'd stopped so suddenly that his brother in arms collided with him.

Peter came up behind them. Together they stared down at what they had discovered; not a cow, a horse or any other four-legged creature. They'd found Percy Routledge, and he was very dead.

23
———

The weekend was over, and she had not enjoyed a good night's sleep. A day at Bertrams Fashion Modes beckoned and she felt nervous about it. She pushed back her worries about losing her job. In an effort to calm her nerves she told herself that she had other more important concerns. Her beloved son was still missing. That was her main worry. The prospect of losing her job wasn't as important as that, though still it niggled at the back of her mind.

It was six thirty on an unseasonal morning of showers and overcast skies when the sound of the postman whistling 'White Cliffs of Dover' preceded the rattle of the letterbox. The first mail of the day had arrived at number twelve Coronation Close, earlier than in pre-war days. Like a lot of others, the postman had war duties as well as delivering the post – which was also important to the war effort.

Thelma slid her feet further into her slippers and went to the window. Although he might be whistling, she couldn't help thinking the poor man had to be run off his feet.

Wrapping her rust-coloured dressing gown more snugly

around her, she went out into the hallway and picked the single brown envelope off the coconut mat, the ragged edge of which took her attention. *Only fit for the fire*, she thought, lifting a corner of it with her toe. Anything fit for burning was welcome and she could do without a new mat for a while. At this time of year, coal was plentiful enough, although industry had first shout on it. Making weapons of all description to fight the enemy came before heating the home.

She noted that her name and address was typewritten on the envelope, fearing it might be something official, something to do with George. News, one way or another, of her son. But although she searched for some sign of it having come from the War Office, there was nothing, and anyway any news about George would firstly go to his wife.

Its importance diminished and fed her disappointment. Brown manilla envelopes usually came from an official source. No doubt more advice from Bristol City Council about what you could throw into the pig bin. They were particularly fond of pointing out that bones should not be thrown away until every morsel of meat – that included gristle and fat – had been used for human consumption. After that, it was the dog's turn. She wondered if they counted how many teeth and how long said dog had gnawed at the bone before it was thrown away. It hardly mattered seeing as she didn't own a dog. It was bad enough feeding herself and her daughters on the wartime rations, let alone keeping a pet.

Morning sunlight coming through a gap in the curtains at the front window would normally lift her spirits, but today there was none. Even having the curtains pulled right back didn't brighten the room. The Sunday picnic on a day of sunshine seemed an age ago – although it was only days.

Floating up into the air on the end of the metal cable of a

barrage balloon had made it a day to remember. She chuckled to herself and cupped her warm cheek with her hand. How embarrassing. She felt her pink cheek grow hotter beneath her palm when she thought about the man who had put his arms round her to get her back down to earth. She said the name. 'Peter van Luntzen.' Rolled it around her tongue.

There had been more than friendliness in his smile and somehow it had made her bristle, not because it wasn't welcome but because she felt an immediate attraction and surely that wasn't right. After all, she was engaged to Bert Throgmorton, wasn't she?

The truth was the Dutch air man had been very forthright and his obvious interest had taken her by surprise. After all, he was younger than she was, but it was more than that. His blue eyes and the toasted wrinkles of his face made her think of sunny pre-war days at the beach. Of being young.

Truth be told, she had felt an immediate attraction to him.

Brushing her fingers through her hair, she reminded herself of how old she was, that she was a mother, that all that romantic nonsense was behind her. Wasn't that the reason she'd opted for good old safe and steady Bert Throgmorton?

Of course it was.

I'm just an old kettle long past boiling point, she said to herself and smiled.

The letter sat on her lap, a dull, boring manilla envelope. She flicked it at a spider that had dared weave a fragile web between the handles of two commemorative cups on the dresser. One cup commemorated the coronation of King George the Fifth and Queen Mary, the other that of King George the Sixth and his queen, Elizabeth. The spider scuttled away.

Cup and saucer in hand, she made herself comfortable in

one of the two armchairs placed either side of the fireplace. It squeaked under her weight, the worn leather creaked, and a spring protested with a sharp twang.

A glance at the mantel clock confirmed that it was only six thirty leaving her plenty of time to get ready for work.

The first sounds of Mary stirring sounded from upstairs. The fact that both her daughters were still here was comforting. Thank goodness they hadn't joined up and left her here alone. Not that Alice could join up, but her Mary was nearly eighteen and free to do so if she wished. So far, she had not, but it didn't mean she might never go or that she wouldn't be called up at some point.

Thelma took deep breaths between sips of tea which helped steady her nerves. At this time of day, she could easily forget there was a war going on; in fact, she could almost believe that peace had come during the night without her knowing.

The wireless was silent, and she wasn't going to turn it on and hear today's talk of casualties, ships or aircraft lost or whether there had been bombing the night before. She wanted this moment of peace – such as it was.

She would also put off looking into the larder to see what evening meal could be made from next to nothing. These were the things that got a person down, even her, who'd always had a bubbly, bouncy personality. Before the war, she'd been strong-willed and strong-minded, the sort of woman who didn't give in to moods. Life, she'd always believed, was for living. What if there were a few bumps in the road? There was no point crying over spilt milk, no point in suffering if she could do something about it. It was just knowing what.

She thought about going to the doctor, but decided she didn't have time. She was just overtired and very worried about

George. That was all it was. Once he was home, she'd be much better. Wouldn't it be wonderful, she thought, if he got back before Maria gave birth to their second offspring. She might even go to church and give thanks if such a miracle happened.

Of late she'd avoided reading the newspaper or listening to the wireless. Both contained nothing except news of battles won, lost or not yet ended. Food was in short supply. Clothes were in short supply. Luckily, her skill with a needle helped enormously, though there were limits. It was almost impossible to darn a ladder in one of her last pair of stockings, and goodness knows it was almost impossible to buy another pair anywhere in the city – in the country, for that matter. As yet, she had not resorted to colouring her legs with gravy browning and tracing a pretend seam up the back of her calves with a brown or black crayon. She had her pride, plus a few old pairs of stockings that she'd managed to darn. The ladders didn't show too badly.

Each day she looked into her dressing-table mirror and saw a face looking back at her that had aged with the years. Mary was working and Alice would do so soon. They were growing up fast. What would she do once they were gone? The prospect scared her, although she might not be entirely alone.

She hadn't entirely given up on marrying Bert, but wished he would get a move on. Growing old together wouldn't be such a terrible thing. She might even be able to give up her job – if it didn't shortly give up on her. Losing her job was another of her worries.

Mr Bertram had said that he wanted to see her when he got back from accompanying his sister to visit her grandchildren who had been evacuated to Tavistock in Devon. Today was the day. He'd given no hint of what it might be about, but she expected the worst.

She drowned her worries with the last drop of tea and prepared to slide her fingernail along the gummed fastening of the envelope, pausing halfway as a sudden probability stabbed at her heart. Could the typewriter that had typed that address on the envelope be from Mr Bertram? Her blood turned cold at the thought that he might not come back from Tavistock and his decision about closing the store and sacking her had been put in writing rather than waiting for a face-to-face meeting.

The lack of merchandise now clothes were on ration had hit Bertrams hard. They'd always been quite an upmarket establishment, but the better-off women that had patronised the store pre-war were almost as wary as working class when it came to parting with their precious clothing rations. There were fewer customers now and of late Mr Bertram walked around with a worried look on his face. Several staff had left and were working in war production, including Miss Paget, the senior sales manager. It was touch-and-go whether they would be getting a replacement. In fact, it was touch-and-go whether they would stay in business. Getting another job would be easy. The war effort demanded more and more, but she had a soft spot for Bertrams. It had given her a chance to indulge her passion for clothes, even though she couldn't afford any of them herself.

All these worrying thoughts made her delay opening the envelope.

'Get a grip, Thelma,' she muttered to herself, finally taking on board that it had to be faced. 'It'll all come out in the wash. Whatever that means...' she grumbled.

A little diversion first, she thought as her gaze alighted on the copy of *Woman* magazine she'd left at the side of her chair. Some light reading might calm her nerves and take her mind off worrying about her job. Anyway, wasn't it trivial compared to everything else? She would manage somehow.

The letters page was a good place to start, women writing in about their families or their love life. Such things might refer to war but predominately it was about romance, husbands, sweethearts.

Placing her now empty teacup to one side, she picked up the magazine. Letters abounded from weeping widows, young wives whose husbands were serving abroad and single girls unsure whether they would ever see their sweetheart again.

Dear Madge,

My fiancé is fighting, I don't know where, and I'm missing him very much. My children have been evacuated and I'm feeling very lonely. There's a nice ARP warden…

Dear Madge,

My mother never approved of Clive, the man I wanted to marry. We waited until I was twenty-one and got married anyway. He got called up and has been away for some time now. My mother-in-law keeps having a dream that he won't be coming back… I'm frightened.

Dear Madge,

I'm fourteen years of age – fifteen in three months' time. Everyone says that I'm too young to fall in love, but I took no notice of them. I love John and we want to get married. Our parents refuse to give us permission to marry…

Dear Madge,

I'm having a baby, but I'm not sure who the father is…

Thelma had always read such letters to the agony aunt with salacious enthusiasm as she might a work of fiction, unsure whether these letter writers really existed. For that matter she wasn't entirely convinced that Madge herself was a real person with a sympathetic ear and a whole pantechnicon of well-founded and sensible advice gleaned over years of experience. Perhaps she too was pure fiction.

So find out.

The thought seemed to come out of nowhere and not only did it seem like fun, but Madge might be a real person and respond to her with some sage advice.

Yes. Why shouldn't she write a letter. About her and Bert and ask *Dear Madge* how she should handle a man who made her a promise to marry but still missed his mother.

After checking her fountain pen was primed with ink and the writing pad was opened at a clean page, she pulled a chair out from beneath the dining table, rested the pad on the table, sat down and began to write.

Dear Madge,

I am a mature woman with no husband and two daughters who are no longer small and will very shortly be off my hands. I have had a man friend for a few years, and he did promise he would marry me once his mother no longer depended on him.

His mother died a short while ago, but as yet he has not suggested we marry; in fact, we've seen very little of each other of late, but then he does have an important job with the city council and out of hours is involved in fire watching and other war duties.

I am finding the situation frustrating, and although I am fond of his company and our relationship as it is, I would like

him to make some commitment. I am not getting any
younger and the prospect of a lonely old age is quite
daunting.

What do you suggest I do? Confront him with an ulti-
matum or should I just break off the relationship and look
elsewhere for a long-term partner?

Yours faithfully, Mrs T. Dawson.

She finished the letter with a swirling signature.

'Now be my friend and reply to me as soon as you can. Time is running out.' She threw back her head and laughed. 'And isn't that the truth!'

A lonely old age did indeed beckon in the years ahead once her daughters had married and left home. In the past, they might have stayed close, and she would have enjoyed the prospect of looking after grandchildren. The war had changed all that. Young women were marrying men from all over the country – even all over the world. Once hostilities had ended those young wives would follow their duty and move to wherever their husbands came from. She'd worried about George when he'd married his Italian sweetheart, but at least his wife was living in his home city and George, bless his heart, had continued to serve in the merchant navy.

'Where are you, George?' Her wistful words seemed to float away. She'd long feared for his safety, and he had been torpedoed a while back, but survived. She'd tried to convince him not to go back, to see if there was some land duty that he could do without putting his life in danger.

'You've done enough,' she'd urged.

'Ma, who else would go out of their way to bring them supplies from all over the world for this country.' He'd treated the whole thing with a casual humour, and she'd been both worried and proud of him when he'd assured her that he'd given Hitler one chance to drown him and he'd fluffed it. 'Had his chance, and he ain't getting another.'

She tried not to worry about him, but it wasn't easy. Worrying only served to make her feel even more lonely. Sharing her concerns with a companion did tend to make things easier.

After folding the letter to *Dear Madge* and putting it inside the envelope, she ran her tongue along the sticky bit and promised herself to find a stamp later. The fun thing over – she'd much look forward to receiving a reply – she turned her attention back to the brown envelope with the typed name and address.

Heaving a big sigh, she ripped it open, unfolded the contents and prepared to be told that if it was from Mr Bertram, she was unemployed – or, if it had come from the war on waste lot, that she'd been fined for throwing away a piece of gristle that even a dog wouldn't touch.

Her face paled and her eyes were round as soup spoons when she read the opening lines. The word 'dear' jumped off the page, hitting her eyes so hard she couldn't stop blinking, couldn't stop disbelieving.

Dear Thelma,

This may come as a bit of a shock, but it's something I've been thinking about for quite some time.

I realise I should say this to your face, but at heart I am something of a coward. My mother said thus before she died, which made me want to prove that I was not. That is why I've joined up, not as a fighting man – they told me I was too old for that – but I have been ordered to report to Aldershot in the payroll unit. As a clerk.

I know we were close, but from my side at least our relationship was purely platonic. I realise I should never have
mentioned marriage. I should never have led you to believe
that we were engaged. Marriage isn't for me. Quite frankly, I
am and never will be the marrying kind. I apologise again for
not telling you this to your face but hope we can remain
friends – should we ever bump into each other again.

I don't know when I shall see you again but do hope you
will forgive me for taking the coward's way out.

I trust all is well with you and the family.

Yours faithfully…

'Yours faithfully!' She spat the words, exploding with
disbelief.

The dawn was creeping through the curtains and the stark
truth about Bert flashed like lightning in her head. He had
never been over-affectionate, and certainly not one for whispering sweet little nothings into her ear. But now she suddenly
saw him anew, saw that the routine, ordinary and rather dull
man had never envisaged whispering endearments or sharing
a bed. And him a man who painted semi-naked ladies as a
hobby!

Thelma stared at the letter and repeated the word 'faithfully' again and again. Solicitors or some kind of business or
official letter writer used the word without really meaning it. It
was just a formal response. With a pang of anger touched by
pain, she uttered the words she would have expected from him.
'"With love" or, at a push, "sincerely"… I could have coped with
that, Bert Throgmorton, but not "yours faithfully"!'

Tears stung her eyes, accompanied by a dry anger that hurt
her throat and made her teeth ache.

She crumpled the letter into a tight ball, her knuckles

turning white with the effort as the room spun around her. Along with it, an old saying sprang to mind. *Hell hath no fury like a woman scorned.* Well, she was that woman and wanted to hit out at someone – mostly the man who had sent her the letter – Cuthbert Throgmorton.

An angry thought came to her. The man did not deserve her. Neither did he warrant the effort of her writing to Dear Madge at *Woman*.

Outraged, she picked up both letters and reached for the poker. Despite the vigorous poking of the remains of last night's fire, there was no flame, only soft white ash tumbling out through the bars of the fire grate. The fire had gone out and she so badly needed some cleansing flames to destroy these letters. To that end, she made her way into the kitchen, lit the gas and watched as they flared and then diminished into flakes of blackened paper.

The day seemed bereft. Someone who had been in her life had, without warning, passed from it. As though he'd died or had never been.

Could the day get any worse?

She said a little prayer. 'I'll cope with anything so long as George is safe. And protect my girls. Keep them safe forever and ever.'

As for Cuthbert Throgmorton. Thelma gritted her teeth at the very thought of him. She couldn't possibly condemn him or wish him blasted to smithereens – which wasn't likely to happen in the army wages department at Aldershot. But she did feel bitter. If everything did go in threes, Bertrams Modes would be next to let her down. There was nothing she could do about it but face it head on and hope to get out of this time of trial and tribulation before very long.

24

The red-brick houses of Coronation Close glowed more brightly when the sun was going down, or at least the houses on the side facing west did. Those facing east were shaded, although they had the advantage of the last rays in their back gardens – advantageous to the vegetables or overly long grass growing there.

The residual warmth of the day had brought neighbours out to their front gates and kids playing hopscotch on the pavements. Two girls were twirling a skipping rope, a third skipping. A group of boys were playing cricket on the green. They were using a rubber ball and an ancient bat. The latter looked as though it might have once been used by W. G. Grace, the great Gloucestershire cricketer. Once hit, the ball bounced all over the place but did not break any windows.

Thelma's elbows were going lickety-split, like bat wings extending out to either side of her as she applied a pair of shears to the privet hedges, which formed the boundaries of all the houses. Although an evergreen, at this time of year they were bursting into flower. Each one was like a small miniature of a lilac blossom and smelt just as sweet.

Engrossed as she was in attacking the hedges, she stopped on seeing a police car take the corner at the end of Coronation Close.

Gossiping women, women cleaning windows or scrubbing the front step looked up too. Cleaning the front step had been a daily – or at least weekly habit – in the bland terraced houses they'd once lived in before being offered a new council house. But there it was. Old habits die hard. Anything official entering their domain was bound to draw their attention. A police car. Gone six at night. What was going on?

There was an obvious answer of course. Something to do with PC Percy Routledge.

Women who were more likely to have been discussing what their neighbours were up to than war news in the newspaper or on the wireless stopped chatting. That their mothers had fallen to silence was noticed by the children. The skipping rope stopped turning and the next 'turn' at hopscotch was paused. The boy meant to hit the cricket ball let it fly past him. Everyone's attention was on the police car.

A uniformed policeman and a plain-clothes man got out of the car and proceeded up the garden path to the front door of number five where the Routledge family lived.

Thelma's arms, one hand holding the pair of gardening shears, fell to her side. She felt a great surge of pity for Margaret Routledge, but relief for herself and her family. Nobody liked hearing bad news.

Jenny, who had been sweeping the garden path, put aside her broom, crossed the green and joined Thelma at her front gate.

'Don't look good,' murmured Jenny.

Thelma only nodded.

Side by side along with the rest of Coronation Close, they watched as the uniformed policeman removed his helmet and the other took off his hat before both entered the opened door of number five.

Thelma and Jenny exchanged looks. They were both thinking the same thought but were reluctant to put those thoughts into words. It was Betty, holding tightly to her mother's hand, who joined them and stated what was uppermost in their minds.

'They've found Percy Routledge. Must have done.'

Mrs West, Betty's mother, had escaped the house and been picking dandelions beneath the trees. Betty had waylaid her before she had chance to wander too far.

Mrs West tried to pull away from her daughter, her gaze fixed on the dandelions which blossomed like small sunbursts among the grass, but Betty was keeping a firm hold.

'I wonder what happened to him,' said Betty, keen to hang around and find out, even though her mother was tugging at her hand and demanding to go back to what she was doing. Not that she really knew what she was doing or was fully aware of where she was.

'Can we go to the park now?'

Her daughter ignored her. Like Thelma and Jenny, her attention was fixed on what was going on across the road. Everyone wanted to know what had happened to Percy. It was the most exciting thing to have happened in Coronation Close for years and everyone had suggestions of what might have taken place.

'You can't help wondering, can you,' said Betty, an animated expression on her face, almost as though this was some kind of denouement in a cheap detective novel.

'If it's the police, it has to be serious,' muttered Thelma.

'Murder!' exclaimed Betty.

Jenny couldn't help noticing that she looked almost hopeful that it was murder. She felt a need to counterbalance this. 'My money's on him having had an accident,' she proclaimed.

Thelma threw Betty a disdainful look, accompanied by a fierce snip with the shears at a twig of overgrown privet. 'Whatever it is, things can't get any harder for poor Margaret.'

The air in Coronation Close had acquired a distinct chill – partly because the sun had gone down behind the houses, but also because of the silence of those who watched and wondered, each holding onto their own thoughts, their own fears.

Mrs West would not give up tugging at her daughter or asking her if they could go to the park. 'I want to go on the swings.'

'Be quiet!' Betty shook her mother's arm and tugged her back so roughly, the old lady crashed into her side.

'Best you take her inside,' Thelma said to her. 'Go on. Then you can come back out.'

Thelma gave her a slight push – a far gentler one than Betty had given her mother.

'Yeah. I'd better. Come on, Mother. It's bedtime.'

Mother and daughter departed, Betty with her shoulders squared and an air of annoyance because she would miss the news. The old lady shuffled along behind in her bedroom slippers.

Mary came up behind them from Thelma's house with a towel around her just washed hair. Her face was shiny with a moisturising concoction she'd made from an ounce of lard and some elderflower blooms that grew profusely in their back garden. 'What's going on?'

'We think they've found Percy Routledge. The police have gone inside number five.'

'Do we know what happened?'

'Not yet, but no doubt we will once Cath knows all about it.'

Just at that moment, Cath came running down the road and without looking from left to right entered her brother's house.

Mary rubbed at her damp locks whilst gazing around the red-brick houses encircling the green and trees at the centre of Coronation Close. More neighbours had gathered around each other's gates – men as well as women, everyone speaking in low whispers, each with their own opinion of what had happened.

Mary rewrapped the towel around her wet hair, her head swivelling as she took in the clusters of neighbours gathered around their garden gates.

Her look was derisory. 'Look at them all. Death and scandal. They love it.' She chuckled.

Thelma slapped her daughter's shoulder. 'That's not a nice thing to say.'

The warning was water off a duck's back. Mary cocked her head. Of late, she'd become more insolent. It annoyed Thelma, but nothing she said seemed to make much difference.

'Ma, you know as well as I do that news travels like drums along the Mohawk around here.'

'Seen the film, have you?'

'Yes.'

Mary had indeed seen the film with Beau and even though it was dark, and they'd been wrapped up with each other, the drums had made a big impression. It was, she thought, like the drumming of her heart when it was pressed against his, when his hand was inside her bodice, his thumb tickling her nipple.

'At least keep your voice down,' Thelma hissed.

One car in the street sent a ripple of excitement through

the neighbourhood, but suddenly there was another gliding into Coronation Close, an ominous presence that turned heads and beetled curious brows. Unlike the police vehicle, it was not shiny black but a dull olive green – the colour used in camouflage and by military vehicles. They recalled that the only other military vehicle ever to have entered the Close had been marked military police and they had come to arrest Mrs Graham's son from number nine who'd gone AWOL – absent without leave. This was not at all like that. Everybody who was supposed to be in the services was accounted for – except George.

A sudden fear squeezed at Thelma's throat.

Jenny sensed her anguish and affectionately lay her hand on her dear friend's shoulder. 'It can't be,' she said quietly. 'Maria would have had a telegram if there was news – one way or the other.'

Hardly daring to breathe, Thelma watched as the car came closer, praying it would not stop at her door. Her legs almost gave way when it slid to a halt in front of them. *This is it*, she thought. *This is the moment when they're going to tell you that George is not coming home.*

'It can't be about George,' Jenny said softly, her gaze still following the action on the other side of the close.

''Course not,' added Mary, her tone not so strident as it had been.

The fluttering in Thelma's stomach remained. There had to be some reason for a military car not joining the police car but stopping outside her house.

A young man in a RAF ground crew uniform got out and opened the rear door to let out his passenger, who bent his head and held onto an off-white fedora. The brim hid his face, one hand seeming to hold it there. The hat was adorned with a thick black ribbon. The suit he wore was also light coloured, like the ones they'd seen on films set in Africa or the Far East.

Once the car door was closed behind him, he straightened, smiled and lifted his hat. 'Ladies. I do not know if you recall me from the adventure with the barrage balloon, Peter van Luntzen, though you may better recall the barrage balloon that had you walking on air.'

Thelma and Jenny exchanged looks of surprise. Embarrassed at being caught with her head wreathed in towels, her hair lank and wet, Mary groaned.

Peter van Luntzen's warm smile alighted on each of them in turn. He also shook their hands.

Was it Jenny's imagination, or did he hang onto Thelma's hand that bit longer than he had hers?

Mary's face turned pink when he kissed the back of her hand.

'Mother and daughter,' he queried, pointing at them in turn.

Mary was quick to respond. 'Yes. I get the red hair from my father.'

'Your dazzling features you get from your mother,' he said to her, his blue eyes hooded but very direct.

'I take it you're not here just to thank us for our help with the barrage balloon.' Thelma jerked her chin to the other side of the green. 'Something to do with Percy Routledge, is it?'

Adjusting his hat so that it sat more firmly on his head, he gave a quick nod, and his expression turned grim. His tone of voice followed. 'I am afraid so. What you saw when you grabbed that young lad and held onto the balloon was not an animal. It was the missing policeman. I am sorry to bring you such bad news but glad you did not see more at the time. It was not a sight I would like any woman to see. My apologies, Mrs

Dawson,' he added, bowing his head slightly, his eyes fixed on
Thelma.

Peter's countenance had a granite pleasantness to it and
although he spoke in a confident, authoritative manner, it was
the kind of voice you could listen to all day – deep, throaty, a
crooning voice, like Bing Crosby or even Paul Robeson.

Thelma asked him how Percy had died. 'I take it he is dead,'
she added in case she had made a mistake.

He nodded grimly; face shaded as his head tilted forward.
'Most definitely. Someone wanted him that way – dead, that is.'

Mary gasped. 'Was he murdered?'

Thelma warned her to keep her voice down before turning
to the man who had wound his arms around her and dragged
her down to earth before she'd floated away to goodness knows
where. 'Mr van Luntzen...'

'Peter,' he said. 'Call me Peter.'

'Peter. Can you give us the details?'

He took a moment to consider whether to state the circumstances of the death. Finally, he obliged.

'Someone hit him with something heavy. We have not yet
found the weapon that was used.'

Jenny felt the colour draining from her face and became
aware that her jaw was hanging open – like a goldfish.

Thelma stated things as she saw them. 'It doesn't surprise
me. Percy was a meddler. It was only a matter of time before he
poked his nose where it wasn't wanted and got his comeuppance. Seems as though it finally happened.'

Her comment brought instant reaction from the Dutchman. His crystal blue eyes fixed on her as though a button had
been pressed. 'Have you any idea who he might have upset?'

Thelma shrugged her shoulders. 'Could have been anyone.
Most of the neighbours for a start.'

He carried on as if that particular piece of information had been filed away somewhere marked relevant. 'Any friends that might have become enemies?'

Jenny answered. 'He didn't have any friends.'

She thought it sounded sad, but, on reflection, Percy, driven by his total devotion to law and order, had not shown any sign of needing friends. To that end, he didn't care much who he upset. All that mattered was his perception that he was carrying out his duty.

Peter van Luntzen's expression showed no reaction. Whatever was going on in his mind stayed there and was not visible on his features.

If they could have read his mind, they would have discovered his disappointment that his questions had not yielded any clue as to who had killed the unpopular police constable. It wasn't entirely unexpected, however. What they needed was a miracle, one of the eureka moments of someone having seen something that would lead them to the perpetrator.

The only miracle so far was that the woman who had first spotted the body – without knowing whether it was animal or human – lived across the road from the murder victim. Thelma Dawson had intrigued him from the first, purely because she'd reminded him of Anselma, his wife. She had the same vibrant presence. Anselma had been a life force, a woman who was as brave as a lion, protective of her family and attractive despite the passing of the years. She'd not been able to fend off the bombs that had turned what had been the thriving port of Rotterdam into a smouldering ruin.

For her and the children's sake, he'd vowed to fight on, at first in the Netherlands working for an infant resistance that had only just begun flexing its muscles. When hope was lost, he'd made the decision to flee and fight on in England, both as a pilot and in intelligence gathering. He found it an easy job to do, but he was weary and lonely.

The night after he'd met Thelma, he hadn't been able to sleep for thinking about her. He'd sought female company since his wife's demise, but never had he met anyone who was so like her in looks and mannerisms. It was as if Thelma were a slightly older reincarnation of his wife that fate had put in his path.

Dragging his thoughts back to the present, he returned to the routine questions he'd been taught to pursue, his training far more intense than that of the policemen who wanted revenge for their dead colleague.

'Have there been any strangers around here of late? People – perhaps foreign?'

'Like you, you mean,' said Thelma somewhat sarcastically.

Peter laughed. 'Yes. Anyone who you believe was speaking English with a foreign accent.'

As Thelma shook her head, it was Mary who answered.

'Yes.'

Both Jenny and Thelma looked at her in surprise. Mary, aware she was now the centre of attention, wrapped the towel more tightly around her wet hair, looking aggrieved that she wasn't dressed for meeting strangers.

Peter was all interest. 'There was a stranger?'

'Yes. On the bus coming 'ome from work. Can't recall which day. But he was asking a lot of questions.'

'What about?'

Mary held her nose high, as though what she had to say was extremely important.

'He was asking about the artillery around here, whether we'd been bombed and about the aerodrome. Kept on about it, 'e did. Us women thought he might 'ave been a fifth columnist, blocked his escape and told the conductress and she got the driver to stop and call the police. PC Routledge turned up and took the man to one side to 'ave a word. I got off the bus there too, hung around and listened to what was being said. That cheeky sod said that we was only a group of hysterical women and Percy Routledge agreed with 'im. They got quite chummy. He said he was working at the aerodrome and that it was all very hush-hush. Percy was dead impressed. Well, he would be wouldn't he. Fancies himself as Richard 'Annay, that bloke in the film *The 39 Steps* who got caught up in a German spy network and saved Big Ben from being blown up. By the time they'd finished, they were the best of friends. Snake in the grass that Percy Routledge! Looked as if he would fall and lick the other bloke's boots if 'e was asked to.'

'Then what?'

'They said they would meet up.'

'Are you sure about this?' Thelma remarked. Mary had always been a bit of a storyteller.

'I heard them say it, Ma,' Mary said. 'Honest I did.'

There was an openness in her expression that Thelma could not ignore.

'All right, Mary. All right, I believe you.'

Peter was all attention, which made Mary feel very important.

'Can you describe this man?'

Mary's little chin bobbed defiantly forward as she nodded. There was bravery in the action and a surfeit of movement that caused the damp towel wrapped around her head to falloff its perch. She put it back in place before answering.

'Brown trilby, khaki-coloured trench coat, a pointy face. A mole under his eye. Not a big mole but big enough. And he pretended he was from Guernsey and could speak French.' She stopped on seeing her mother's surprised look.

'Since when have you spoken French?' she queried.

As always when Mary looked sheepish, her lips twisted from side to side. 'My friend Beau is Canadian. French Canadian. He's been teaching me.'

Thelma's jaw dropped. 'Has he indeed.'

Although feeling he wanted to know this woman better, for now it would have to wait. Peter carried on. He had a job to do and needed every bit of information he could get his hands on. 'How tall was he?'

Mary thought about it as she looked him up and down. 'About your height.'

Peter seemed to devour the information, nodding thoughtfully, his brow creased as though sifting through it all.

Thelma looked nervously from the Dutchman to Mary. 'Is my daughter in danger from this man seeing as she might be the only one who knows what he looks like?'

'It is possible. But please, do not be alarmed. We have cordoned off the area surrounding the airport and made enquiries of people working at the aerodrome and in the few houses thereabout. There are many people working at the aerodrome, but most have been there a while and have passed security checks – not that everyone tells the truth about their background. That does not mean they are not above suspicion. But...' His voice slowed as he looked directly at Mary and thought carefully about what he was about to say. 'We have picked up one man who was staying at a local farmhouse. I would like you to come with me and see if he is the man you saw on the bus.'

Mary gasped. Her mother might be worried about her being in danger, but as far as she was concerned, she'd never felt so excited. It was as though she was one of the characters on the big screen, involved in something dangerous and exciting. The most exciting thing she'd ever come across in her life, in fact.

'Is he the killer?' She couldn't help sounding quite thrilled about it.

Peter gave a so-so sideways shake of his head. 'He might be. It all depends.'

'On me?'

'To some extent, yes. If he is the man you saw talking to the police constable, then he may indeed be the man responsible for PC Routledge's death.'

Mary's eyes were bright with excitement, but then that was hardly surprising. What she said next was less so.

'Can I dry me hair first?'

25

The sun had gone down. Night was falling, a dense dark night by virtue of the fact that there were no streetlights even in the made-up area. The car they travelled in, its headlights shaded for security reasons, motored on through the ever-increasing darkness.

Thelma reached for and clutched her daughter's hand. 'Don't be nervous,' she whispered.

'Nervous?' Mary gave her mother a nudge with her elbow. 'I'm not nervous. It's exciting. Don't you think?'

Thelma sighed heavily. Not sharing her daughter's confidence, she turned her head and looked out of the window but saw nothing except her own reflection.

There were no lights at the aerodrome either, the buildings solid blocks of blackness.

'Pitch black here too,' muttered Thelma.

'We only turn the runway lights on when an aeroplane is coming into land or taking off,' explained Peter.

On arrival at a brick-built office, Thelma and Mary were escorted out of the car, an armed guard either side of them.

'Mind your step,' said Peter. 'Here. Follow the light from the torch.'

Their footsteps crunched over a mix of gravel until they were in front of the building when their footsteps made contact with freshly laid tarmac.

'Voila,' said Mary as they stood in front of a green metal door and waited for Peter to open it.

'What,' hissed Thelma.

'Here we are,' Mary whispered. 'It's French.'

A blast of warm air came out into the chill night from within the building. The first room immediately inside the door was small and square. A young man in uniform was seated behind a desk that had three phones on it and a filing tray containing no more than three or four brown manilla folders. He got to his feet and saluted. 'Sir.'

'I need the interview room. Is it empty?' asked Peter, his accent mildly attractive.

'It will be, sir. Lieutenant Broom is asking a few things of the farmer and his wife.'

Peter took a few steps towards another door. 'I will check.'

'I can do that if you like, sir.'

'No need.'

The man sat back down then got up again. *Like a blasted jack-in-the-box*, thought Thelma as she took a step back.

'It's no trouble, sir.'

'I've already told you that there is no need. You stay at your post and man the phones, Corporal.'

'Yes, sir.'

The corporal – a RAF corporal judging by his uniform – pulled a face behind the Dutchman's back as he went off to check for himself. Thelma heard him say what sounded like, 'Bloody foreigners.'

'Foreigners here fighting for us,' she said hotly, leaning into him and poking him in the chest.

Peter came back accompanied by two people – a man and a woman – who looked as if they spent a lot of time outdoors. Both had ruddy faces, the woman's unblemished by face powder or even a greasy coating of petroleum jelly. The man wore boots, the soles of which were heavily clogged with mud. The woman, no doubt his wife, was wide in the beam. They looked like country folk. There were still a few farming families hereabouts despite the incursion of the council house estate. Some farmers and landowners had made a fair packet from selling the land for housing. Obviously, these two had not.

The man was shaking his head. 'I can't believe what I saw in that barn. Can't believe it.'

'Never mind. Your cooperation was much appreciated. Corporal, please take statements from these good people and then arrange for a car to take them home.'

The corporal picked up a phone and began to dial. His voice was clipped and commanding as he ordered whoever was on the other end to send a car.

Whilst he was doing all this, the woman eyed Thelma and Mary with a surprised look, almost as though she wasn't quite sure what had happened.

Peter diverted their attention as he extended an arm to the door from where the old couple had come out of. 'This way.'

The second room was much like the first one: square, bland and lit by a single lightbulb hanging from beneath a conical lampshade. Thick curtains covered the windows. The room was gloomy but light enough to see what you were doing.

Peter led them to another metal door in the corner of the room. Like the car that had brought them here, it was painted in matt olive green.

As they entered, they saw that they were not alone in the room. A guard wearing a uniform they didn't recognise stood next to the door, his stance alert as he awaited instruction.

At a nod from Peter, he took a key from the ring hanging at his belt and opened the door to a smaller room.

'Goodness,' muttered Thelma and then laughed. 'A room, another room and now another.'

It had a chilly atmosphere perhaps due to the metal doors, the lack of furniture, the blank expanse of empty walls. No posters, no clock, nothing to alleviate its bland state of nothing. Her attention was drawn to an iron grille in one corner.

The guard who had accompanied them shouted out, 'Prisoner. Step forward.'

As with the other room, there was only a single light flooding light into the centre of the room. Set against the furthest shadows of the room was an iron-framed bedstead, a small square window some way above it.

A long, lean figure got off the bed and took half a dozen steps to where the light shone brightest.

Mary covered a gasp with her hand.

Her mother touched her arm, her fingers soft as feathers. 'Is that him?' Thelma whispered.

Mary recalled the brash manner of the man on the bus. He'd been smiling and he'd been respectably dressed. Clean. She remembered that much. Now, his hair looked in need of a barber, his face in need of a razor. There was defiance in his eyes, an arrogant set to his jaw. He hardly seemed to notice anyone else in the room until his narrowed eyes opened a little wider when he espied Mary. She stood staring wide-eyed, not moving, not saying a word.

Peter came to stand beside her. 'Is this the man?'

Despite her mother's arm around her, Mary felt a tremor of

fear running down her spine. The man hadn't invoked fear when she'd first seen him, in fact patriotism had surged over her, perhaps because everyone had stated their opinions about him. The possibility that what they said was correct and that he was indeed an interloper and spy had seemed feasible.

'Mary?' Her mother gave her a nudge with her elbow.

As though awakened from a short but deep dream, Mary nodded. 'Yes. That's the man from the bus.'

'Are you sure?'

Another jerk of her head. 'Yes.'

'This is definitely the man you saw talking to Police Constable Percy Routledge.' It was a statement rather than a question. Peter van Luntzen wanted all the boxes ticked, all the i's dotted and all the t's crossed.

'Yes.' Even to her own ears, her voice sounded small and just a tad frightened.

There was no reaction from the prisoner, just a blank stare as though he couldn't quite recall who she was – which was probably true. The incident of their meeting had been brief and there had been many other people on the bus. It was quite possible that the only person he would have recognised from that day was Percy Routledge – and he wasn't around to give evidence.

'Thank you,' said Peter, reaching his arm around his charges. 'That will be all.'

Out in the front office, the farming couple had just finished making statements. Mary and her mother heard them say the man had told them he was working at the aerodrome.

'We didn't know he was a Hun,' said the man and spit on the floor. 'Bloody Bosh. 'Ad enough of them back in fourteen to eighteen.'

Peter gave the splash of spit a look of disgust before giving the corporal a telling look. Thelma interpreted that as an order for the mess to be cleared up.

The farmer's wife was wringing her hands and vocally explaining what she'd already written. 'He rented one room from us with food, plus the loft out above the barn. He told us he was doing paperwork for the job he did at the airport.'

'What kind of job would that have been?' Peter asked them.

The old couple looked at each other and shrugged.

'He never said.'

Once they'd signed their statement, the corporal escorted them outside, where a car awaited to take them back to the farmhouse, the chickens and the few animals they kept.

Peter van Luntzen pulled out a chair for Mary and another for her mother. 'Please sit down. You can dictate your statement to me if you wish, or you can write it yourself. Keep it simple. The best way is to think of that incident as a series of steps you are taking across stepping stones. One at a time.'

She remembered she'd been on her way home from work with Pauline. Her friend had not taken any active part in the incident, her head full of the likelihood of her boyfriend proposing to her. Mary brought the event on the bus to mind. She'd been thinking about Beau when the man had boarded the bus, went upstairs at first, then came back downstairs. She recalled him smiling and lifting his hat. After that, he began asking questions, which at first seemed trivial until one of the women on the lower deck of the bus pointed at a poster just above someone's head warning about careless talk.

Yes. Mary remembered it well and before details were forgotten she wrote carefully in shopping list style, things to be remembered. Once one woman had expressed her suspicions, the subject had spread like a snowball picking up speed as it rolled downhill.

She congratulated herself on her efforts until Peter peered over her shoulder and suggested she now carry on with the conversation she'd overheard between the man and Percy.

Mary bent back to her task, sticking her tongue through the corner of her mouth to aid concentration.

She noticed there was ink on her finger and thumb when she put the pen down. For some reason, it made her think of Percy's blood. Poor man. He wasn't likeable, but he hardly deserved that.

Peter picked up the statement, his eyes rapidly reading what she had written and looking satisfied when he'd finished. 'A very good effort,' he said to her. He waved the piece of paper. 'Not just this statement. Your instinct to stay and listen to the conversation of the policeman and this man was commendable. Very quick thinking.'

'I was suspicious.'

'And downright nosy,' her mother added, positively glowing with a look of both humour and pride.

Peter laughed. 'Being nosy is a distinct advantage in my line of work, although we don't call it that. We call it observation.'

Thelma asked if Margaret Routledge would be told about all this.

'I mean, it's terrible to learn that your husband has been murdered. Do you know who this man is?'

Peter wouldn't usually have divulged any more information. On this occasion, he wanted to show them how little things shared with the authorities could bring an end to this terrible conflict. That's what he told himself, but ingrained in his openness was his yearning not to turn Thelma and her daughter out into the night, never to speak to them again. He had a great need not to lose contact with them as he had with his wife and children – forever as it turned out.

'Not exactly,' he said, taking a moment to get his thoughts in order so he could better answer Thelma's question, 'though we know that he's not from Guernsey. French is not his native language. Your daughter was right there. We do not yet know his real name. More enquiries need to be made. What we do know is that he was recording flights in and out of the airport.' He paused and took a deep breath as though considering whether to go further, whether to disclose exactly what the airport was used for, the only civilian airport left in the country. Not military. That in itself gave disclosure a wider remit. 'You might as well know that this airport is used by VIPs. People who need to get to neutral countries in order to continue their specialist work. Not all are shady characters. There's also film stars, royalty and people needing to go on to other countries without being noticed. And safely, of course.'

Sensing he didn't take all-comers into his confidence, Thelma expressed her surprise. 'Oh. I didn't know that.' She was gushing but didn't care.

He smiled at her. 'Best you do not know too much. For your safety.' He turned to the corporal. 'No need to order another car, Watkins. I will drive these ladies home.'

Just as they were about to depart, a young man in a dishevelled uniform that looked as though he'd been crawling in bushes entered along with a blast of night air. He was swinging what appeared to be a lump hammer from his right hand. 'We found it,' he said, a satisfied grin on his softly furred face. He raised his right arm.

Thelma swallowed at the sight of it. Mary grimaced but couldn't help staring in fascination at the hair and blood on the heavy metal head.

A furious look came to Peter's face at the lack of tact shown by his subordinate. He jerked his head at both the young man and the offending article. 'This is not the time! Get it out of here!' He cupped Thelma's elbow with his hand. 'Come. I will drive you home.'

For the first time since they'd met him, there was anger in the Dutch pilot's voice and a sense of urgency in the way he escorted them out of the building.

'I apologise for that young fool showing you such a horror. It should never have happened.'

'Poor old Percy,' said Mary, sounding genuinely sorry for his demise. 'I mean, he wasn't my favourite person, watching when I got home late and all that. But he didn't give me that bad a telling-off.'

'No,' said Thelma, her red lips curled in a surly smile. 'That was my job.'

They travelled steadily through the darkness, the shaded headlights picking their way from the airport back to where the first houses bordered the road home. Out came the torches once they'd reached there.

Thelma hung onto the car's open door as she looked across the green to number five. The police car had long gone. She imagined Margaret Routledge all alone.

'I should go over there and see how she is. Poor woman. There alone.'

'She's not really alone, Ma. Her children are there.' Mary had already opened the garden gate, keen to get into the house, up the stairs and go to sleep until it was time to get up and go to work.

'And Cath. I expect she's over there.'

Somewhat reluctantly and sadly, Thelma followed her daughter to the front door by the pool of light thanks to the torch Peter was training on her feet.

Thelma was so drained, so shocked at what had happened today that she let him escort them both up the garden path.

At the front door, he stopped and said, 'This must have been very difficult for you. But it is all over now. I apologise for any discomfort caused. I trust you will not have bad dreams on account of today.'

'Will there be a court case?' Thelma asked, whilst Mary looked on, aching for her mother to put the key in the lock so she could bolt in and up the stairs. There was so much to think about, so much to tell Beau tomorrow night.

The moment her mother had unlocked, Mary said a swift goodnight and dashed up the stairs without pulling across the blackout curtain and turning the light on.

Thelma was left on the doorstep with Peter van Luntzen. The torch shining up between them picked out what seemed to be a sad smile, a mouth twisted with indecision – should he go or should he stay?

A cat ran across the garden. A dog barked from some way off.

Surprise still sizzled in Thelma's mind. There was so much to take in.

'Well, Peter. You're certainly something of a surprise.'

'War teaches us many skills.'

'It does that.'

She should rightly tell him to go. Neighbours not in bed would be eyeing the darkness, looking for sultry shadows that might or might not be where they should be. A man standing on her doorstep at this time of night would cause tongues to wag.

'You'll get me a bad reputation,' she suddenly said to him. 'A man on my doorstep at this time of night. They'd have seen us leave tonight and will be aching to see what time we got back – and what we're up to now.'

He laughed in a good-humoured yet reserved fashion. 'Does that worry you?'

'My behaviour has always been the subject of gossip.' She shrugged. 'I used to mind, but not now.'

The Dutchman stirred something inside her that she hadn't experienced for years. He was no Bert Throgmorton, steady, dull and ordinary, the man she'd thought she would settle down with. Peter was nothing like him; in fact, he was exactly the sort of man who had led her into trouble in her youth, the sort she couldn't help falling for, a man with a hint of devilment about him. But not now, surely? She was in her forties. The best years were behind her.

Or were they?

'I take it we won't be hearing from you again.'

'Not in this matter. We have your statements. More enquiries will be made before a decision is taken on how to proceed. The proceedings might well be in secret – due to circumstances – and other things I cannot go into.'

She smiled into the blackness of night. 'I'm glad to hear it. It's been quite an ordeal for us – and for other people in Coronation Close.'

'I understand.'

Their conversation could easily have ended there. She sensed he had more to say.

'I am alone in this country. My wife and family were killed in the bombing of Rotterdam. You too are alone. I know it is presumptuous of me, but I wondered whether we could meet in a social manner. Go for a drink?'

For a moment, Thelma was speechless, unsure of how to respond, until the truth hit her, the truth she'd already considered. Time was running out and it was her life and up to her to make the most of it.

'Would you like a cup of tea?' she asked and waited for him to say no. Which would be a great disappointment.

'Not tea.' In the fading light of the torch – the batteries were getting low – she saw a slow smile spread across his face. He brought out a square bottle from his pocket. 'Can I tempt you with a bottle of gin?'

Thelma felt her face splitting in two with the breadth of her smile.

'I'm easily led into temptation. Come on in. Let's give the neighbours something to really talk about.'

26

On the following evening, Mary gave her mother a knowing little smirk before leaving the house to meet up with Beau.

Thelma noticed. 'What's so funny?'

Mary shook her head and eyed her mother via the reflection in the hallway mirror. There was a bloom on her mother's face. The corners of her mouth had been downturned for quite a while – understandable, of course, what with George gone missing. 'Nothing at all. Have to say that man Peter was nice. Didn't you think so?'

Her mother turned abruptly away. 'I don't know what you mean.'

Thelma hadn't allowed for the fact that Mary could see her blushing face via the mirror above the mantelpiece.

Mary was still smiling at the bus stop. She'd never thought much of Bert Throgmorton, her mother's most recent boyfriend – though calling him a boyfriend was stretching it a bit – the boy bit especially. He'd been as grey a character as his hair, as exciting as the newspaper he hid behind in a chair. This Peter, a pilot no less, had more glamour in his little finger than dear old Bert had had in his whole body.

Was her mother so naïve as to think she hadn't heard them, hadn't seen them last night? Peter had not come in just for a few minutes. Their voices still carried at two in the morning. Mary had checked her sister Alice wasn't up and about. On seeing her curled up next to the teddy bear she still took to bed, Mary had ventured back downstairs, one foot carefully placed on each tread so her footfall wouldn't be heard.

Peter and her mother had stood close beneath the fly-speckled bulb in the tiny hallway space, no more than a breath between them. Their voices were low, words whispered and dissected with low ripples of laughter. It was easy to surmise that they'd spent some time getting to know each other. At first, Mary had felt quite offended that her mother and the Dutch pilot might have become more closely acquainted. Her mother was not a girl in the first flush of youth. She was *her* mother and should behave as such. It was the job of older women to focus on their children, not indulge in romance – or let it develop into anything intimate – anything she and Beau and other boyfriends got up to.

Her main feeling was one of confusion. Peter was nothing like Bert. Bert had resembled an old fireside chair. He didn't say much, didn't do much either except for his painting and sculpting. Now he wasn't doing any of that.

On thinking further, she realised that what she was seeing between her mother and Peter was something she hadn't seen before, something she could empathise with. There was mutual attraction. Sexual attraction.

She repeated everything she'd seen to Beau when she met him at the pub, including the whole story of Percy Routledge and the Dutchman's reason for calling in. She was particularly excited when she told him of having to identify the man from the bus.

'Wow. It sounds exciting and good luck to your mom. Sounds as though they got on like a house on fire.'

'But they're old!'

Beau frowned. 'Are they? I didn't think age came into it. My grandparents for instance—'

Mary cut him off. 'She's my mother! She's too old to be romantic.'

'I don't know about that. Just because she's your mother shouldn't make a difference, after all she was just a girl like you at one time. Ain't that right? And ain't it right that everybody needs somebody?'

'He's younger than her.'

'Should it make a difference? I mean, older men marry younger women. If it can work that way, why can't it work the other? What's that old saying, what's sauce for the goose is sauce for the gander.'

Mary fixed him with a look that could have cut through ice. 'Beau Blackbird, you don't know what you're talking about...'

'As I was saying, my grandparents are still in love. My parents are both dead, so I don't know how they were, though my grandmother says they remained in love all their lives.'

'But that's just it. They're still together after all these years with the people they first fell in love with. My mother has been by herself most of her life so that makes it different.'

'She must be lonely. Are you or your brother and sister going to be there all her life?'

'My brother's missing...' Mary sharply reminded him.

'I know that. Just hear me out. Are you going to be a spin-ster and live with your mother for the rest of your life? Or are you going to fall in love with a handsome young man and move with him to wherever the guy has to be?' He winked. 'You never know, I might be that handsome young man.'

His jokiness was infectious and brought a grin to her face. He'd most certainly opened her eyes to an obvious truth. Her mother was an individual, a woman before she'd become a mother, with the same emotions that she had. And now she was lonely and in need of someone to converse with. Even to cuddle up to.

She held her head to one side like a cheeky sparrow eyeing a fat worm that would do nicely for lunch.

'So, what makes you think I'm going to leave home and settle down with you on the other side of the Atlantic in Canada?'

He made a clicking sound with his mouth. 'It's as obvious as the nose on your face. Mine too come to that. I love you and you love me.'

'Oh really!'

'Now,' he said after downing his half a beer in three gulps. 'I think it's time we plighted our troth.'

She drew in her chin and eyed him speculatively, her eyes big and unblinking. 'That's part of the wedding service.'

'I know.' He reached for her hand, a cheeky grin stretching his mouth. 'Are you up for it?' he whispered.

Mary got the message, and she wanted what he wanted, to find a dark place where they could pursue the passion each of them felt for the other. Even when they weren't touching each other, it was there, a ticklish feeling that dived down her belly and between her legs.

However, she had no intention of having him know that. He'd be insufferable if she did that, assuming that she was under his thumb. Playing hard to get was the name of the game and she liked holding him off – until she couldn't stop herself.

She conceded that her mother and Peter, who she did think quite handsome for his age, were too old for romance but they might end up good friends – just like Bert had been. She didn't want to imagine them in bed together – even wearing nightclothes. They were too old.

'I still think that it's all about friendship at their age,' she declared with the air of a woman who'd lived many more years than she had.

'Yeah. Old people do get lonely,' said Beau as though he too had lived long enough to know this was a fact. 'A nice chat over a nice cup of tea suits them.'

She knew he was mocking her. 'They weren't drinking tea. They were drinking gin.'

He raised his empty glass and said, 'Cheers to them.' Shoving the glass to one side, he leaned forward over the beer-stained table and whispered, 'I don't want anything more to drink. I just want you.'

Mary felt as though her cheeks had suddenly burst into flame. She eyed him sidelong as she contemplated whether to keep him waiting or give in to her own desire to find a quiet place and have him to herself.

'I'll think about it.'

'Oh, come on, babe. Live for the day. I might not be around tomorrow.'

She rolled her eyes. 'Give over. I've heard that old chestnut a thousand times.'

A thousand wasn't quite true, but it was a common enough phrase for a guy who wanted a moment to remember. Did she want the same? She wasn't quite sure, but sometimes when she looked at his tawny coloured skin and jet-black hair, she was ready and willing to give into him again, to follow her heart and her body – wherever that was going.

She'd imagined being married to him, living in a log cabin in a valley with a lake close by and surrounded by mountains, the air crisp and clean, miles away from the nearest township, with all its traffic, noisy crowds and towering buildings. He would go off to work chopping down trees and she would do housework, make hot meals to fill his belly in time for when he got home, clothes for them and their children. She wasn't sure how many children, though four seemed a nice round number.

She knew very well that the vivid dream of a different country and a different life was not really the reason she would give in to him so easily. It was other things. She couldn't see herself living without him. His muscles were iron hard, and she lost herself when he kissed her, caressed her or whispered sweet nothings in her ear, sometimes in French.

Leaving the pub behind, they made their way to the favourite spot close to the river where the stony paths led them into semi-destroyed buildings, protected from the wind and prying eyes, the place where they'd made love for the first time a few weeks ago. The path to it could only be found with the aid of a torch. Their surroundings were as close as they could get to romantic: isolated, dark, and nobody else around. They fell on each other the moment they got there.

'One day I'd like to be with you in a proper bed,' she said to him, her whispers rushed, her breath hot. Whispers became gasps when he removed her knickers. 'Don't tear them. My mum made them for me.'

'I'll buy you a new pair if I do.'

'No. Not new. Just get me some parachute silk.'

She groaned when his hand slid up the inside of her thigh, one finger forward of the rest of his hand.

Their lovemaking was fast and furious, energised by the needs of youth and nature's centuries-old intention to propagate the species. Not that they cared about any of those things. They were living in the moment and in these troubled times that was all that mattered.

Afterwards, once she'd adjusted her underwear and brushed her hair away from her face, he lit up two cigarettes, passing one to her and keeping one for himself. The ends of the cigarettes glowed red as they inhaled deeply, each with their own thoughts. They lay close, their bodies tight. Like Siamese twins, thought Mary. Two people joined together at the hip, longing for a time when they would live in a world that was theirs and theirs alone.

'Do you really love me?' she suddenly asked him.

He exhaled a cloud of smoke. 'Yeah, babe. Of course I do.' The smoke lingered in a perfect ring, like a halo hanging in the air.

'Enough to marry me?'

'Ain't I already said that? I did suggest it, but you said—'

'That I weren't ready. Or something like that.' She said it flippantly, as though it didn't matter much one way or the other. Only now it did. Nobody but her knew it did. Not friends, her mother – or Beau. She found it hard to admit it, even to herself.

Even though it was dark she sensed him looking at her in an attempt to read her expression, to see if she was funning or being serious.

'I thought you said you needed to get your mom's permission because you're not twenty-one.'

But things had moved on. Her period was two weeks late. Now how to break it to him. With care, she thought, unusual for her, but she had to betray the news gently – very gently.

'That's right. Although...' She paused to let it sink in, making a statement with her eyes to see if he could guess that they had made another human being – which seemed very likely. What would he say? What would he do? It had been the very first time and she still found it hard to believe. Still, two weeks overdue was all it took. She'd been surprised. Other girls often let their boyfriends go 'all the way' and never skipped a beat. Here she was, only a short time over but convinced that she was in trouble.

'Better get going,' she said, brushing the bits of foliage that clung to her clothes.

He flicked away the remains of the cigarette, grasped her shoulders and brought her round to face him. He switched on the torch and trained it onto her face. She blinked at first, then held her eyes wide open and imagined the effect of her features half hidden in shadow. 'Are you saying it's on? We can get married?'

Mary gave a little cough – not so much to clear her throat but to make what she had to say sound the most important declaration he would ever hear.

'Ma might think we have to.'

Would he understand what she was saying? It had been six weeks since her last period and she was never late. Her appetite was still good, but the first overtures of morning sickness came on with the slightest whiff of a slice of bread sizzling in a panful of lard.

'Do we?'

For all his masculine passion, Beau sometimes came across as a bit of an innocent. Despite what he might think, he was still a boy. The news would either commit him to her or send him running.

'I'm overdue.' She said it quietly. It could be a false alarm. All the same she had to say it, perhaps to some extent because she wanted it so. Being in the family way – or the pudding club as friends her age called it, would make up her mind about everything.

Beau did not respond but stood there, his hands remaining on her shoulders.

The heaving of a big sigh was followed up by her repeating what she'd just said. 'I'm overdue. Do you understand what I mean?'

'Oh God.'

The torch fell from his hand. The light went out.

'Now look what you've done.' She bent down to retrieve the torch from where it had landed amongst the rubble and weeds.

'Babe!'

'I'm not a babe. I'm Mary.'

'Honey!'

Her sigh was heavy with exasperation. 'Mary. My name's Mary. And just to emphasise what I'm saying, I'm not the bloody virgin Mary. I'm Mary Dawson and the fact that I'm in the family way has nothing to do with God but everything to do with you.'

'We're having a baby!' His exclamation echoed around the bare brick walls as it finally sunk in. He sounded proud enough to burst.

'That's what I've just told you, haven't I?'

He tugged his cap firmly upon his head. 'Then that's it. I'll go see the commanding officer and get permission right away...'

'No.' Folding her arms in that forthright manner of hers, she half turned away from him.

'No?'

'I don't want you to marry me just because we must. I don't want to force you.'

'I don't understand.'

He didn't just sound surprised, he sounded mortally wounded.

'I want you to marry me because you want to.'

'But I do.'

Mary had thought about it carefully. Yes, it was a shock to find herself in this predicament, but getting married was supposed to last a lifetime. 'But is that out of lust or love?'

'What? How can you doubt me? I love you.'

'And lust after me...'

'That's all part of the same thing as far as I'm concerned.'

'It won't always be,' returned Mary in a sombre tone. 'Life is a long time.'

'You can't bring up this baby without me.'

Mary lowered her eyes. She felt his consternation. He just didn't understand why she was acting like this. She didn't herself. 'I can if I have to.'

'But what's your mom going to say?'

Mary imagined her mother's fury, which for some reason only made her the more determined to do things her way – just as her mother had – with all three of her children – all with different fathers. 'I think she'll understand.'

It was a long shot. There was no guarantee that her mother wouldn't be highly aggrieved.

He told her not to worry, that everything was okay. Although, of course it would be her decision.

'Of course it is,' she retorted hotly.

He wasn't to know that she was testing him, goading him. She loved him – or thought she did – but he had to want to marry her for herself, not because they'd fumbled in the dark and had been landed with the consequences. Goodness, but her feelings and thoughts were so terribly confused. And she still had to tell her mother.

27

'Jack of all trades,' Thelma muttered to herself as she clothed a naked mannequin in a utility-style skirt – six pleats only – big boxy ones as ordained by the bigwigs who were responsible for laying down the rules as to how much material could be used to make a garment. Women were suffering – and in more ways than one.

She was feeling nervous. Mr Bertram had finally returned from Devon and wanted to see her. So far, he hadn't called her into his office, but it was just a question of when.

In times past, this wouldn't have been her job, but Mirabelle, the window dresser, had joined the war effort ages ago along with half the female staff at Bertrams. It was a case of all hands to the pumps.

Pairing a mauve and yellow short-sleeved blouse with the checked skirt seemed like an innovative idea. The two items were just about the same colourways. What did it matter if the patterns were a world apart? Taking a step back so she could better judge her work, Thelma was relieved to see that they looked quite good together and she congratulated herself.

Later, she would go outside on the pavement and see how it looked to the customers.

Backing out of the shop window was no easy task. The door was narrow and there was a step to negotiate behind her before she was back on level ground. Once she was, she breathed a sigh of relief, although inside the tension was still there thanks to receiving Mr Bertram's summons. Only a fool couldn't see the absence of customers. Pre-war the shop had been heaving but not now. People were more discerning, and wealthy people were wary that an ostentatious display of wealth might look unpatriotic. Besides that, even the better off were in uniform and everyone else rationed. There were rumours of the building being sold off, of Mr Bertram retiring. None of it boded well for her. Would she still have a job after today or was the writing already on the wall?

She'd prefer to get it all over with. *But when?* she asked herself.

The answer she'd been waiting for suddenly materialised.

'Mr Bertram says he's ready to see you now. Can you please report to his office.'

The speaker was Mavis Brent, a young trainee who had yet to grow into the black and white uniform provided by her employer. It had been worn by the previous employee, who had had to get married, so job and uniform had been left behind. Obviously, by the time said employee, one Angela Coulter, had left, the uniform had stretched a little thanks to Angela's run-in with a Polish flight sergeant and the resultant bump he'd left her with.

'Is everything going to be all right?' Mavis said in a hushed and slightly worried manner.

'Of course it is,' Thelma said brightly. 'I expect he wants to make me senior sales manageress.'

Mavis threw her a look of surprised blankness. 'I thought you already were.'

She had to admit that Mavis had a point. In the absence of their retired shop floor manageress Mrs Apsley and young salesgirls leaving for marriage, uniform or munitions factories, Thelma had covered the work of most departments. She'd even done a stint in the accounts department, totting up who owed what, sending out overdue bills to women who thought that if they kept away from the shop, they might extend their credit – or not pay at all.

She was about to learn her fate. It scared her, but if she had to choose between being without a job and her son being alive, she would choose the latter. As for Bert... ultimately, that was neither here nor there. She was a bit hurt, but the situation was not insurmountable. A delicious shiver ran down her spine when she thought about Peter. She just couldn't help herself. Being a few years older than him, was she being a silly old fool to think there might be something more than friendship between them? Her instincts told her that it was so. She was seeing him again. Despite all the reasons not to, she couldn't help herself.

Brushing bits of lint from her skirt and swallowing her trepidation, she made her way to Mr Bertram's office, knocked on the door, waited to be called in, then took a deep breath when she was.

Mr Bertram was dwarfed by his desk, a smoothly golden affair, its glorious colour accentuating the darkness of his pinstriped suit. His hair was snowy white and combed carefully across a freckled pink scalp.

He invited her to sit in one of the two deep tub chairs dating from the twenties, their powder blue upholstery encased in golden blonde wood that matched the desk.

His fingers intertwined on the desktop, untwined and retwined again, like strands of thick string made flesh that could not keep still. Whatever he was about to say was making him nervous. Thelma wanted to tell him to stop doing it and get on with telling her that she'd been a good employee but due to circumstances beyond his control, he had no option but to give her the sack. Might as well get it over with.

'Good morning,' she said. Quite frankly she couldn't recall whether she'd already said that or whether he had done the same. She wasn't used to being all a-flutter. It wasn't part of her character to be nervous.

'Ah. Yes. Good morning. Is it morning or just turned afternoon?' He took a fob watch with a silver chain from his waistcoat pocket, studied it and, once assured that it was still morning, went back to his endless fidgeting. 'Um. I called you in here... I called you in here...'

His fingers continued to dance around each other, clasping and reclasping until his right hand broke the cycle, one finger pushing his spectacles back up his considerable nose. Beneath his nose sat a bristly moustache, predominantly grey, which was relieved with tufts of nicotine yellow. Mr Bertram smoked a pipe.

'It's like this...' He spoke slowly to more carefully gather his thoughts into some sort of order before he could carry on.

Thelma felt a barely suppressed urge to leap across the desk, give his narrow shoulders a good shake and tell him to get on with it.

Before she had chance, a pen was picked up, dipped into the inkpot and then laid back down on a wooden rest adjacent to an oversized pad of blotting paper.

'As you may know... as you may know...'

Her patience broke. 'Yes. I might know if you told me what it is,' she snapped.

Taken by surprise and not ready with any tangible response, his head jerked up. He looked directly at her as though she'd just woken him from a deep sleep. 'What? Yes. Yes. Of course. I do apologise.'

'I need to know where I stand Mr Bertram. Do I have a job or don't I?'

'Ah. Well, that's what I want to talk to you about – in a roundabout way. Basically, it comes down to this. The shop is too large for our current trade.'

'Yes. I know that.' She said it expectantly and waited.

Suddenly relieved, he licked his lips and carried on. 'It's like this, you see. What with the war on and the scarcity of material and suchlike...'

This was it. Thelma had to accept that she was for the chop.

'Right.' The tub chair she sat in was heavy so stayed put when she sprang out of it. She leaned over his desk, her face, hot, red and out of patience. 'If you're going to sack me, please get on with it. I suppose I can always get a job welding or such-like. It can't be much harder than using a sewing machine and I can certainly treadle my legs off on that with a good wind behind me!'

'What?' Mr Bertram's eyes protruded as though they'd come out on stalks or long springs like a cartoon character at the pictures.

'Mr Bertram! Would you please get to the point. I don't have all day.' She pointed towards the office door. 'There's a shop out there that isn't going to run itself.'

Any other employer might have shown her the door, but confrontation was not part of Mr Bertram's character. He also valued his staff.

Their gaze met. She thought she saw something like surprise in his eyes, his lips held slightly ajar, the bristly moustache hanging over it like the thatch of a cottage canopy.

'I've a proposition,' he pronounced on a great exhaling of breath. 'The shop is not properly facilitated at present. As you are no doubt aware, Mrs Dawson, we just can't get the stock. And as for staffing...' He spread his hands helplessly. 'Everyone's gone to war – well, almost everyone.'

Thelma waited for the hammer to fall. *Thank you. You're out. I'm sure you could get a job anywhere.* Her hands grasping the back of the curved wood of the tub chair, she prepared herself, shoulders stiff, legs braced.

Mr Bertram continued. 'We still have our wealthier clients, but they are curtailing their spendings habits, which means only part of these premises are being utilised to their full capacity. One half of the shop is plenty enough to contain the quality items we have always been famed for supplying.'

Thelma wasn't quite sure where this was going. She needed confirmation. 'You're going to close one half of the shop?'

'In a way.' Suddenly, perched behind the imposing desk, Mr Bertram beamed from ear to ear.

Unsure how to interpret his expression, Thelma jerked her chin. 'Go on.'

He took a deep breath. 'Our client base has shrunk. We could try to get new clients, but not everyone can afford our high-end garments. But all the same, there are people in need and in the present circumstances perhaps we can do our bit for the war effort. With that in mind, I thought we might open the other side of the shop to second-hand items, refashioned items, adult clothes cut down to suit children, that kind of thing. All items that fill the make do and mend criteria. I've even heard it said that some women have cut down a pair of cricket flannels to make skirts or shorts for children. Quite amazing. Quite amazing indeed.'

Thelma was taken aback. Dividing the shop in such a way was not at all what she had expected to hear. It had most certainly taken her by surprise, and she had to admit it was quite novel. There was a place for second-hand clothes, but she wasn't sure it was in a shop like Bertrams – even half a shop! It certainly needed some thinking about.

Mr Bertram's pale eyes bored into her expectantly, almost like a little boy seeking approval for his stamp collection or exam results. 'Mrs Dawson, you're a valued employee. I would like your opinion. What do you think? Please. Be honest.'

Thelma took a deep breath and exhaled it with a whoosh of outward breath. What did she think? One big question came to mind. 'What are our ladies – our well off and regular customers – going to think? They're used to us giving them exceptional service – as befits their status...' Even though he intended dividing the shop, their 'ladies' would be mixing with the lower orders in his eclectic vision, the poor mixing with the well off. She felt the need to explain further. 'They might not take too kindly to be mixing with people not of their own class. A parlourmaid, a cook and a lady's maid are about it for them.'

'Ah!' said Mr Bertram, raising his finger like a magic wand in front of his face. 'That's just it. I have sounded out several of our more open-minded ladies. Some of our customers have relatives fighting with the forces and feel that doing their bit might also in some way be of benefit to their menfolk. Our customers understand everyone must do their bit,' he said in the prissy way he favoured. 'They know how difficult it is for families on restricted means to manage during the current situation and are willing to help. Some have promised to raid their wardrobes and attics in a bid to find unwanted and dated items of clothing that with a bit of alteration might be cannibalised. I was thinking we could even offer an alteration service for those who can afford it, and with that in mind...' He looked at her with all the enthusiasm of a hound aching to go for a walk. 'As you've stated yourself, Mrs Dawson, you're very handy with a sewing machine. Past employees and customers have been known to remark how smartly you are always turned out and many knew that you made and altered things yourself. You're a credit to Bertrams, Mrs Dawson. A credit indeed.'

Thelma was dumbstruck and aware that this was a time to eat humble pie. She'd come in here thinking she was being fired and instead was praised. Once she found her voice, she agreed it was a good idea and that she would be happy to help. 'I will do everything I can to make it successful.'

'You will continue on your present wage – I would like to give you an increase, but...' He spread his hands helplessly.

'I quite understand.'

An increase in wages would have been much appreciated, but first and foremost she still had her job and for that she was extremely grateful.

'When do you want me to begin rearranging things?'

All signs of nervousness vanished, relief beaming on his face. 'Might I suggest you give yourself time to think about how best to divide the shop between couture and charity?' He nodded. 'Yes. Give yourself time to think how best to approach it.'

All manner of possibilities immediately raced through her head in vivid detail. That half of the shop selling high-class dresses attracting at least one pound ten shillings and seven coupons would be best housed on the half of the shop with the highest ceiling, from where a sparkling chandelier flung spangles of light. The other half, where underwear, night attire and hosiery were presently displayed and sold, would be turned over to items not costing much more than a couple of shillings. Being second-hand, there would be no need for coupons. Bits of material for home sewing, items already cut down or refashioned, seams let out, pretty collars and cuffs added to matronly items from earlier in the century... So many possibilities, so many colours and cut-outs and recycled yards of material from grandma's old bustles. Like Derby Day, she thought not without amusement.

'Thank you, Mr Bertram,' she said. 'I won't let you down.'

Head in the clouds, Thelma went back down the stairs, her feet seeming to float three inches above the ground whilst her fingers tapped along the curving balustrade.

As it was Wednesday closing, she went home with a spring in her step – a far cry from the way she'd slumped in that morning.

28

Not fancying lunch, Thelma sat down at her kitchen table with a piece of paper and a pencil and began to draw a plan of how she would rearrange the counters and the mannequins. Now how to divide the shop into two halves? As yet, she wasn't sure, but despite Mr Bertram assuring her most of their wealthy clients were keen to 'do their bit' to help those less fortunate than themselves, she suspected there would be exceptions. The class divide was still alive and kicking. Perhaps this war would alter all that, she thought. After all, people from diverse backgrounds, places all over the British Isles and from all different countries, had been thrown together to fight a common foe.

Her agile mind went back to the task in hand. What would make an attractive but effective barrier between the two? At present, she had no answer.

Think about it, she said to herself. *Just think about it. A solution is sure to come.*

Nothing came quickly, so she occupied herself making one of her specialities for the evening meal. Corned beef hash. One tin of corned beef, two onions, one pound of potatoes and one pound of carrots. Vegetables boiled, drained (the seasoned water left to cool for tomorrow's soup). Tin of corned beef tipped into the potatoes and briskly mixed to form a nutritious and quickly heated meal. Apple rings, cured and kept all winter, topped with a little custard would be pudding this evening.

Home front sorted; she went back to her plans. Throwing herself into the project helped her cope with not having heard anything from George. It was hard to push the problem completely out of her head, but if she didn't occupy herself, she would go out of her mind. Best to hope. Best to imagine him coming in the door with a cheerful George countenance.

Every so often, she paused what she was doing and asked herself the same old questions she'd asked a hundred times before. Where was he? There should have been a telegram by now, surely. Other possibilities persisted to creep into her mind. Had he jumped ship in some foreign, war-free port? God forbid, had he met an enticing temptress and decided to abandon his family?

She shook her head. No. She knew her son well. He wouldn't do something like that.

She re-concentrated her efforts on the plans for Bertrams Modes.

It was four o'clock in the afternoon when Jenny came over. Like Bertrams, Robin's shop up in Filwood Broadway closed at lunchtime on Wednesday, so meeting up in the afternoon was a natural progression that had turned into a habit.

Jenny came in humming a Vera Lynn song.

'What are you sounding so happy about?' queried Thelma.

'It's Wednesday afternoon. This is the day when we unburden ourselves of all our worries.'

'Might start the ball rolling by making a pot of tea.'

Jenny leaned closer to see what Thelma was doing. 'It's a drawing.'

Thelma beamed. 'Half of Bertrams is being made over for second-hand, make do and mend items. And I'm in charge.'

'That's wonderful. If anyone is good at make do and mend, it's you. I take it brand-spanking new items will still be available.'

'They'll be in one half of the shop. The make do and mend in the other.'

'What a brilliant idea. I've brought a smidgen of tea with me. I've only used it once.'

Like everyone else, Jenny had brewed a pot of tea when she'd got home from work at lunchtime. Once the pot was empty, she'd tipped the loose leaves onto a plate to dry for an hour or so before wrapping them in newspaper. They would do service again for a second time, providing a cup of tea each for her and Thelma. No sugar, of course, and just a splash of milk. Rationing had become a way of life. It occurred to Thelma that they'd still adhere to frugal habits even when the war was over.

Jenny made her way into the kitchen and put the kettle on the gas before coming back in. 'How's Maria?' she asked.

'As well as can be expected.'

'No news then on that front?'

Thelma shook her head, eyes still fixed on the scribbled plan for two new shops made from one. 'None.'

Jenny lingered by the door between the kitchen and living room searching for a sign of hope in her friend's face. 'And you?'

A rueful slip of a smile played about Thelma's lips, which were smudged cerise – the remains of the red lipstick she wore to work. 'I'm managing. Not everything's bad.'

Jenny studied the glossy dark hair, the face that was still

heart-shaped and firm even though Thema was in her forties. No wonder the Dutch pilot had made a beeline for her.

'Go on,' said Thelma suddenly raising her eyes. 'I know you want to ask me something else, and I know what that something else is about.'

'Right. I'll say it then.' Jenny flounced cheerfully around the table, placed her hands palms down and asked, 'When are you meeting Peter again?'

'Whenever I want.'

Thelma had given the matter of Peter van Luntzen great thought, finally concluding that seeing as she was unattached, it was nobody's business but her own.

'I know it's going to cause gossip – him being younger than me for a start – but I really don't care.'

'I don't blame you, love. Strike while the iron's hot. Live in the moment. Tomorrow might never come and all that.'

'That's my intention,' Thelma declared with a flourish of one hand, waving it dismissively as she would any critical comment she might receive. *And she's bound to receive some*, Jenny concluded.

When the tea arrived, Thelma slid the scribbled plan and notes – no more than short sentences – beneath the pile of sewing that had been pushed to one side. 'I need some kind of barrier between the posh bit of the shop and the other bit. I was thinking of potted palms, but that wouldn't be quite enough to give privacy to both halves.'

'We might have something at the shop,' said Jenny. 'Some kind of screen or shelving unit; curtains even. It's amazing what Robin's collected. Leave it with me.'

The smile was small, but Jenny was glad to see it and sensed that this business at Bertrams had raised Thelma's spirits. Obviously, there was still the uncertainty over George coming home. Bert abandoning her hadn't helped. He'd hardly been a ball of fire, but he had been some kind of company.

'Seems a nice man, that Mr Bertram.'

'He is. Took me by surprise, that's for sure. I thought I would run a few things up to get the whole thing going. Underwear for a start. Then I could cut down kids' and baby clothes from adult clothes. That should work. Do you think you could give me a hand?'

'I'd love to, but bear in mind, Thelma, that I'm not as skilled as you.'

'Don't you worry. I'll be looking over your shoulder.'

'And there you were thinking you were for the chop and instead you've ended up as shop manageress. Who would have thought.'

Thelma took the cup of tea in both hands and had a moony look on her face. 'There were so many things going wrong, so many things to worry about. I'm still worried about George, but perhaps things are on the turn. Things are getting better, and doesn't everything go in threes? Number one, I keep my job, number two...'

Jenny caught her blushing. 'You've lost one man and gained another.'

Thelma gripped her teacup close to her mouth and eyed Jenny over the rim, her cheeks turning pink again. 'Do you think I'm being foolish? After all, he's a few years younger than me.'

'How many years?'

Thelma thought about it before answering. 'Five or six.'

Jenny shrugged casually. 'It's nothing and, anyway, if older men can marry young girls, you can do the same.'

The cup went back into the saucer. 'I feel so blessed.' The eyes that gazed into those of Jenny were both intense and full of wishful thinking, plus unshed tears. 'But I'd swap it all to have my boy home safe and sound.'

Jenny reached across and patted her hand. 'Of course you would. But you need to stay strong, Thelma. After all, Maria and the newborn will have need of you. There's them and a future out there.'

Thelma looked up at the ceiling, then back to the pillow slips she'd made from cut-down sheets. The middles had been threadbare, but the ends had been good. She'd made four pillowcases from two old sheets, make do and mend at its finest.

She shook her head. The smile came despite the fear that was always there, morning, noon and night. 'I live in hope.'

'Who knows what might happen next. Mr Bertram certainly took me by surprise. Things could get even more surprising. He might bequeath the shop to you in his will.'

Thelma laughed. Jenny laughed with her, determined to keep the cheerful atmosphere going as long as she could.

'As if. I'm not that lucky.' Thelma's smile faded.

Jenny swiftly sought a spot of humour. 'Will the cheap side have any decent stockings? Mine are in shreds. Just a host of ladders held together with a few strands of silk.'

She showed Thelma one leg and then the other. Both were in a dire strait.

Thelma laughed. 'We have a few pairs of pre-war silk stockings left and quite a few pairs of lisle stockings.'

Jenny pulled a face. 'I hate lisle stockings. They're too thick, too heavy and don't darn as easily as you'd think they would. Still, you've been given a wonderful opportunity,' said Jenny, clapping her hands together. 'Make do and mend really being taken seriously.'

'I must admit, you could have knocked me down with a

feather. It was the last thing I expected. I did mention that our usual customers might not like hobnobbing with the peasants, but he said he'd had quite the contrary response. Most of the younger women are in uniform – smart uniforms of course,' she said with a smile. 'But the older women feel they want to do their bit too, so they're all for it.'

'I am surprised.'

'So was I.'

Jenny looked at the treadle sewing machine, which was always threaded ready for the next worn-out item to be made useful again. Thelma was giving new life to old-fashioned garments that their mothers – or even grandmothers – used to wear.

'There's more,' said Thelma. 'He thought we could offer an alteration service – or in fact I could cut things down for those who aren't handy with a needle. I'm in charge of the whole scheme. It's up to me to plan out how it'll work.' Her eyes shone with excitement; her face happier than Jenny had seen in a long time, and Jenny felt in danger of crying. She was so happy for her friend.

Thelma said, 'All I want now is for George to come breezing through the door, then my cup would be running over.'

'It would indeed. But at least you've still got your girls.'

A gentle fanciful look came to Thelma's face. 'Here's hoping I'll live long enough to see them walking down the aisle. Wouldn't that be a thing!'

29

The moment Jenny saw the folding screens, she knew they were exactly right for Thelma's project at Bertram Modes. Japanese ladies in silk kimonos of rich hue were depicted in a garden of pale greens, pinks and blues. They were old but in very good order.

'Robin,' she exclaimed breathlessly as she ran her fingers over one of the gilt and lacquered folding screens. 'They're beautiful.'

In response, he placed his arm around her shoulders, pulled her close and kissed her cheek. 'So are you, sweetheart.'

She snuggled up to him but whilst rubbing her cheek against his clean-shaven chin, her gaze remained fixed on the screens. 'Where did you get them?'

His arm stayed around her shoulders, warm and comforting. 'Some old colonial sort up in Clifton. His butler told me he'd brought them back from Hong Kong some years back when he retired from the army. The whole house was being emptied.'

'I take it he'd died?'

'He had indeed, and his daughter had relocated to America. Florida, I think.'

'Nice for some,' said Jenny, her brow furrowing in thought. 'I won't say I'm not jealous of those who can afford to sit out the war on the other side of the world while the rest of us manage – or just about manage.'

Robin shook his head sadly as he wondered how much of the old man's history was caught up in the screens. The colonel didn't sound as though he'd been a bad sort and had fought for his country in old battles from the Great War and back in the previous century. He'd sensed that the butler had not approved of the house being emptied and locked up. For a start, the butler would be losing his position. 'I thought Sir Cyril would have gone on for a few more years. I was his batman in the army days. I knew his wife too. Lovely woman. Her daughter's unlike her. Not one bit.'

Jenny fingered the embroidered silk. There was a little fading, a little fraying, which only seemed to enhance their exotic appearance. 'Were they very expensive?'

'I didn't pay much for them, but then who wants stuff like this any more? I got them for the price of a bundle of firewood and a sack of coal. A pittance.'

'A bargain.'

Robin grimaced. 'I don't know about that. Now I've got them, what am I going to do with them?'

Jenny turned to face him. Eyes shining, she placed her hands on his shoulders and fingered one corner of his mouth with her index finger. 'I think I know who could make use of them.'

'You do? Well, that's a relief.'

She went on to tell him about Thelma's good fortune.

'She could certainly do with it. I take it George is still missing?' he asked.

Jenny nodded before her eyes slid sidelong. 'Is Simon around?' she whispered.

'Yes,' he replied and failed to control the scowl cross his face. 'He's gone upstairs to his room.'

'Because he saw me coming?'

'Of course not.'

Robin seemed quite piqued. Of late he was finding it harder and harder to admit to his children's shortcomings one of which was that they treated Jenny with undisguised dislike, an attitude instigated by their artful mother.

Jenny shook away the negative thoughts. Robin coped with things as best he could. Making it seem as though nothing was wrong, she said, smiling sweetly, 'Can you put these back for Thelma?'

'I'll put them in the van right now and get them to Bertrams in the morning. How would that be?'

She kissed him on the nose. 'Wonderful.' And then on the lips.

* * *

'Mrs Dawson?'

The colour drained from Maria's face when she saw who it was who had knocked on her front door; a young lad in the uniform of a post office despatch rider holding a telegram in his hand. Her knees buckled. She caught hold of the doorpost in an effort to remain upright. A despatch rider meant only one thing.

Silently, her mouth too dry to speak, she took the telegram and thanked him.

'Me mum asked if I could bring it round.'

She frowned. 'Your mum?'

He nodded. 'I've finished me shift, but once me mum discovered where you'd moved, well – she reckoned it should get to you as soon as possible. Somebody said that a Mrs Dawson lived in Coronation Close, but me mum said it couldn't possibly be her. The one in Coronation Close didn't 'ave a husband. One of the neighbours told her it had to be the Italian girl and that you lived here.'

Not quite understanding what was going on, Maria stood with mouth agape. 'I'm sorry. Where is it you live?'

There was pity in the boy's eyes as he took in the question and answered that he lived in Montpelier. 'Me mum said that you used to live there too. In the rooms at the top of the 'ouse. Is that right?'

'Yes.' She said it softly, voice only just above a whisper.

'There was somebody else in our place before we moved in there and other people on the top floor. Then it was empty for a while. We reckon this was left on the doormat and the rooms being empty for a while, nobody noticed. We just moved in, and my mum said we should get this to you straightaway. I had me motorbike 'andy, so I slung me leg over it and came straight round. Thought you might be waiting for it. Looks important. On His Majesty's Service in fact.'

Maria stared at him and at the envelope. It looked as though it had already been opened, then stuck back down.

'Sorry about that,' said the telegram boy, his eyes flickering with embarrassment. 'Me mum thought it was about me dad. But it ain't. It's for you.' His smile widened. 'Looks like your old man forgot to change your address when you moved out. Daft bugger.'

Maria felt as though a metal band was tightening around

her chest, so tight that her lungs wouldn't let out the air she had just breathed in. Her hand shook. Her eyes stared at the envelope; her lips slightly parted. She feared what the missive would say.

'You wanna go ahead and open it,' the telegram boy said softly. Although he considered himself a tough lad answerable to nobody, he felt for anyone who was waiting for news about a loved one. After all, the boy had delivered enough telegrams to understand how she was feeling. On this occasion, he'd delivered good news. On other occasions, he had not. He was glad that this was a good one. He knew this because his mother had already opened it and cried with joy. It would have been even better if it had been news about his father, but good news was that for everybody. 'I'll leave you with it then. And it's good news. I can tell you that much.'

He took backward steps to the garden gate, waiting for her to stop looking like a statue and open the envelope. Hadn't she heard what he'd said.

'It's good news,' he repeated.

With a wave and a cheery smile, he was gone, the exhaust from his motorbike staining the night air with intrinsic puffs as it sped off out of Redruth Road.

The words finally sank in. Hands trembling, Maria slid a finger along the jagged gap where it had already been opened. Then she stopped. She was too full of exultation to open this by herself. She had to take it around to Thelma.

Clara next door was more than willing to look after her little tot when she told her the reason she had to run round to her mother-in-law.

'Love to. Good practice for when my nipper puts in an appearance. Is it good news you've got there in your hand?'

Although her eyes were awash with tears, Maria managed

to nod and utter a small, pitiful yes followed by two more, louder and louder. 'Yes. Yes.'

She wanted to go on saying yes, but all she could do as she ran around to Coronation Close, her hair dark and tousled flying out behind her, was laugh and cry at the same time.

Maria was still laughing and crying when she dashed round the back of the house, pushed open the door and ran into the kitchen. She waved the brown envelope at Thelma, who took it immediately. Her hands shaking, she read the most magical words she'd ever read in her life.

```
The War Office is pleased to inform you
that Able Seaman George Arthur Dawson is
alive and well.
```

'Blimey,' said Thelma, sinking into a chair. 'I was about to tell you about the lovely screen Robin Hubert delivered to Bertrams for dividing the shop in two halves. Nothing compared to this, nothing at all.'

'He's coming home,' cried Maria, dancing around the room and sending the coronation china displayed on the dresser rattling.

'He's coming home,' cried Thelma, dancing with her, tears of joy running down her cheeks.

Her prayers had been answered and if there really was a heaven, then whoever was up there had kept their promise. Her boy was coming home.

30

It was afternoon and the red-brick walls of the shops girdling
Filwood Broadway looked brighter than they did on cloudy
days. It seldom found its way into Robin's shop, which saved
him having to pull down the canopy that ran the length of the
front windows. The interior remained cool and the jumble of
old tables, chairs, sofas, wardrobes and a red velvet covered
Victorian chaise longue kept the faded patina they'd had when
he'd first bought them.

The shade at the front of the shop deepened towards the
middle and back, where the narrow staircase wound up to the
first floor living room. This was also the location of the largest
bedroom and small bathroom, where a cast-iron bath rubbed
shoulders with a washbasin resting on a wrought iron stand.
The stairs wound up further to the two attic rooms, one that
served as a linen cupboard, the other containing two single
beds. These were the beds where his children slept when they
came to stay.

Robin's son, Simon, arrived unexpectedly on the bus from
Montpelier surprising his father. 'Simon. I wasn't expecting

you, not two Saturdays following.' He paused. 'How's it going at Bawns Garage?'

'Fine.'

'Do you need more money for tools?'

Quite frankly, Robin was so pleased to see him, he would, at that moment, have given his son anything he wanted.

'No. Not really. I came to see you, Dad. I thought we could have a night—'

The pleasure in his face disappeared when Jenny came out of the back office, her cashbook tucked beneath her arm.

'Hello, Simon.' She flashed him her best smile though inside she truly wished he wasn't here.

Just the sight of her stiffened his features.

Mouth downturned, he grunted what passed as a warm greeting in his adolescent world.

Robin seemed oblivious to his changeable moods. He was just glad to have him here. 'You're staying tonight? Your bedroom's ready. I've made a cheese and potato pie for supper. There's plenty for two.'

There was a sad neediness in the way Robin threw words at his son, wanting the boy to respond, to interact and say how grateful he was; anything to show some sign that there was love between them.

'Okay.'

'We'll talk later,' Robin called after him.

Jenny watched the whole episode with something bordering on pity, but also anguish. Robin always seemed so capable, but when it came to his kids, he could give in easily to whatever direction the wind was blowing.

Simon threw a terse okay over his shoulder before tugging open the door leading to the stairs up to the next floor.

After throwing his small suitcase on the bed, he pressed his face tightly against the window so that his nose was squashed and his forehead cooled by the glass.

A fly dared skitter between him and the frame. It was in the wrong place at the wrong time. Simon squashed it with his fist.

He shrugged off his blazer. His mother made him wear a blazer even when it was hot, even now he was no longer at school.

'Good boys wear blazers. They don't go round in scruffy corduroys like someone I can mention.'

Even without mentioning, he knew she'd meant his father.

A few breaths of air from the open window cleared his head and cooled his thoughts. He felt calmer now. He'd wanted some private time with his father. Why didn't he see that? His mother had assured him that it was a good idea to arrive unannounced and that his father wouldn't hesitate to send 'that woman' away immediately. But he hadn't done. Not yet anyway. And he wouldn't. Somehow, he knew he wouldn't.

Not only was he disappointed, but he was also angry.

He placed the change of underwear and pyjamas he'd brought with him in one of the drawers kept purely for his visits. The lower drawers held items from the pawn shop side of the business – those items not redeemed. He always found it interesting having a look through these, his prying fingers exploring the motley collection of silver-plated salt cellars, spoons and toast racks that nobody bothered to use. Amongst the household bric-a-brac, he touched something more solid. The cigarette lighter was a rare find, an item that to his impressionable mind identified someone as a man. No furtive lighting of matches and stealing a cigarette from his mother's obligatory packet of Woodbines.

On closer examination, he traced the slightly worn initials *H. E.* etched into its shiny surface. A quick shake told him its fuel chamber was full. With a flick of his thumb, up shot an inch-long flame.

Its yellow brightness was reflected in his eyes. He imagined it being bigger than it was, leaping a foot high, a mile high, not just a paltry inch. He'd seen Hollywood stars in films offer ladies a light for their cigarettes with a lighter like this.

He slipped it into his pocket, settled his countenance, prevaricating whether to ask his father if he could have the lighter.

Dinner wouldn't be ready yet, but he made his way down-stairs hoping that his father would be alone now and that he would throw his arms around him.

The staircase was dark, but he didn't care. He was excited and aching to be his father's son, to have conversations with each other that women couldn't understand. Man talk. He listened before opening the door at the bottom.

The sound of a woman's laughter blended seamlessly with his father's throaty voice sounded from down where the stairs spilled out through a door and into the back of the shop. He stood totally still, one foot paused above the next tread, the other poised at an angle on the one behind him – like a runner on the starting blocks waiting for the sound of the starting gun.

The woman laughed again, not so loud as before, as if to do so was quite outrageous.

His father said something he couldn't understand, a stran-gulated sound between heavy breaths.

Leaning forward, Simon cracked open the door just enough for him to see through without being seen.

His eyes, as brown as his mother's, opened wide and a fiery heat spread up from his neck and over his cheeks.

Father and Mrs Crawford were melded tightly together, as if they weren't two people at all but one undulating mass.

His mother's words rang in his head – not like a bell – more like the point of a knife being run down a sheet of glass, a sound enough to put anyone's teeth on edge. 'Tell me if you see them gum sucking and canoodling.'

He'd asked her to explain what she meant.

'Kissing. You know what kissing is, don't you? Well, that's what gum sucking is.'

He'd acknowledged that he knew what kissing meant, but what was canoodling?

His mother had wrapped her arms around herself and made sucking sounds whilst wiggling her body and thrusting it forward in a way that had made his jaw drop and his eyes big as gobstoppers.

'All over each other. Arms all around each other. Like a two-backed monster.'

He'd been too bashful to ask if she meant what men and women did when they made babies because he wasn't that sure that Arthur Crabbe, a school mate, had been telling the truth. Arthur liked everyone to think that he knew everything in the world about being naked and doing things Simon, quite frankly, thought was disgusting. How could their parents do things like that?

Mentioning to his mother what Arthur had said had earned him a clip around the ear and a threat to wash his mouth out with carbolic soap if he repeated the performance.

But Arthur Crabbe was right. Here it was, in front of his eyes, his father and Mrs Crawford doing everything his mother wanted him to report on. Gum sucking! And what was worse, canoodling.

His bottom lip curled in disgust, but also fear and loathing because he'd remembered what else his mother had said.

'One day he'll be off with her, and you'll never see him

again. Good riddance as far as I'm concerned – so long as 'e leaves us well provided.'

Tears had stung his eyes and just for once he'd dared to talk back. 'My dad wouldn't do that.'

His father wouldn't do the things she'd said – that's what he told himself, but here he was, the father he'd been taught to treat with contempt. The contempt was only to please his mother. Beneath the surface, he loved his father but seeing him canoodling with Mrs Crawford distorted his feelings. He felt betrayed and couldn't watch any longer but was unsure whether to confront the pair of them.

His feelings were too bruised, his face too wet, streaked with tears. Going backwards up the stairs wasn't easy – especially seeing as he didn't want to be discovered.

Somehow, he made his way up the staircase and carefully negotiated the landing without the floorboards creaking. Once safely ensconced behind the closed bedroom door, he was tempted to throw himself on the bed, where he could bury his face in the pillow and give full vent to his disappointment and his anger. Perhaps it was the voice of his mother crackling somewhere at the back of his head that stopped him doing that. Many slaps and even the odd punch had landed on the back of his head. That was why he always envisaged her right behind him telling him what to do rather than advising him.

'If I've got to beat some sense into you, I will. Believe you me.'

Of course, he believed her because she often did it. He clenched his fists and ground his teeth, determined that he wouldn't cry out loud and draw attention to himself.

The window of his bedroom faced west. The sun was low in the sky but strong in his room glowing like fire on the windowpanes and the cheap chest of drawers set against the wall where he had found the lighter. He found it again now and when he pressed his thumb against the trigger, a bright yellow flame sprang into life. He watched it for a while until his thumb went numb. Once the numbness had passed, he flicked the trigger again. The flame was constant, unerring and ready to be used over and over again to light a cigarette – or anything else for that matter.

His jaw set, Simon eyed the small flame. His eyes were narrowed and there was a throbbing in his head and a sick feeling in his throat. His father had disappointed him. His mother had said that he would. Dark thoughts curled around in his mind. He didn't just feel hurt, he felt angry, although it didn't seem to fully belong to him.

Although she wasn't there in person, his mother was in his head, her hand slapping him and telling him what to do. Simon wanted to please her whilst at the same time assuage the hurt he was feeling. Perhaps if he did something to please her she would treat him better. What pleased her the most was to have him hurt his father, destroy the life he had – and then perhaps his parents would reunite.

It occurred to him that if his father didn't have the shop, then Mrs Crawford wouldn't work there and, perhaps, he might move in with his mother. If that happened perhaps the uncles would stop coming. There were too many of them. Some gave him a crumpled bag of boiled sweets which were in short supply.

Yes. Getting rid of his father's shop would mean no more 'uncles' taking his mother out drinking, laughing and mauling her in front of him, finding one of them in bed with her in the morning. Mother and father together again. Bliss.

* * *

That night after Mrs Crawford had gone home, Simon sat at the dining table eating a cheese and potato pie. His father wasn't that great a cook, but this was one of those meals that Simon found himself enjoying. There was plenty of cheese in it.

'Eat up, lad. I know it's your favourite.'

Simon prodded a cheese covered slice of potato with his fork. 'I ain't that hungry.'

'I'm up for seconds if you don't. I'll gobble it all down, I will, if you don't do it justice. You've got more cheese there than I have.'

Robin was speaking the truth; he'd purposely layered more cheese on his son's potatoes than on his own. Besides the fact that the boy was growing, he wanted to see him smile. It didn't happen that often nowadays.

Resting his elbows on the table, Robin folded his hands in front of his chin whilst studying his ginger-haired son. There had been times when Simon had been at school that he'd wanted to be there to help him with his reading and doing sums, especially mental arithmetic. Robin found it easy to add and subtract in his head but knew his son did not.

Doreen had said Simon was thick – not quite right in the head. 'You'll have to beat reading and writing into that one – I'm telling you.'

He suspected that was what she did, although, when questioned, Simon had shaken his head. Going on about it and questioning him again wouldn't help. Doreen was a bully. Robin only wished he'd known that early on. His life might have been so different. Might have gone to sea. Might have joined the army. Might even have been in with a chance with Jenny and whipped her away from under Roy Crawford's nose.

At least Simon now had an apprenticeship and in time might escape his mother's clutches.

Robin stopped himself from grimacing in front of his son. Happiness must prevail between them. He'd do anything for that. Just plain old happiness.

He painted a cheery smile on his face. 'I've got custard tart for afters. Made it myself. Pastry, jam from Mrs Aldridge, her that goes blackberrying out on Whitchurch Lane. Wonder them aeroplanes out there don't blow the fruit off straight into her basket.'

His jokey manner didn't raise even a tiny smile.

'How about you and me taking a walk out there tomorrow afternoon? Along Whitchurch Lane? There won't be any black-berries until the autumn, but at least we can get as close as we can to the fence and look at the planes. What do you think?'

He'd fully expected to see a glimmer of interest on his son's face but was disappointed. The only thing he did discern was a locking of his youthful jaw in a way that an older man might do if he'd come to a serious decision or a secret not to be told.

Simon continued to poke the prongs of the fork at the barely touched cheese and potato pie. His eyes were downcast, the corners of his mouth downturned.

He reached for his son's plate. 'Are you sure you've finished?'

Simon dropped his arms to his sides, his sullen look turning even more sullen.

'No pudding?'

A shaking of his head.

Robin got up and took both plates to the draining board and scraped what remained into the pie dish in which it had cooked. Nothing in this war could be wasted. The dish was placed on the cold slab in the larder.

He turned back to Simon, who still sat with head bowed at the dining table. He'd tried so hard to please the boy, to make him feel welcome, but nothing he'd tried had worked. Now an anger he rarely allowed to take him bubbled to the surface – but coldly.

'Your face is as long as a fiddle. No reading then? No listening to the wireless?'

Simon didn't answer and stayed stiffly resolute.

Finally, the anger – and the accompanying hurt – took over. Robin flung out his arm. One finger pointed at the stairs. 'Then you might as well get to bed. I work hard all day in this shop and can do without your miserable face! Go on! Get to bed!'

In response, Simon kicked the chair back. Head still bowed and fists clenched, he headed for the stairs. His footsteps thudded all the way up, not at the usual volume but with purpose, bringing his feet down as heavily as possible so that Robin would be in no doubt that he was in a mood and his ire was directed towards his father.

The sound of a slamming door came from overhead, sending flakes of loose limewash showering from the ceiling, which Robin eyed with dismay.

He slouched into a dining chair. Elbows resting on the table, his head sank into his cupped hands. He had no appetite for reading the newspaper or listening to the wireless. All he wanted to do was engage with his son. Although it wasn't strictly true, he blamed himself for the fractured evening.

The water tap dripped into the sink. A fly buzzed around a few crumbs on the draining board. Both sounds amplified the silence.

Pushing the chair back, Robin headed into the shop, unbolted the front door and stood staring out at the diminishing daylight. Once that was gone, the whole of Filwood

Broadway would dive into darkness. The blackout would reign supreme. And he would be alone.

His thoughts turned to Jenny. He would be glad to get the weekend over with and have her here in the shop, tending to her accounts, chatting with customers, giving him delivery details so he could load up the pushcart, or the van if it was too big an item.

Going back into the shop where the remains of the daylight could not reach brought on a shallow melancholy that he couldn't shake off. To drown his sorrows, he got out a bottle of parsnip wine some old dear had given him, dusted off a glass, sat down and prepared to alleviate his painful feelings in the only way he could think of.

The wine turned out more powerful than anticipated. The old dear concerned must have stockpiled a lot of sugar – possibly from before the war. His eyelids began to flutter and eventually shut. The empty bottle lay on the floor beside his chair. The wine had done its work. Robin was oblivious to the world as darkness fell around him.

For some odd reason a series of railways posters flashed through his head; the kind seen on many railway station hoardings depicting happy families playing on a beach, a smiling young woman in swimsuit and bathing cap posed to throw the red and white beachball. In his dream, she finally threw it before another poster flashed up, this time of a train crossing a viaduct in Scotland. Come to bonny Scotland. Come to the Cornish Riviera. Come to London by train.

He'd always liked trains. As a boy, he had done as other boys had done, collected the details of trains as they'd chugged along the railway line down in Victoria Park on their way to Temple Meads Station. He and the other boys had stayed out all day, and even when they'd expressed their intention to go home, Robin had wandered along to the main station and sneaked in without buying a penny platform ticket. That was where the posters advertising seaside, countryside and cities to visit had drawn his attention and stayed in his memory.

There was also the smell of the station and the chuffing trains, plumes of steam and smoke shooting upwards from their funnels, gathering like clouds against the glass roof that arched over several platforms. The white steam had smelt of a wet warmth; the smoke had smelt of coal dust, gritty on the tongue and choking to the nostrils.

He could smell it so plainly, so strongly, that for a moment he thought that reality had overtaken his dream, that he was once again a boy eagerly breathing in the addictive concoction of coal and heat. The hot humidity of it fell over his face, but although he breathed it in, sought that old smell of yore, it wasn't there. Not the coal dust or taste of grit in his mouth and yet he felt he was being smothered. There was also a sound he couldn't quite grasp, a crackling noise. At the same time, the heat increased. Now the smoke no longer smelt of steam locomotives. The sound and smell of a railway station turned strange and unrecognisable. In response some sense of survival kicked in, a realisation that he was in the present and something wasn't right.

A sea of smoke filled the room, stinging his eyes as he opened them, causing his chest to tighten before convulsing with a series of coughs. The cause of the increased heat became apparent and the source of the crackling sound that had invaded his sleep made him stagger from his chair.

Both arms held across his face, he staggered out into the shop to be confronted by a wall of flame. Legs of chairs were like Roman candles, the old, dry wood burning easily, worst of all the horsehair stuffing of old armchairs and sofas was like a series of fire grates devoured by the relentless flames.

The shop door was on the other side of this inferno. Faced with no prospect of escaping through the shop and beaten back by the flames, Robin's top priority was finding an escape route. But first to get Simon out of his bed.

Stumbling through the darkness, he fell onto the handle of the door at the bottom of the stairs, tugged it open and began to make his way up.

The door had formed a barrier to the smoke and Robin took great gulps of air clasping his chest as he climbed upwards.

'Simon! Wake up. Wake up!' Robin shouted urgently.

He stumbled up the last of the stairs on his hands and knees, not because he was still affected by smoke, but he couldn't get to the top fast enough.

'Simon.' He almost fell through the bedroom door, clung onto the handle as he coughed and spluttered his way forward. The room was in darkness, and he'd made enough noise to wake the boy.

Fearing the worst, he dragged himself to the bed, fumbled for the switch of the bedside light. Meagre as it was, the twenty-watt bulb gave him enough light to see that the bed was empty, the bedding thrown back and nothing left to tell him that his son had been sleeping here.

The curtains at the window were not drawn. Both hung limply until moved by a light draught. Robin sprang to the open window. The tiled roof of the lean-to below sloped gently down to a gutter. Below it, he could see the outline of the push-cart he used for delivering small items of furniture. At present, all it held was a mattress.

Had Simon escaped this way? If he had, he was safe. Going

out the front way through the shop was impossible. He had to have gone that way. Suddenly he realised that the shop held no value to him. It was all about his son. It always was.

A sudden crashing from downstairs, possibly more piled-up furniture, spurred him into action.

'Simon.'

Robin ran back down the stairs. The door at the bottom had crashed shut behind him. When he pushed it open a blast of hot air, smoke and behind pillars of flame licked towards him.

Slamming the door shut, he shot back upstairs and, closing the bedroom door behind him, climbed out of the window, slid down the roof and dropped onto the mattress.

Despite his gut feeling that his son had also escaped by this route, he still feared the worst. Landing awkwardly, he winced with pain and limped away, his ankle twisted, one leg trailing behind the other.

'Simon,' he shouted again.

The sound of people came from out front. So did the distant jangling of a fire engine.

'Robin, mate. You all right?'

The speaker was a Colin Peake he sometimes had a half with at the pub.

'I'm looking for my boy. Have you seen him? He had to have come this way from around the back.' He shook his head. 'Nobody could get through the front.'

Colin patted his shoulder. 'Don't you worry, mate. He'll turn up. Like you said nobody with any common sense could come through the front way. And your boy's a bright lad.'

Robin made a move to go back in. 'I need to see. Just in case.'

Colin held him back. 'No, mate. Leave it to the firemen.' He

jerked his head to where a fire engine decked out in camouflage colours came to a halt, a bunch of uniformed men in dark
green helmets piling from the back.

Robin blinked. 'They don't look like firemen.' His voice
shook as he said it and, although he was aching to rush back in,
Colin was a navvy and his hands as big as shovels.

There was a firmness to his voice. He wouldn't be allowing
Robin to rush in and do something that was stupid, but at the
same time he was reassuring. 'They're firemen, old but not the
proper firemen from the fire station. They're from the airfield.
The ARP phoned them from his unit. Closest they were. Made
sense they'd get here quicker than anyone else.'

It was hard to stand there and watch as fire hoses were
rolled out. Someone asked Robin if it was his place and was
there anyone left inside.

Eyes glazed and fixed on the flames, he nodded. 'It's my
place.' He jerked away from Colin. 'My son was in there
with me.'

For a moment, Robin saw a pitying look on the fireman's
face before he turned away and shouted orders, checked hoses
and sources of water.

A crowd had gathered. Murmurs of explanation and
sympathy trickled like water through the onlookers. Some were
still in their nightclothes. Others had alighted from the late-
night bus.

The obvious question was asked. 'Was it a bomb?'

'Didn't know there'd been a raid.'

There hadn't been, although Robin wished there had. At least
he would have someone to blame. As it was, the open window
and the empty bed kept coming to mind. So did his son's disposi-
tion earlier in the evening when he'd been surlier than usual.

As the flames were overcome by water, two firemen volunteered to go forward.

The officer in charge ordered them to be careful.

They took tentative steps, leaping back when a joist, black and still smouldering, crashed to the floor.

The chief officer pointed. 'Turn that hose on there.'

In response, a jet of water, strong enough to knock a man over, gushed from the mouth of the hose, so powerful in fact that it took two men to hold it.

When the water finally stopped and the hose retracted, the officer called for volunteers to go inside.

'He don't mean you,' said Colin, his fingers resuming their pincer-like grip.

'Robin. Robin. What's happened? Was it a bomb? A gas leak?'

In a flurry of tumbled hair, a coat pulled over her nightdress, Jenny was there looking up at him wide-eyed, her face full of concern.

Seeing Robin's arm go around Jenny, Colin's big hand fell away.

Robin looked down into her face. For some reason, he felt calmer now she was here, though the fear for his son was like a bunch of nettles stinging his throat.

He shook his head and swallowed before he could speak. 'I don't know.'

'At least Simon's not inside.'

He stared down at her. 'How do you know that?'

'I went to meet Tilly off the bus earlier at the end of the journey – you know where it turns round before going back into town. I saw him sitting inside downstairs. I waved, but he didn't wave back.' She frowned. 'I'm sure he saw me.'

The firemen began using rakes and a sweeping brush to clear up the debris that had fanned out over the pavement.

Robin called to the senior officer. 'There's no need for anyone to go inside. It seems my son left earlier.'

'Are you sure?'

Jenny confirmed that she had seen him.

'Good,' the man exclaimed.

His attention was suddenly alerted to one of the men raking the pavement.

'Just found this.'

The fire chief took something small and shiny from the hand he'd raised above his head. 'This yours?'

Robin stared at the shiny object. He thought he recognised it but had to know for sure. Earlier in the day, he'd placed a cigarette lighter in one of the bedroom drawers in the attic room. Robin fingered the etched initials, *H. E.* It had been pawned only a short while ago.

'What is it?'

Robin looked at Jenny, thought about telling her his immediate suspicion but couldn't bring himself to declare it out loud.

'I dropped it,' he said, shoving it swiftly into the depths of his trouser pocket.

Jenny could tell by his face that he was lying but wouldn't challenge him. It was the first time she could ever remember him lying to her and it hurt so much she turned her back on him and walked away with tears in her eyes. Doreen had won. Again.

31

Forty-eight hours later, Jenny was at Thelma's, her nostrils stinging with the sharp tang of scorched timbers.

Her eyes stung too, not so much from the fire but Robin's reaction. Deep down he knew that his son had started the fire but held no grudge. Up until this moment Jenny had always believed that she and Robin could win through his family problems and eventually beat Doreen's ongoing vindictiveness.

It seemed to her now that it had all been in vain. She had been harbouring a false hope, hugging it to her breast like a drowning man might with a lifebelt.

Number twelve Coronation Close was heaving with people. The star attraction was George. His arm was around Maria. At his knee, his little girl was looking up at him as though unsure of who he was, this man she'd seen so little of.

'Here's to my George,' shouted a jubilant Thelma.

Everyone raised their glass. Peter van Luntzen was there. Thelma had warned her son beforehand that she had a new man friend.

'Good for you, Mother. If I weren't yer son and married already, I'd marry you meself.'

Thelma gave him a shove. 'Go on with you!'

If she could be any happier than she was at this moment, she didn't know how. And she found happiness a funny business. During the worrying time when they hadn't known her son's fate, she hadn't broken down. Not a tear had trickled down her cheek – if it had she couldn't remember it. But now he was home the tears were not far away, although of course they were tears of joy, of relief that he'd finally returned.

Everyone around them was happy too, including Mary for whom the possibility of pregnancy had been a false alarm. Nevertheless, her darling Beau still had it in mind to make an honest woman of her. She was still holding off.

Thelma was in two minds whether she wanted her daughter wedded. She instinctively knew that Beau would want to go home after this war was over. Depending on whether they were still together, he would want Mary to go with him. Thelma would prefer her daughter to stay home.

Jenny Crawford was the only one who smiled with her lips but held sadness in her eyes. The fire at the shop had shocked everyone, but it had affected Jenny the most. Thelma felt her anger and her disappointment.

'Where's he staying?' Thelma asked her.

Jenny shook her head. 'I don't know. Perhaps he's gone back to Doreen.'

Thelma made a guffawing sound. 'I don't believe that for a moment.'

Jenny kept her feelings under control, after all this was a party of joy, but she only stood it for so long.

'Thelma, I think I might go now.'

'Why?'

'I'm happy for you, Thelma. Everything's turned out as you hoped it would, but me... well... I can't help feeling like an old sourpuss.'

'Jenny, you're my friend. You've been my friend since the moment you moved in from Blue Bowl Alley. Stay. You've supported me of late now I want to support you.'

Jenny smiled a little soulfully. 'I much appreciate your concern, but I have to get through this by myself. Though let's be fair, it's nothing compared to what you've been through.'

Seeing the sadness in her eyes, Thelma conceded that Jenny needed some time alone. Robin had disappeared. The shop was gone which also meant Jenny's job was gone.

'Shall I see if I can get you a job at Bertrams?' she asked.

Jenny shook her head. 'No. Something will turn up. There's plenty of war work about.'

Thelma watched her walk across the road to her own house, and although the fire at Robin's shop had nothing to do with war, she couldn't help concluding that the circumstances of war had led up to it.

She closed the front door, her spirits soaring as she returned to her living room and the lively bunch eating, drinking and making jokes about Adolf Hitler and all his dire team.

* * *

Nothing was known for days, although it had to be said that Jenny had not made enquiries. She was still angry with Robin. He had continually denied the fact that his children had been primed by his estranged wife. He'd lied to her about the fire and knew just as she did that his son had been responsible. Robin could have been killed.

Deep down, she was beginning to forgive him, but she needed to see him face to face to do that.

Thelma was there to give her advice. 'Best get on with it. It's all you can do.'

The very day George was due to report back to his ship was the day when Jenny finally received news of where Robin had gone.

The very same telegram boy who had brought the news to Maria that George was alive passed a telegram addressed to Mrs J. Crawford into Jenny's trembling hand.

The sight of it made her feel queasy. 'But I don't know anyone who would...' Jenny had been going to say that she had no close relatives in the armed forces – that was where most telegrams emanated from. As the truth hit her, she stopped herself, thanked the boy and gave him a threepenny bit.

Two lines.

```
Have      joined      the      merchant      navy.
Forgive me.
```

It was signed by Robin.

The world spun. The summer night turned cold. Was it because autumn was on its way. No. She didn't think so.

Thelma was the only person she showed it to.

There was silence between them at first, then a reaching out, a shared feeling of loss and of fear.

'We're living through tough times,' Thelma eventually said. 'All we can do is take each day as it comes until finally it's over.'

'Life or the war?' Jenny remarked bitterly.

'The war,' Thelma exclaimed. 'Just the bloody war.'

She turned slightly as a heavy hand landed on her shoulder.

'We should regard this war as a turning point in history.' The voice belonged to Peter Van Luntzen. He turned his head and looked down into Thelma's eyes. 'We have been and will be presented with many lessons by it. Let us hope we learn those lessons. I dread what might happen if we do not.'

* * *

Jenny put on a pretty dress of pale blue. As a finishing touch she pinned a silk flower on one of the lapels. With many others she was attending an interview at a munitions factory. She'd heard how noisy it could be, how mind numbing, but at this moment in time that was what she wanted.

The women were of all ages, several looking closer to her own age. They were from all social classes, the wealthier middle-class women dressed in clothes purchased before the war had started and still looking smart. Jenny wondered if any of them had shopped in Bertrams.

Most of the women were working class. She wondered at their reasons for applying for work. Some had no doubt been called up by the powers that be. Others might have no children at home and were bored. Some harboured the illusion that packing bullets would go some way to winning the war.

Whatever, here they were waiting in line until they were called into an office or a cubicle to give their details and be told something about their job.

'What's the difference between us going into a cubicle and into that office over there,' said one straight-talking young woman.

'None whatsoever,' came the swift reply. 'We're just trying to get everyone dealt with as quickly as we can.'

There were smiles and comments.

'I fancy going into the office. It's more private.' That was one commonly spoken comment.

The queue filed forward, most peeling off into the cubicles.

The office door opened, and a man emerged holding a pen in one hand and a folder in the other.

'Mrs Crawford. Mrs Jennifer Crawford.'

Jenny stepped forward but stopped when she saw who was standing there. Whatever hopes and confidence she'd had flew out of the window. He still had dark blond hair with only a few silvery streaks. Charlie Talbot was as sleekly groomed, a man of another class and a time when she'd thought herself in love with him.

'Can I come back tomorrow?' she asked one of the other people with the job of enrolling women for war work.

The puzzled-looking woman said that she could.

'Are you feeling ill?'

'Yes,' said Jenny. 'Yes, I am.'

She apologised to those she jostled in the queue in her hurry to escape. There was no way she could go into that office, no way she could be alone there with Charlie Talbot, the man she'd once fallen in love with.

'How did it go?' Thelma asked her when she got home.

'I didn't feel very well. They said I could come back tomorrow.'

Thelma eyed her quizzically. Eventually, she said, 'Well there's a turn-up. Never mind. Try again another day.'

And that, thought Jenny, *is what I intend doing.*

* * *

On the other side of Coronation Close Margaret Routledge was planning her future. For the first time in a long time she would be left to her own devices, to do whatever she wanted to do, to look and dress as she wanted to. Percy was gone. Her son was gone.

Her two surviving children were asleep upstairs. The house was silent around her. Like a tomb, she thought. That was how Percy had liked it. Everything in its place. And her in a straitjacket.

Well now was the time for change! A change to what she wanted.

She got up from the armchair. She threw the cushion onto the floor. She did the same with the cushions from the sofa. A vase given to them by Percy's grandmother went smashing to the floor. It had been his favourite. She'd thought it hideous.

Pictures that he'd liked came down from the wall. She placed them on the sofa. She'd deal with them tomorrow rather than wake everyone up. But they would go. Oh, yes, they would go!

The mantelpiece drew her attention, the clock that ticked too loudly that Percy insisted was wound up before it ever had chance to wind down.

Yes, she thought, her hands folding around it.

The clock might have gone crashing into the fireplace then and there if her reflection in the mirror hadn't drawn her attention.

Her complexion was pale, her mousy brown hair tied back in the severe bun her husband had insisted was the only acceptable style for a respectable married woman.

Pulling out the pins one by one, she let her hair tumble onto her shoulders. She pulled some forward around her face and was surprised at how different she looked.

'This is the real me,' she said softly. Her eyes glittered. Her pale lips smiled. *But you could look better*, said the voice inside her head. And she knew that voice was right. And when she did look better, when she applied face powder, lipstick and eye make-up, what then? What would her life be like?

She didn't need her inner voice to tell her that her life would be different. She knew it would be so because she would make it so.

* * *

MORE FROM LIZZIE LANE

Another book from Lizzie Lane, *A New Doctor at Orchard Cottage Hospital*, is available to order now here:

www.mybook.to/NewDoctorBackAd

ABOUT THE AUTHOR

Lizzie Lane is the author of over 50 books, including the bestselling Tobacco Girls series. She was born and bred in Bristol where many of her family worked in the cigarette and cigar factories.

Sign up to Lizzie Lane's mailing list here for news, competitions and updates on future books.

Follow Lizzie on social media here:

ALSO BY LIZZIE LANE

The Tobacco Girls

The Tobacco Girls

Dark Days for the Tobacco Girls

Fire and Fury for the Tobacco Girls

Heaven and Hell for the Tobacco Girls

Marriage and Mayhem for the Tobacco Girls

A Fond Farewell for the Tobacco Girls

Coronation Close

New Neighbours for Coronation Close

Shameful Secrets on Coronation Close

Dark Shadows Over Coronation Close

Tough Times on Coronation Close

The Strong Trilogy

The Sugar Merchant's Wife

Secrets of the Past

Daughter of Destiny

The Sweet Sisters Trilogy

Wartime Sweethearts

War Baby

Home Sweet Home

Sixpence Stories

Introducing Sixpence Stories!

Discover page-turning historical novels from your favourite authors, meet new friends and be transported back in time.

Join our book club
Facebook group

https://bit.ly/SixpenceGroup

Sign up to our
newsletter

https://bit.ly/SixpenceNews

Boldwood

Boldwood Books is an award-winning fiction publishing company seeking out the best stories from around the world.

Find out more at www.boldwoodbooks.com

Join our reader community for brilliant books, competitions and offers!

Follow us
@BoldwoodBooks
@TheBoldBookClub

Sign up to our weekly deals newsletter

https://bit.ly/BoldwoodBNewsletter